Temptation. . . .

A few dozen dresses, tops, skirts, and shoe boxes were scattered over the bed, the furniture, and hanging on a rolling clothes rack where gossamer hems and dangling sashes floated in the breeze from the open windows. Grace gaped at the feminine chaos, her gaze flitting from sea green chiffon to orange floral print to black satin. There was not a single item that looked like something she had ever worn, and they were all . . . *beautiful*! She'd never worn pretty things; she hadn't had the money, or the places to wear them.

Then a haunting sense of guilt crept over her at her own lusting reaction to the *Vogue*-worthy collection. Shopping for trendy, sexy, expensive dresses was not a politically correct activity in her home, landing somewhere between reading *Cosmopolitan* and learning to pole dance on the list of Things Serious Women Do Not Do.

Grace went to the rack and ran her fingertips over the sea green chiffon, feeling the forbidden desire tremble through her.

Great-Aunt Sophia's Lessons for Bombshells

ALSO BY LISA CACH

Have Glass Slippers, Will Travel

A Babe in Ghostland

The Erotic Secrets of a French Maid

Available from Pocket Books and Gallery Books

Great-Aunt Sophia's Lessons for Bombshells

LISA CACH

GALLERY BOOKS

NEW YORK   LONDON   TORONTO   SYDNEY   NEW DELHI

G

Gallery Books
A Division of Simon & Schuster, Inc.
1230 Avenue of the Americas
New York, NY 10020

First Gallery Books trade paperback edition June 2012.

GALLERY BOOKS and colophon are registered trademarks of
Simon & Schuster, Inc.

For information about special discounts for bulk purchases,
please contact Simon & Schuster Special Sales at 1-866-506-1949
or business@simonandschuster.com.

The Simon & Schuster Speakers Bureau can bring authors to your
live event. For more information or to book an event contact the
Simon & Schuster Speakers Bureau at 1-866-248-3049 or visit our
website at www.simonspeakers.com.

Designed by Akasha Archer

Library of Congress Cataloging-in-Publication Data

Cach, Lisa.
    Great-Aunt Sophia's lessons for bombshells / Lisa Cach.—1st Gallery Books
trade paperback ed.
        p.   cm.
    1. Aunts—Fiction. 2. Nieces—Fiction. I. Title.
    PS3553.A3125G74 2012
    813'.54—dc23

                                                    2011051758

978-1-4165-1331-5 (trade paper)
978-1-4165-5382-3 (eBook)

Manufactured in the United States of America

10 9 8 7 6 5 4 3 2 1

To Melanie,
who got me out of frumpy dresses

Acknowledgments

Many thanks to my editor, Micki Nuding, for both her patience and her genius with an editing pencil.

And thank you, my darling C.H., for duties performed on the high seas.

Great-Aunt Sophia's
Lessons for Bombshells

CHAPTER
1

PEBBLE BEACH, CALIFORNIA

"Gracie, you've got the luck of the devil."

Grace Cavanaugh rolled down the passenger window of the old Volvo, taking in the fresh sea air and the view of rocky shoreline, the lush green golf course grass, and cypress trees bent by the wind. "I had no idea it was so gorgeous here! All I've ever seen of Pebble Beach on TV is the golf course."

Catherine's elfin face was pinched with envy. "I can't believe you're getting *paid* to hang around in a beach house for the summer."

"Hey, not just hang around," Grace said, cheerful from her good fortune. "I'll be providing necessary companionship for a lonely old lady."

Catherine snorted.

"Admittedly, in a house at the beach." Grace laughed, feeling free and happy for the first time in what felt like years. The June sunlight was warm on her pale arm, a deeply welcome change from the cold gray clouds of Seattle. Three months of California summer stretched before her, gloriously free of teaching undergrads, free of rent, free of grocery bills and roommates, free of everything but working undisturbed on her dissertation and sharing a few undemanding hours of companionship with her almost-ancient-enough-to-be-dead great-aunt. She felt like a kid again, on the last day of school. "It's too good to be true, isn't it?"

Catherine arched a black brow. "Better not say that—it means you've overlooked something."

"*Pshh.*" Grace waved the thought away. "Everything's going to be fine."

The car glided through a gentle curve of 17-Mile Drive, the scenic loop road that residents of Pebble Beach drove free of charge, but which tourists paid nine bucks to do. At the gated entrance to the drive, the guard had handed them a preprinted pass with Grace's name and the date for the dashboard.

"What *could* go wrong, anyway?" Grace asked, the thought taking unwelcome hold. She pulled a lock of red hair to her mouth and started nibbling. When this cushy summer job had appeared so conveniently, she'd felt a surge of joy and relief so powerful that it had washed away her usual caution. Now and then there was a faint buzz of misgiving in the back of her mind, but she'd gleefully smothered it.

"The only things I could possibly be worried about are whether she has freezer-burned food dating from the Reagan administration, and how well we'll get along," she said. "I only met Sophia once, when I was ten."

"What was she like?"

"She scared the bejesus out of me."

"Yeah?"

"We were at my uncle's house for Easter, back in Connecticut where I grew up. It was the snooty side of my family, so I was on edge to begin with. Sophia was visiting from California. She held court in the living room like Queen Elizabeth, sitting stiff and straight in a high-backed chair, with ropes of fake pearls around her neck and half a dozen enormous rings on her bony fingers. Her hair—pure white—was parted on the side in that 1940s style, like Lauren Bacall, with a swoop of waves down one side. I'd never seen hair like that on anyone, or so much costume jewelry, either."

"So what happened?"

"My mom dragged me over to be introduced. Sophia looked me over as if she was evaluating a dog in the show ring. Then she turned to my mother and said, loud enough for the whole room to hear," Grace said, sitting up straight and pitching her voice high and haughty, "'Darling, that girl needs a training bra. Do you want old men ogling her tits?'"

Catherine burst into laughter. "She didn't!"

Grace went on in the same haughty voice, "'I hope to God you're doing a better job teaching her about birth control than you are about lingerie. Boys are going to be getting into her pants sooner than you think.'"

"No!"

Grace crossed her arms over her chest. "I was *ten*. I was so embarrassed I ran outside and crawled under a hydrangea."

Catherine chortled.

"I was afraid to come out because I thought everyone would be staring at my breasts. They were only anthills, but Sophia was right, they weren't flat like a child's anymore. So I stayed under my hydrangea until it was time to go. Ruined my dress. Missed the egg hunt. Cried my eyes out."

"I wonder what got into her?"

"Too many Bloody Marys, I bet. I refused to go to school until Mom bought me a bra, which did *not* endear Sophia to my mother. She started referring to Sophia as 'that crass old tart.'"

"*Your* mom said that?"

"I know, Earth Mother herself. Which tells you how mad she

was. She thought Sophia had turned natural comfort with my body into shame."

"The serpent in the garden of your innocence."

"Pretty much. But I'm twenty-six now, a grown woman getting her Ph.D. in Women's Studies." Grace assumed a prim expression. "I am safe from corrupting influences."

"I'm the only one who's even *tried* to corrupt you in the last five years," Catherine muttered, then darted a look of hope and hurt at her.

Grace felt a stab of pain and discomfort. "Don't, Cat," Grace pleaded. A year ago, Catherine had tried to seduce her. Catherine's hurt at the rejection was a constant threat to their friendship, and Grace wished they could both forget that it had happened. "We agreed not to ever speak about that."

An awkward silence fell between them. Ahead, a group of equestrians appeared on a path leading out of the cypress trees. Catherine stopped the car to let them pass, the horses' hooves clopping across the road. "So," she said, her voice brittle, "didn't you say Sophia used to be an actress?"

"A B actress, for a couple of years in the forties," Grace said, relieved to change the topic. "She wasn't in anything important. I don't remember what she looks like beyond that hair and jewelry, so I keep picturing her as an aging Bette Davis swilling a martini, cigarette between her fingers, insults dripping like acid off her lips."

The horses now gone, Catherine pressed on the gas. "She's probably got dementia and sits watching Animal Planet all day."

"Or maybe not." Hoping to lighten the mood, Grace narrowed her eyes and waggled her fingers at Catherine as if casting an evil spell. "Maybe she invited me here so she could mess with my mind. She wants to continue the evil work she started at that Easter party long ago."

Catherine rolled her eyes. "You said she was going to have hip surgery this summer and wanted to have family nearby."

"It's a cover story. No, what she really wants is to break my spirit, then pimp me out for porn films. Maybe she's starting a production company in her garage."

"You wish. I bet you'd enjoy it." They came to a stop at an intersection, a sign beside the road offering half a dozen arrows pointing to different destinations. "What's the address?"

Grace clenched her jaw and looked down at the Google map in her lap. "I think we turn right." Catherine was a loyal and generous friend but as sensitive as a hormonal house cat. It might be hours before she could be cajoled back into a good mood. Catherine had been cheerful and entertaining during the fifteen-hour drive from Seattle, and Grace didn't know why she had to wait until right before their arrival to get in a snit.

A few minutes later they turned down a driveway that twisted through a grove of cypress and pine, and Grace caught glimpses through the trees of a golden stone house and the brilliant blue sky beyond. A final turn brought them through a pair of stone pillars and out into a courtyard, an Italianate mansion rising like a fortress before them.

"Stop!" Grace squealed.

Catherine jammed on the brakes, jerking them both against their seat belts.

Grace stared at the looming house. This couldn't be it. *No way* this could be it. No one in the family had ever said that Sophia had money, and it was the type of thing they would know.

Grace looked down at her map again. "We must have made a wrong turn. Or maybe she gave me the wrong house number." She dug through her backpack looking for her phone. "Maybe I should call."

Catherine parked the Volvo next to a vintage Jaguar convertible, its maroon paint and polished chrome gleaming in the sun. The Volvo's engine gurgled to a stop.

"What are you doing?" Grace yelped. "Don't stop! Turn around, get us out of here before someone calls security and we're arrested for trespassing!"

"Why are you so sure this isn't her house?"

"Because!" Grace riffled through the papers crammed in her pack until she found the letter from her aunt. "It says right here, 'beach house.' This is not a beach house. I see no driftwood garden ornaments, no old floats hanging from a deck, no wind chimes. Therefore, *not* a beach house."

"It's a house. At the beach. And didn't you just say that when you met Sophia she was dripping with jewelry?"

"I thought it was *fake*! She was a two-bit actress, not Elizabeth Taylor!" Grace stared at the house in front of her, anxiety tightening her nerves. "I hate being around rich people."

"What? Why?"

"They look down on me. They know I'm not one of them." That had always been the story with her cousins, the sneering, dismissive branch of the family that saw Grace's parents as depressingly meaningful hippies, with their academic careers, natural-fiber clothing, and fondness for organic co-op farming.

Catherine snorted. "It's all in your head. Rich people don't care what you do. They're too busy with their own screwed-up lives."

Grace shook her head. Everyone silently assessed whether someone was like or unlike oneself, better or worse, higher on the social ladder or lower. She herself did it, an unconscious evaluation that took in subtleties of dress and health, posture and speech, education and culture, or the lack thereof. She relaxed if she was roughly equal, or higher. So did everyone else.

But no one liked being the lowest dog in the pack. Her rich cousins in Connecticut had laughed at her clothes, at her hair, at her going to public school, at her earnest activist parents with their green Subaru and National Public Radio bumper sticker.

"Besides," Catherine went on, "what have you got to be embarrassed about? You're brilliant. Bet you no one here is half as smart."

"Thanks." But being smart wasn't the issue.

"And you're beautiful."

"I'm thirty pounds overweight. I look like a pig." The Taco Bell burritos she'd had for lunch rolled heavily in her gut, and the waistband of her khaki capris dug into her flesh.

Catherine heaved a sigh tinged with delight. "Gracie, if you of all people can still fall prey to the fake marketing-based ideal of beauty in this country, and base your sense of self-worth on it, then there's no hope for any woman!"

"It's not my self-worth that's in question, it's my worth as judged by others, and how they'll treat me as a result. Which *can* affect my sense of self-worth over time."

"I don't know whether to keep reassuring you or to kick you in the butt."

"Butt kicking is probably quicker," Grace grumbled.

"Then consider yourself kicked. Come on, let's go meet Bette."

Grace took a deep breath and got out. How bad could it be, anyway? Aunt Sophia's letter had made it sound like she would be a guest more than an employee. She would be a valuable member of the household, introduced to visitors as the brilliant grandniece, admired for the generous spirit that had brought her here to tend to an elderly woman in need.

Or maybe she'd be more like a Brontë heroine: plain, impoverished, and relegated to the shadows, pining for the manly hero who was forever inaccessible.

She'd be pressing a cool cloth to Sophia's fevered brow, a brooding hero telling her what a brave young woman she was—

The front door opened and a middle-aged brunette poked her head out. "Is one of you Grace Cavanaugh?"

Grace waved her hand, gathering her courage as she walked over to the woman. "Hullo! Yes, that's me."

The woman had a thick, blocky torso that was not helped by her brown silk blouse and tweed skirt. Her hair was bobbed at her chin, a line of gray showing where her roots had started to grow out. Her mascara had smeared under her small, dark eyes, and her gold-rimmed glasses looked strangely old-fashioned. Her whole outfit looked old-fashioned, as if she was dressed as a no-nonsense secretary from a 1930s film.

The woman looked Grace up and down, then chuckled. "Well, of course you are."

What the hell was that supposed to mean? "And this is my friend Catherine Ruggieri. She gave me a lift."

The woman spared Catherine a glance and a nod. "Darlene," the woman said, holding her hand out to Grace. "I'm your aunt's personal assistant."

"I didn't know she had one. I thought she'd retired a long time ago."

"Oh, she doesn't work anymore, but Sophia won't sit still until she's dead."

"I hope that's not anytime soon."

"It won't be. She's got too much of the ornery bitch in her to die off quickly."

Grace blinked in shock. "Uh, er, uh . . ."

Darlene raised an eyebrow. "I hope you're not the sensitive type; you won't last long around here if you are."

Grace squeaked a laugh. "Me? Oh no, I'm thick-skinned!"

"Mm," Darlene grunted, unimpressed. "Your aunt is being

attended by her doctor at the moment, so get your things and I'll show you to your room. You can clean up before you meet her."

"Sure. Thanks. Um, and would it be all right if Catherine stays the night? She still has to drive down to San Diego, and it's too much to take on today after how far we've come . . . ," Grace trailed off as Darlene stared at her without expression.

"It's not *my* house," Darlene said into the silence.

"I guess I'll check with Aunt Sophia, then?"

"I guess you will."

Grace turned and rolled her eyes at Cat, who was smothering a grin. Together they dragged Grace's possessions out of the back of the Volvo, the car rising on its springs as it was freed of the weight. Loaded down with backpacks, book bags, and suitcases, they could barely stagger to the front door and into the foyer.

Darlene's brown leather pumps clicked on the checkerboard marble floor as she quickly led the way to a curved stone staircase.

"*What* is her problem?" Catherine whispered.

"Shhh," Grace hissed, "she'll hear you."

"So what?"

"I've got to get along with her for the next three months, that's what!" Grace set her old wheeled suitcases on the floor and dragged them, the things as heavy as rocks. A horrid screech came from one of the suitcases, and after a few hard tugs it fell over. Grace looked back in annoyance and saw an empty metal bracket where a wheel had once been. A gray gouge cut across a black marble tile, ending at the dead suitcase.

Grace's stomach sank to the cold stone floor. "Oh, crap."

Darlene stopped and turned, her eyes sharp, then click-clacked back across the floor. She looked at the gouge, then at Grace.

"I'm so sorry!"

"It's *not* my house."

"I'll tell my aunt—"

Darlene shook her head, a sharp denial. "This isn't the type of thing to bother her with. *I'll* take care of it," she bit out. She turned on her heel and once again set out for the stairs, moving up them without a backward glance.

Grace's shoulders slumped. It had taken her only minutes to screw up. She was nervous and embarrassed, and she avoided Catherine's eyes as tears stung her own, afraid that any sympathy would undo her. She set her jaw against her tears, righted her bag, and hoisted it off the floor.

She was a few steps up the staircase, deep in a silent monologue of self-chastisement, when the sound of quick, solid footsteps behind her penetrated her inner storm cloud. Catherine made a startled noise, and a moment later Grace felt the heavier of her suitcases being pulled from her grip. She instinctively tightened her hold and jerked it back toward her.

"Here now, beautiful young women shouldn't be carrying their own bags," a deep male voice said.

Grace looked down at the broad, strong hand pressed against hers on the handle of the bag, then raised her gaze to meet startling turquoise eyes fringed with black lashes.

"I promise I won't steal it." He winked.

Grace opened her mouth, but all that emerged was a gurgling sound. A flood of heat rose to her cheeks. He was the most ruggedly handsome man she'd ever seen, tall and broad and with a square jaw and heavy brow that had testosterone written all over them. Sex appeal wafted off him like cologne off a hot lightbulb. He steamed with it.

Grace's grip loosened, and he took the bag, slinging it under one arm as if it were a loaf of bread. He grinned and reached for her other bag, his arm brushing against the small of her back. A shiver stroked over her body, and her breasts tingled. She dropped her eyes.

And then he had her bag and had pulled away. "Which way, my darling Darlene?" he asked, and with their three suitcases ran easily up the stairs.

"The Garden Room. Don't go barging in on Sophia; she's with Dr. Andrew."

"When do I barge? I'm meek as a maid."

"And chickens dance the cha-cha," Darlene said sourly, leading them all down the hall and opening a door.

"I taught them myself," the man said. "Wonderful sense of rhythm, chickens."

Darlene shook her head, a hint of a smile softening her mouth, and waited in the hall while he deposited the bags inside. Grace followed him in, her book bag bumping Darlene as she passed.

"Sorry," Grace muttered.

Darlene exhaled through her nose, her lips tightening again.

The Garden Room was full of light, one wall composed of French doors that showed the tops of cypress trees and the blues of the sky and ocean beyond. Grace was only vaguely aware of yellow-flowered wallpaper and a canopy bed; the man setting down the suitcases sucked up her attention, even as she pretended to look at everything but him.

"Excuse me," Catherine said, dropping her own things and disappearing into the bathroom.

When Grace sneaked a peek at the man's face she found him staring at her, looking puzzled.

"Declan O'Brien," he said, and put out his hand.

"Grace Cavanaugh." She shook his hand, but he didn't release it. He sandwiched her hand between both of his, his thumb rubbing the back of it, his fingertips pressing gently against the inside of her wrist. Each stroke of his thumb sent shivers up her arm.

"Do I know you?" he asked. "Where do I know you from?"

She pulled her hand out of his grip. "Nowhere. I've just arrived from Seattle. Sophia is my great-aunt."

She could see comprehension work its way across his face. After a stunned moment he laughed. "Well, of course you are!"

"Yes, of course I am," she repeated, bewildered again. "Are you a friend of Aunt Sophia's?"

"Financial adviser. And friend, too."

Suspicion snaked into her mind. He seemed too young and good-looking to be a financial adviser, and too charming. She hoped he wasn't taking advantage of her aunt. He seemed like a salesman/womanizer/fast-talker type. She'd bet he owned a speedboat, or some other noisy, motor-powered, penis substitute.

Catherine emerged from the bathroom and Grace introduced her, noticing how Declan quickly scanned her friend's lithe, compact body and high, small breasts. Catherine was a natural beauty, her olive complexion smooth, her curly black hair luxuriant in its loose ponytail. Grace always felt like pale boiled haggis in comparison.

"How long are you visiting?" Declan asked Grace, turning back to her.

"All summer. I'll be watching over my aunt," Grace said, crossing her arms. *Yes, that's right, Slicky McSlickerson, I'll be watching if you try any schemes on a relative of* mine.

"Watching over her?" He laughed. "Is that a joke?"

"No joke."

"Well, I hope you enjoy your time here. You're very fortunate to have an aunt like Sophia." He nodded to them both and then was gone, taking all the energy in the room with him.

"I'll send someone to fetch you when Sophia is ready to receive guests," Darlene said. "Don't bother her on your own." She pulled the door shut with a slam.

Grace blinked, then went to the bed and plopped down on the edge. She felt like her stuffing had been knocked out. With a groan she collapsed backward and then covered her eyes with her forearm. Fifteen minutes ago she'd been laughing with joy at the prospect of her summer here in Pebble Beach. It really *had* been too good to be true. "Oh God. This is going to be a very long summer."

The bed shifted as Catherine lay down beside her. "So you have an ocean-view room in a mansion filled with vipers. It just goes to show: there's nothing good in this world without the bad to go with it."

"Then let me hope Great-aunt Sophia is a perfectly average old woman."

"Somehow, Gracie . . . I just don't think that's what you're going to get."

CHAPTER

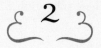

Half an hour later someone knocked on the door, and at Grace's call of admittance a pretty Hispanic girl came in. She looked about sixteen and was wearing a pale gray maid's dress, white sneakers, and a white headband to hold back her long glossy hair. Like Darlene, she appeared to be wearing a costume from an old movie. "Hi!" she said, with an uncertain smile.

"Hello!"

The girl's eyes went back and forth between Grace and Catherine, then rested on Grace. "You're the niece?"

"That's me. Grace. And this is my friend Catherine."

"Lali. Short for Eulalie." She came farther into the room. "Can you believe my mother had the nerve to name me that? What, was I, like, born in 1890? I'm so glad you're going to be spending the summer with us. Last year I was bored out of my mind working here, with no one near my age to talk to all day. No girls, anyway, just the guys working in the garden and on the pool, and occasionally some repairmen. Not that I don't like seeing guys around without their shirts on, but you can't exactly gossip with them, you know what I mean? They're always staring at your boobs." She grinned. "Bet you get that a lot."

"Er, not really."

"Then you just don't notice. Believe me, they're looking."

"I hope not."

"Really?" Lali shrugged off the imponderable. "Anyway, I'm supposed to tell you that tea is being served on the terrace. Mama made me say that, 'Tea is being served.'" She rolled her eyes. "As *if*! It's as pretentious as these silly uniforms. What is this, the nineteenth century?"

"Your mother works here?"

"She's the housekeeper and cook. Has been since before I was, like, even *born*. Ever since she took that Cordon Bleu course, though, she's had pretensions. Says she's a chef, not a cook. C'mon, I'll show you the way."

They followed her out, barely keeping track of her stream of chatter. Boys, her junior prom a few weeks earlier, more boys, girlfriends, clothes . . . "Good Lord," Catherine whispered, "is she ever going to shut up?"

"At least she's friendly," Grace whispered back. She was grateful for a friendly face, grateful, too, for the distracting monologue. She'd been feeling uneasy for the last half hour, waiting to meet her aunt and imagining how horrible it was going to be. All indications hinted that Sophia had not gotten softer with age.

Lali led them through a plush, pale Louis Quatorze living room and pushed open a French door. "Ta-da! The terrace. And tea. Ooh, and Declan. Hi, Declan!" she called out the door. They heard the murmur of a response. "He's so cute," Lali said sotto voce to Grace and Cat, and sighed. "He's way too old for me, but a girl can dream, can't she? Can you imagine what it would be like to have him be your *first*?" Lali widened her eyes at them. "Can you?"

"I'm trying not to," Grace said, as visions of a naked Declan rose in her mind.

"At least you're closer to the right age for him. He calls *me* 'jail bait.'" Lali grinned, then giggled. "*Jail bait*. See ya later, 'gators!"

"While, crocodile," Grace called after her.

Catherine stared at Grace.

"What?"

"Do not regress to that age. I don't want to pick you up at the end of the summer and hear you punctuating your sentences with 'like.'"

"Like, why would I do that?"

"Like, hell if I know. Hell if I know why anyone would want that sleazeball Declan to touch them, either."

"We don't know for sure that he's a sleazeball." They'd spent half their time in the bedroom discussing the possibility. Financial planners had a lousy reputation since the market crash.

"That type *always* is." Catherine tilted her head, examining Grace. "You're not attracted to him, are you?"

"God no!"

"He'd treat you like crap."

"Cat, I'm *not* attracted to him. He wouldn't be interested in someone like me anyway."

"Wouldn't he?" she asked cryptically.

Grace ignored her and stepped out into a world of sunlight and blue sky. The terra-cotta terrace ended thirty feet in front of her at a stone balustrade, beyond which the earth appeared to fall away into endless blue. To her right were broad stairs leading down into gardens. To her left a wooden pergola covered the terrace, sheer linen panels draped over its roof and down its posts. In the filtered shade beneath were a long table and several iron chairs strewn with flowered cushions. Declan O'Brien sprawled in one of them, while a tall, slender young man with light brown hair held a chair out for Sophia as she sat.

"Thank you, Andrew," Sophia said. "I could wish that your gesture was inspired more by chivalry than by a conviction of my frailty, but it is appreciated nonetheless."

"It will take more than osteoarthritis to make me ever think you're frail."

"Shh! Please don't use that word to me. 'Arthritis.'" She shuddered elegantly. "It's an old person's disease."

"Miss Cavanaugh!" Declan said, standing. "What a pleasure to see you again. And Miss Ruggieri."

All eyes turned to them, but it was Sophia's face that Grace watched. The hair was the same as she'd remembered, still pure white, still parted on the side and falling in neat waves to her shoulders, now topped by a wide-brimmed, light green straw hat. Her pale skin was creased with age but her fine bone structure turned the wrinkles into flourishes for high cheekbones and a graceful brow. She wore blush and lipstick in a delicate rose pink, but had been more generous with the dark mascara and eyeliner, emphasizing eyes that were the same clear green as Grace's own, albeit faded.

Sophia drew in a breath and placed her long-fingered hand to her heart, over a string of pearls and the floaty neckline of a retro silk tea gown that wouldn't have been out of place at a garden party at Windsor Castle. "And there you are, child, all grown up. Come closer, darling, and let me look at you." She held out her hand.

Grace came forward and took it, wary. "It's very good to see you again, Aunt Sophia. Thank you so much for asking me to spend the summer with you."

Sophia didn't seem to hear her, her green eyes looking Grace up and down, then resting on Grace's hair. Sophia touched a strand of it, then put her fingertips to her own lips. Tears filmed her eyes. "Just look at you. Such a beautiful face, such glorious hair."

Grace shifted, unbalanced by the unexpected compliments and sentimental tears. Maybe Sophia *was* suffering some dementia. This was not the woman she remembered. "Um, thank you."

Sophia released her hand and waved her away. "Don't mind

me," she said. "My evil doctor has been giving me steroids, and they make me overemotional."

The light-haired man made a noise.

Sophia nodded toward Catherine. "I see you've brought a friend?"

Introductions were made all round, and the tall young man was revealed as Dr. Andrew Pritchard. Lali appeared with a wheeled cart, and they made small talk about the drive from Seattle as the tea and cakes and sandwiches were served. Declan was given the equipment for a whiskey and water on ice, and served himself while the others took cookies and strawberries.

"How long are you staying in town, Grace?" Andrew asked.

"All summer. I'm here to help Aunt Sophia while she has her hip—er," Grace cut herself off, remembering Sophia's dislike of anything that made her sound old, and a hip replacement said nothing but "old." "To help her with any, er . . . procedures she may undergo and need to recover from."

Sophia laughed. "She makes it sound like I'm having liposuction. Perhaps that's what I shall tell everyone. There's less shame in a bit of fat removal than a complete replacement of failed body parts."

Grace didn't think anyone would believe it. Sophia was blade thin, with barely enough fat to keep her from looking skeletal.

"I suppose I should have told you that I'd invited her, Andrew, but I didn't want to see you feeling smug. Her presence is an admission that I have to have that damned surgery."

Grace caught Andrew looking at her. He dropped his eyes and poked his fork at a wedge of melon. "The sooner you do it, the easier your recovery will be."

"Yes, yes, I know. Do you hear him, Grace? That will be one of your first duties, keeping Andrew from treating me like a child who doesn't know well enough to take her hand out of the fire."

"Don't listen to her," Declan said. "She needs scolding. One might almost say she invites it."

"*He* will be your second duty," Sophia said. "He's worse than Andrew. I didn't reach this age by being obtuse about my own well-being."

The two men gazed with doting eyes upon Sophia, but Grace thought she had caught a thread of real annoyance in her aunt's tone. What she didn't know was whether the men's patronizing was justified, and Sophia's annoyance merely the petulance of a child who must be told no. "I promise to silence all *unnecessary* admonishments."

Sophia lifted an eyebrow, her eyes meeting Grace's with appreciation. "Carefully said, my dear."

The woman didn't miss a beat.

"I've met Grace only once before," Sophia said, addressing the men. "Although she is in part named after me. Grace Sophia, correct?"

Grace nodded, and felt Catherine looking at her. "I didn't know that," Catherine said, offense in her tone at not being privy to all the details of Grace's life.

Grace shrugged. Her maternal grandmother had suggested her middle name, even though Grace's mother had known little of Sophia beyond family tales of her independent—some said willfully rebellious—spirit.

Sophia went on, "She was a child then, and I had nearly forgotten about her when this past Christmas she sent me one of those strange personal newsletters people are so fond of composing these days."

Grace squirmed in her seat. That newsletter had been a whim, inspired by a bout of depression in the gray winter of Seattle, her usual optimism and academic energy lost beneath a blanket of clouds and loneliness. She'd wanted to connect with family, any family. Her mother had sent her a list of the addresses of relatives and family friends, and she'd sent the embarrassing missive to them all. It had been full of false cheer and tiresome personal anecdotes desperately embroidered to make her life sound more interesting than it was. She'd included a photo of herself on the observation deck of the Space Needle, wind blowing her hair against a backdrop of heavy clouds.

"Inviting her to Pebble Beach for the summer seemed a way to fulfill both our needs. Grace is getting her Ph.D. in—what was it, dear?"

Grace's shoulders slumped, dreading what was to come. No male reacted well to mention of her field, and mentioning it all but guaranteed a nasty discussion of its faults and dubious merits. "Women's Studies," she said, and she felt the shift in atmosphere immediately. Andrew's expression turned uncertain, while the line of Declan's lips betrayed distaste. He took a sip from his glass as if to clean "Women's Studies" from his mouth.

She knew what they were thinking: she must be either a lesbian or a ballbuster. In either case, no one worth pursuing romantically. She'd had five years of defending her choice to potential dating partners, and had learned to accept romantic defeat before she began. Even math majors got more action than she did. "I hope to get most of my dissertation written while I'm here."

"What's your thesis?" Declan asked, with the same tone used to ask if one knew what the mold-furred blob in the back of the fridge might be.

Grace squished a little lower into her chair. "The working title is 'The Belle of the Ball Cries Alone: How Beauty Brings Unhappy Endings in the Emotional Lives of Women.'"

Silence settled upon the tea party. A breeze soughed through the trees. A bird chirped and then flew away.

"Oh, dear," Sophia said faintly.

"Her work is brilliant," Catherine said, leaning forward and looking around the table. "Most of the beauty debate we hear about in the media is where the ideals come from: are they innate, or are they the product of advertising and the ubiquitous images of movie and pop stars? Do women improve their appearance for themselves, for men, or for other women?

"Gracie is taking a different slant, looking at the emotional result for women who, for whatever reason, are perceived as beautiful. And the results ain't pretty. Gracie is proving that to be beautiful is to invite misery into your life."

"What a perfectly depressing thought," Sophia said.

"Here, here," Declan agreed, raising his whiskey glass. "Give those miserable beauties to me, and don't you worry about them."

"That's exactly the type of statement that causes pain for women," Grace said, anger straightening her spine. "You don't give a damn about their inner lives, it's what you see that matters."

"He's not serious," Andrew said, looking embarrassed for the other man. "He's giving you a hard time."

"Like hell I am! Of course what a woman looks like matters. You're lying if you say anything else, Andrew. You're no more of a saint than the rest of us."

"I'll agree that there's an evolutionary bias toward beauty, but for most human males, in the end the conversation we have across the dinner table matters more to us than the view."

Declan turned sideways in his chair and leaned back as if trying to get a better view of the creature next to him. "What planet are you from?"

Andrew's soft gray eyes met Grace's and she told him across a platter of cucumber and salmon sandwiches, "If I can make my ideas the basis for a national discussion with young women," Grace said earnestly, "we might be able to save a whole generation of women from valuing themselves on appearance alone. If they can see that the beautiful girls are the ones with the most unhappiness in store for them, they can be better judges of the worth of beauty in their own lives. Right now, all they see is that women like Scarlett Johansson and Angelina Jolie get all the attention. They don't see the failed marriages and personal instability. They don't see the misery that their beauty has brought them."

"Grace, darling, you relieve my mind," Sophia said.

"Do I?" Grace asked, surprised.

"Yes, dear. I had thought you dressed the way you do from a lack of taste. I see now that your boxy T-shirt—with, what does it say? UN-DAM THE SALMON?—is an expression of your sexual politics, as are those unflattering capri pants and running shoes. You believe that if you were to make better use of the physical gifts God has granted you, you would be setting yourself up for unhappiness."

Grace blinked down at the salmon spread across her breasts. "But I like this shirt."

"Darling, no one can like that shirt. The last thing you should be encouraging a man to think of when he looks at you is the smell of fish."

Declan choked on his drink. Andrew turned scarlet. Grace gaped at her aunt.

"Grace is beautiful no matter what she wears!" Catherine said. She put her hand over Grace's.

"If you were any friend of hers and of her thesis, you wouldn't say such things," Sophia said gently. "Do you want her to have a miserable life?"

"I wish her every happiness! As would you, if you knew her."

"I do wish it for her, even without knowing her. Now, Catherine, what are you yourself studying?" Sophia asked, all innocent mildness.

Declan emptied his glass, ice cubes clinking. "Christ," he muttered, and nudged Andrew. "Want one?"

Andrew shook his head.

Grace wished Declan would ask her the same question.

"My area is power differentials in same-sex relationships," Catherine explained. "Specifically, how that manifests in domestic violence between women."

"Ah. Indeed. And I take it that you are, yourself, a lesbian?"

Grace went rigid and flashed a look at Sophia.

"Don't worry, Grace, I'm not going to fall over in shock. Homosexuality is nothing new."

"No, it's not," Catherine said. "And yes, I am a lesbian."

"So what was it that turned you into one?"

Grace whimpered. Declan topped up his glass. Andrew looked longingly at the decanter, apparently having second thoughts.

"I beg your pardon?" Catherine asked.

"There was some trauma in your young life, no doubt. Some abuse at the hands of a male?"

"It's very kind of you to be interested, Aunt Sophia," Grace broke in, trying to deflect her. "Cat has done a lot of work with women's shelters, both in Seattle and her hometown of San Diego. I think she—"

"Did your father beat your mother? Did a cousin rape you? I haven't yet met a lesbian who didn't have a trauma in her past."

"Sophia," Declan warned.

"I can answer for myself," Catherine barked, and Grace could feel the anger vibrating off her. "Shall I educate you, ma'am, on the origins of homosexuality?"

"By all means," Sophia said, and wove her fingers together

into a bridge, resting her chin upon them like a child prepared to hear a bedtime story.

"People are born homosexual. Events do not turn them, no more than any amount of preaching can turn a gay person straight. It's as natural as the grass and the trees, and is found in all of nature. Even some animals are gay, and you can't pretend that trauma turned them so."

"So a straight person cannot be turned gay?"

"Of course not."

"Then why, my dear, did you try to sleep with my niece?"

Andrew dropped his cup. Declan hit his knee on the underside of the table, making the dishes jump. Cat gasped and turned furious eyes on Grace.

"I never said a word to anyone! I swear it! Sophia took a shot in the dark."

Catherine snarled. "This is why you don't want to spend the summer with me, isn't it? You're afraid I'll make another pass at you. Or were you afraid that you might give in and enjoy it this time?"

Grace said nothing, unable to deny it. She *had* been looking forward to being away from Catherine for a few months.

"There's no need to blame Grace for spilling your secret," Sophia said. "It was clear for anyone with eyes to see. You're in love with her, but she won't have you."

Catherine's lower lip began to tremble.

"Don't blame yourself," Sophia soothed. "Grace *is* beautiful. She can't help it if the thought of touching you makes her stomach turn."

"What do you know of love, you sadistic old bitch?" Catherine spit. "I don't see anyone here who loves *you*!" Catherine shoved back her chair and ran for the house, her sobs carrying on the breeze.

"Cat!" Grace called, shoving back her own chair.

"Don't bother, darling. She'll be fine. You'll only encourage her if you chase after her. It's what she wants."

Grace shook her head. "You deliberately humiliated her."

"She humiliated herself by mooning over someone who had rejected her. She'll be better off for facing the truth." Sophia took a sip of tea. "Don't go after her."

"No matter what she feels, she's my *friend*." Grace turned on her heel and followed Catherine.

CHAPTER
3

Declan felt Sophia's grip on his arm tighten and knew she was in pain. "This is far enough, isn't it? Shall we go back inside?"

"No. Andrew said to walk as much as I could bear, and I can bear this. Besides, I've always loved the gardens at twilight. It's enough to make me forget a twinge of discomfort now and then."

Declan knew it was more than a twinge. Andrew had shot steroids and lubricants directly into Sophia's hip socket today in hopes of alleviating some of her pain. The more she moved, the better off she'd be, but Declan had a hard time watching the ripples of pain under the mask of placidity she wore on her stunning face. He looked instead to the sunset, glowing orange through the black silhouettes of trees. The cool garden paths wound across a private rocky headland of three acres, a piece of land that was now worth tens of millions but that Sophia had sworn she'd never sell.

And why would she? Only a fool would sell a heaven on earth.

"I'm trying to figure out why you treated your grand-niece and her friend so badly," he said when they'd walked a bit farther. "Grace will probably leave in the morning, if she hasn't already."

"What have you decided my motives were?"

"I'm not sure I should say. None of them are flattering."

"Then I'm sure they're all wrong. Come, tell me what nefarious purpose I had in mind."

He sighed. "At first I thought you were chasing her away because if she left, in your mind it meant you wouldn't have to have the surgery."

"That would have been both illogical and cowardly."

"I know. So I moved on. I decided you were striking back for what you took to be an attack on yourself. Grace's thesis is a slap in the face for someone like you."

Sophia laughed. "Her thoughts on beauty are those of an insecure child. They say much more about her than they do about me. Besides, you know me better than to think I would sink to giving tit for tat."

"No, you're of the 'dish served cold' variety of vengeance takers."

"*Pshh*. I'm above it all."

Declan laughed at the blatant lie, and they walked on to a view at the edge of the cliff. A wooden staircase was bolted into the rock, twisting down several stories to a narrow strip of beach. A fisherman stood on one of the rocks at the water's edge, casting into the sea. It was probably Ernesto, Lali's grandfather. "Do you think he catches anything?" Declan asked.

"I don't think that's his goal; he's more Buddhist monk than Hemingway. Catching a fish would disrupt the Zen."

They watched Ernesto for several minutes, the motions of his rod as hypnotic in their regularity as the rolling of the waves. "Stubborn old bastard," Sophia murmured.

They turned away. "Grace looks like you," Declan said. "It's hard to see at first because of the weight, but it's there."

"I know."

"Is that what it was? Were you angry with her for looking like you and being so young?"

"I'm angry at her for looking like me and *wasting* it!" Sophia snapped, suddenly vehement. "Women's Studies! Good Lord, can you think of a more useless way to spend her time?"

"Yeah, but not a less appealing one. Would you rather she ran off to Hollywood to be an actress, like you did?"

"At least I was out in the world. I wasn't moldering in a library, trying to convince myself that anyone prettier than me was unhappy. What type of life philosophy is that? The girl is a coward."

"That's why you were so hard on her?"

"I had to see how deep it ran."

"What was your answer?"

Sophia smiled. "We'll see in the morning, won't we? But I'll bet you a bottle of Johnnie Walker Blue that she stays."

Declan thought about it for a minute. "I always lose my bets with you, but you're on."

They turned back toward the house, retracing their steps. It was dark now under the trees, small landscape lights along the path guiding their way. Strategically aimed uplights limned the branches of the older, wind-twisted cypresses. A glimpse of the house showed a warm orange rectangle of light spilling from the Garden Room, and the flicker of a shadow as someone passed in front of the window. So she hadn't left yet. Declan felt a moment of pleasure despite the threat to his Johnnie Walker Blue and his uneasiness with the situation.

He'd only ever heard Sophia make vague, disparaging remarks about her extended family, and he couldn't fathom why she had invited Grace to spend the summer. No other relatives had ever come to visit, and his impression had been that she preferred keeping it that way.

Nor had he ever seen her be so unpleasant upon first acquaintance.

It wasn't unusual for Sophia to take a young person under her wing—witness his own history with her—but he had the feeling that there was something different about her interest in Grace. Something unhealthy, even, and possibly harmful. Maybe those drugs Andrew was giving her were interfering with her thinking.

He couldn't trust his own take on the situation, though, given how much Grace's appearance unnerved him. It was disturbing to see the ghost of Sophia's features in a young, overripe woman who so obviously needed a good workout between the sheets. When he'd first met Grace on the stairs, he'd assessed her as "do-able," and in that moment when their eyes had met he'd known he could have her if he wanted. But she was Sophia's grand-niece, and even worse, she was getting a Ph.D. in Women's Studies. He'd downgraded her to "only if I was drunk," although the lesbian subtext with Catherine had briefly revived his interest.

"How is your love life?" Sophia asked, with uncanny timing. "Are you still dating the corporate attorney?"

"Her, and a few others."

"Anyone special?"

"One or two who want to be special, but no, no one serious."

"I'm beginning to worry, Declan. You're thirty-four. If you don't feel even the faintest urge to settle down . . ."

"Then what?"

"I hope you're not one of those men who has to come to it the hard way."

"Shotgun wedding? They don't do those anymore. It's all paternity suits and child-support payments."

She shook her head. "I hope you're not one of those who have to suffer a great personal loss before he can find the space in his heart to love a woman."

"I've been in love!"

"Not since you were twenty. It's not the same."

"But I love *you*. Surely that puts me in the safe zone?"

She patted his arm.

"You're serious, aren't you?" he asked.

"You're still young. I may be wrong."

"I'm not ready, that's all. I've got too much to do. I'm still building my firm, and there's the development project I'm trying to bring together . . ."

"You'll be down here a lot this summer, working on that project, won't you?"

"Ye-es . . . Why?"

"I don't want Grace to spend the next three months indoors, waiting on me or writing her ridiculous dissertation. I'd like you to take her out whenever you're down here."

"*Date* her?"

"Do you *want* to date her?"

"God no!"

"Then just take the girl out, Declan. Show her around. Take her kayaking or rollerblading or whatever it is young people do these days."

"Rollerblading?"

"Take her golfing. Anything. She doesn't know anyone here, and she doesn't strike me as the type of girl who's going to zip into Carmel and find herself a pack of friends to go do things with."

"I don't think she likes me. She may not want to spend any time with me, however innocent my intentions."

"She'll go," Sophia said.

Declan helped Sophia up the stairs to the terrace, feeling the weight she put on his arm. A cold trickle went through his heart as he remembered that she was eighty-five. Her vibrance usually made age irrelevant, but in this moment at the edge of night, he realized there was no guarantee she would make it through her surgery.

He felt a shot of hatred for Andrew Pritchard. Who was he to badger Sophia into a hip replacement? It could very well do more harm than good.

He took Sophia into her library, a small room with a large flat-screen TV square in the middle of a wall of books. A laptop and a phone sat on a small desk beside a well-worn velvet couch with mismatched pillows. The fireplace was surmounted by a life-size portrait of Sophia in her prime. Red hair fell in waves to her bare shoulders, and a dark green strapless gown hinted at abundant cleavage, while the waist nipped in, accentuated by a black belt with a diamond buckle. She was posed half lying on a recamier with a leopard skin tossed over it, and the invitation in her eyes said that she would either purr for a man or devour him; it was his choice.

Sophia eased down onto the sofa, then saw where he was looking. "A few pounds less and in the right clothes, it could have been Grace who sat for that."

"Her jaw's different, and the expression in her eyes would give her away."

"I suppose you're right. The posture, too."

"How much do you really know about your niece?" Declan asked, leaning against the mantel.

"What a suspicious question to ask! You make it sound like she's here to murder me and steal my riches. I don't suppose it will make you feel any better to hear that I know next to nothing about her, will it? Of course I plan to write up a new will and leave every earthly possession to her, and then tell her about it right before I put her in charge of my medications."

Declan scowled. "Very funny."

"Don't be an ass. She's as innocent as she looks. Her mother is one of those 'natural' women with underarm hair and a unibrow. I don't think much evil grows from composted ground."

"People are people, even the ones who act whole-wheatier than thou." A thought hit him. "Grace would be a good match for Andrew! She's got him half hooked already. Why not ask *him* to show her around instead of me?" The two would be a punishment for each other.

Sophia tapped her bottom lip with her fingertip, thinking. "He wouldn't be an easy fish to land. Almost as difficult as you, in his own way. He's the type who will nibble at the bait but never bite."

"And what do I do?"

"You steal the bait and swim away."

"You make me sound like a cheat."

"Perhaps no one's had the right bait to make you forget the hook."

Declan looked again at the painting. Since he'd met Sophia, he'd compared every woman he dated against his imaginary vision of what she'd been as a young woman. From the age of eighteen, he'd been looking for someone with the beauty, intelligence, and raw sexuality of that imagined Sophia.

He tried to imagine Grace in Sophia's place in the portrait, sitting awkwardly upon the leopard skin, her brow wrinkled in worry as she pulled up her bodice to cover more skin. That puritan Dr. Andrew would probably like her self-consciousness. It would give the weasel courage.

Declan was suddenly sorry that he'd made the suggestion to throw the two together. He could see it: self-righteous Grace married to puritanical Andrew, Sophia dying, and all her assets ending up in the hands of two life haters who were the complete opposite of everything Sophia had ever stood for.

Declan had no interest in Sophia's money for himself—frankly, he hoped she'd take care of her household staff and then leave the rest to charity—but he didn't want Andrew to get his lily-white paws on it. The young doctor's air of benevolent omniscience had always annoyed him, like a rough tag in the back of a pair of jockey shorts. He thought Andrew would have made a better priest than doctor.

"I've been worrying about Andrew finding a woman almost as much as I have been about you," Sophia said.

"Admit it, you think he's gay."

Sophia rolled her eyes. "He's not *gay*. And even if he was, I'd still be worried that he didn't have a partner."

"It's not a mystery as to why he's alone. The guy's a downer."

Sophia shook her head. "He's shy and introverted, and he takes both life and his work much too seriously. If I handle them correctly, I think Grace could be engaged to Andrew by the end of the summer."

"Why would you want that?" Declan asked, appalled.

"For their mutual happiness, of course."

"I don't think their sort can *be* happy."

"What nonsense. Love makes everyone glow. It would bring joy into both their lives."

"Well, I wish you luck," Declan said.

"It's not luck I'll need, it's your help."

"Mine?"

"I know there are competitive feelings between you and Andrew. I won't ask him to show Grace around; that duty will remain yours, and I want you to make a good show of it. It will make him jealous, and prompt him to act where he would otherwise dither. He *is* attracted to her, that much is obvious."

"If we're so competitive, maybe I'll try to keep Grace for myself to prove I'm the better man."

Sophia's eyes narrowed. "Don't play with my niece's heart, Declan, and don't touch her. She might believe you care. We both know that isn't possible."

The words hurt. Sophia seemed to think he wasn't even *capable* of loving a woman. "Isn't there a danger Grace is going to think I'm attracted to her if I keep taking her out?" he asked.

"Be your worst self with her, as sexist and womanizing as your dark side desires. Your type is anathema to hers."

He felt insulted, even as he recognized the truth of her words. Somehow it seemed fair that he should find Grace's personality type repulsive, but not vice versa. He suddenly wondered if Sophia thought he wasn't good enough for her niece. "Dr. Andrew hasn't had a girlfriend in all the time I've known him," he said flatly, changing tack. He was increasingly feeling that he didn't want Sophia's plot to succeed. "Your plan isn't going to work, no matter how jealous I make him."

"Care to put another bottle of Blue behind that attitude? I say that they will be engaged by the end of August."

Declan laughed. "There's no way in hell that's going to happen. Yeah, I'll take that bet. It'll be a chance to win back the bottle I'm going to lose tomorrow morning."

Sophia laid her hands gracefully in her lap and smiled sweetly up at him. "Or not."

CHAPTER
ε 4 з

Grace took a sip of chamomile tea and grimaced. Did Catherine really like this stuff? She shrugged and fished the tea bags out of the mugs she'd prepared and carried the cups out of the quiet kitchen, shutting off the lights as she went. It was almost midnight, and the household had retired for the night. She'd been cooped up with Catherine since teatime, the only relief coming when Lali brought them a dinner tray.

Catherine had refused to eat any of it. "I'm too upset," she'd said. "I've lost my appetite. But *you* go ahead if you're hungry." As if being hungry meant Grace was heartless.

"You know I'm a stress eater," Grace had pleaded, staring at the gnocchi in brown butter sauce with spinach and bacon *lardons*. She usually tried to eat vegetarian, but bacon was her tempter in the desert. It was just so savory and salty and *good*. There hadn't been consolation in the meal, though, with Cat lying on the bed, facing away from her, her shoulders tight, the room silent.

It had been a long evening of consolation and argument, Catherine's dramatic distress pushing Grace further and further away until she felt like an actor pretending to care. At this moment, it was beyond her how women could stand to fall in love with each other.

She didn't know how men put up with them, either. Really, why would any guy bother? Was the sex really worth it?

She felt guilty sometimes for feeling a kinship with men who complained that women talked too much about their feelings. There were times she wanted to yell, "Just get *over* it, for criminy's sake! Let it go!"

Cat had been drowsing when she left the room; maybe she'd fallen asleep by now. Grace dawdled in the dark entrance hall, the moon lighting the space in shades of gray. The solitude and emptiness were a relief. She didn't want to go back to her room, where the air was fuggy with emotions.

She set the mugs on the bottom step of the staircase and wandered into the living room, her feet feeling the cool marble of the hall change to warm, polished wood, and then the soft, rich pile of an Oriental carpet. The shadows were darker in here, the furniture black silhouettes against the moonlight coming through the French doors to the terrace. She saw the outline of a grand piano and walked over to it, sliding onto the hard bench. The keys gleamed dimly in front of her. She curled her toes over the cold metal of the dampening pedal and softly picked out the notes to Beethoven's *Moonlight Sonata*.

She wished that Cat had just dropped her off today and left. Aunt Sophia might still have gone on the attack, but Grace would have weathered it without making a scene. And if tea had continued, she would have had more time to talk to the adorable Dr. Andrew.

She sighed. Now *that* was the type of man she'd been hoping to meet for years. Educated, caring, so cute she could eat him, and he'd seemed to understand where she was coming from. *That* was the type of man who would emotionally support her and her goals.

Not like Declan, who would undermine them with his obtuse incomprehension. She abandoned romantic Beethoven and
dove into the lugubrious violence of Rachmaninov's Prelude in
C-sharp Minor. Declan obviously had no respect for women, or
interest in their thoughts. He'd probably marry someone with
implants and a Botox addiction.

He was everything stereotypically male: misogynistic, arrogant,
and so sexually attractive that it was embarrassing to look at him.
She almost felt embarrassed *for* him; men weren't supposed to
attract that much attention for their looks. It made her strangely
queasy, like seeing male models posing for underwear ads.

She'd read research about what women found attractive in a
male face, and it had turned out they liked two types, for different
reasons: a macho male face with a square jaw and heavy eyebrows
for sex, but a man with softer, more androgynous features to
marry and raise children with.

She congratulated herself on being evolved enough never
to have fallen for the jock/asshole type of guy. The thought of
letting some inconsiderate jerk invade the most intimate places
of her body, no matter how good-looking he was, had always
made her cringe. The nice guys were undoubtedly better lovers,
anyway.

Although, hadn't there been another study saying that women
had more orgasms with the sexier-looking men?

It had been a flawed study, obviously. Andrew would be a far
more generous, perceptive lover than smug, arrogant Declan. Andrew might be her Mr. Right. When you found the right guy you
knew it immediately, didn't you? That's what everyone who'd had
true love said; you just *knew*.

Her fingers moved to a new position on the keyboard, and she
sang along in a whisper:

Another bride, another June
Another sunny honeymoon
Another season, another reason
For makin' whoopee

A throaty male laugh rose from the darkness. Grace shrieked, her fingers crashing on the keys.

A dark shadow moved on the sofa. "Don't worry. I'm not going to ravish you, no matter how hard you plead."

Grace's heart thumped to life again. "D-Declan?"

"Keep playing. I can't wait to hear the verse about the pussy-whipped groom sewing and washing baby clothes." He sang in a deep baritone that sent shivers over her skin:

But don't forget, folks, that's what you get, folks
For makin' whoopee

Grace crossed her arms protectively in front of her, feeling naked in her pajamas, her breasts unfettered beneath the thin, well-washed T-shirt. "I wouldn't have guessed that you'd know the words to a song from the 1920s."

"I wouldn't have guessed your hands could elicit such passion," he said, and paused. "From a piano. Were you thinking of me while you played the Rachmaninov?"

Grace spluttered. "Not in a positive way!"

The shadow laughed. "Good or bad doesn't matter, only the strength of your feelings."

"Are you drunk?"

"Maybe."

She slid off the bench and started toward the door. "I'll leave you to sleep it off, then."

"Coward."

"I'm not a coward for not wanting to hang around with a drunk chauvinist pig."

"Sure you are."

She laughed. "You don't object to being called a chauvinist pig?"

"Your opinion doesn't come as a surprise. And I still think you're a coward. Think of all the information you could pry out of me while I'm in this vulnerable state."

"There's nothing I want to know."

"I'm insulted! And wounded. Severely." She heard him pat the cushion next to him. "Come sit down and make me feel better."

"Oh, please."

"Aren't you at all curious as to why I've spent the evening passed out in your aunt's living room?"

She was, a little. She wavered. "Why do you want to talk to me?"

He was silent for a long moment. "I don't know."

If he'd said anything else, she might have left. Instead, she moved toward an easy chair. As she passed by him, his hand shot out and grasped her wrist. He tugged and, caught by surprise, she dropped onto the couch next to him. "Hey!" she protested, scrambling away from him.

Something soft hit her and she squeaked.

"Have a pillow," he said.

She clutched the throw pillow to her chest, but he made no further move to touch her. She could make out only the barest hint of his features, and he didn't seem to be looking at her. Reassured, she drew her knees up and leaned against the arm of the couch, watching him. Her bare toes were only a few inches from where his hand rested on the cushion, and she was careful not to let them touch. "Do you often spend the night on Aunt Sophia's couch?"

"No, never. It's surprisingly comfortable, though. I probably would have slept till morning if you hadn't woken me. Has your friend been trying to persuade you that it would be a mistake to stay here?"

"Yes."

"Are you going to listen to her?"

"No."

"You should," he said.

"Why?"

"You're not too bright if you have to ask that."

"Sophia doesn't scare me."

"Liar, liar, pants on fire."

"How can you know?" Grace demanded.

"Because she scares *everyone*."

"Even you?"

"Yes."

"It's not very manly of you to admit it."

He laughed. "I don't need to prove my manhood to you."

Grace chewed her lip. She got the feeling that Declan thought she was immature. Naive, even. "You said you were both her financial adviser and her friend. You don't sound like a friend."

"'Friend' probably wasn't the most accurate choice of words."

Grace drew in a breath. "You're not her . . ."

"Her . . . ?"

"Her, *you know*," she whispered.

A laugh burst out of him. "Her boy toy? No, Grace, I'm not a gigolo."

"Oh."

"You sound disappointed."

She squirmed, feeling like a twelve-year-old talking to a dissipated adult. "Well, if you're not her friend, then what are you?"

"I think 'surrogate son' might be closer to what I meant."

She had trouble imagining it. Neither seemed to have enough love in them to spare any for other people. "But you're afraid of her?"

"What son isn't afraid of his mother?"

"Most, I should hope! My brother isn't afraid of our mom."

"You wouldn't know."

"There's nothing for him to be afraid of. She loves him with all her heart."

"Exactly!"

"Exactly *what*?" she asked, bewildered.

"Maternal love is a ferocious thing. It devours men whole and spits them out without their balls."

"You *are* drunk. It's nurturing and supportive, and if that's not what you get from Sophia, then that's about you and her, and not about maternal love. And if it's so horrible, why would you stay with her?"

"Masochism. Addiction."

She rolled her eyes. "I didn't figure you for a drama queen."

"If you stay here, you'll get sucked in, too," he said.

"You make Sophia sound like a mob boss."

"It's not a bad simile."

The conversation flagged and they were both quiet. Grace remembered Catherine waiting for the chamomile tea, and hoped she'd fallen asleep. Surely Cat would have come looking for her by now if she was still awake. She would be shocked to find Grace sitting with Declan in the dark.

Why *was* she sitting here with him?

It was the late hour and the quiet of the house, she decided, and the concealing darkness. He was less threatening when she couldn't see him. She was reminded, though, of her first boyfriend and the evening they'd spent together on the couch in the basement of his parents' house, watching movies. They'd started the evening with a foot of empty space between them, Grace achingly aware of every slight movement he made toward her, every "accidental" placement of hand or leg, every shift of body. It had taken one and a half movies for their hands to meet and then entwine, the two of them sitting with eyes glued to the screen, pretending that their hearts weren't beating in their throats.

Declan shifted, his hand bumping her toes. She pulled her foot back, but his hand followed, his warm, rough palm sliding up over the top of her foot to grasp her ankle.

An electric thrill shot up her leg. "What are you doing?" she squeaked.

He pulled her foot into his lap. "I dated a massage therapist for a while."

"So?" She tugged at her foot, but he wouldn't release her. His thumb found the tender skin beneath her arch and started to rub in slow, delicious circles, sending a tingle of pleasure directly up her leg. She squirmed in embarrassment and feebly tugged again at her foot. Somehow, he'd hit upon a spot that was creating echoes of sensation in a decidedly less innocent body part than the sole of her foot. "You have a foot fetish or something?" she asked, trying to hide her embarrassing reaction.

He chuckled, the sound rumbling over her in the darkness. "The massage therapist was a big believer in reflexology. Do you know what that is?"

Grace murmured a negative sound, unable to speak further. His touch felt so very good, and if she closed her eyes she could forget who was creating such divine sensations. She sank down against the arm of the couch, glad of the darkness and determined not to let him know how very good his touch felt.

"Reflexologists believe that areas on the feet and hands correspond to other parts of the body. So if I massage a specific spot on your foot, you can feel it elsewhere."

She opened her eyes in alarm.

"It's mostly nonsense, of course," he said, stroking the spot on her foot with exquisite tenderness.

"Of course," she echoed weakly.

"You don't feel this anywhere else, do you?"

"Like where?" she squeaked.

"Oh . . . your spleen. Your small intestine. Maybe even . . . your pituitary gland."

She chortled in relief. "No."

"Good. I wouldn't want you to think I had intentions on your pituitary gland."

She stared at him in the dark. *Did* he know what he was doing to her?

He found her other foot and brought it to join the first in his lap, both his thumbs working on that spot in slow, short strokes. Her eyelids fluttered, her eyes rolling back in her head. *Oh God, it feels so good. . . .* It really *had* been too long since she'd been touched by a man.

She felt a moan of pleasure start in the back of her throat and swallowed it. But those strong thumbs, stroking her just there. . . . *Distraction! I need distraction!* "You never answered why you're sleeping on the couch," Grace said hoarsely. "Don't you have a home to go to?"

"In San Francisco. Surely you don't think I should drive there in my present condition?"

"How drunk are you?" She couldn't smell anything on him.

"Enough to sit here with you."

She couldn't claim the same excuse. "How did you meet Sophia?"

"I have football to thank for that."

"Did you meet at a game?" It was hard to picture Sophia in the stands, face painted in team colors, yelling whatever people yelled at football games.

"No. She was friends with one of my football coaches at USC. She used to have a house in Beverly Hills, and when she needed a couple of young, strong, good-looking guys, she called Coach Griggs."

"Needed good-looking guys for what? Her harem?"

"Your mind sure runs easily to sex." He slid his palm up her calf, inside the leg of her pajama bottoms, and gently played his fingertips against the delicate skin at the back of her knee. He was turned sideways toward her, his dark shadow hovering over her. "I may have to take another look at what goes on in Women's Studies programs."

"What are you doing?" Grace breathed, hyperaware that she wore no underpants and that there was no obstacle, however flimsy, on the path between his hand and . . . everything else.

"This is supposed to be good for your, uh, liver," he said, fingers stroking with hypnotic regularity on the tender, soft skin behind her knee.

"You're making that up."

"Does it feel bad?" he asked. "For your liver, that is."

"N-n-noo . . ."

"Waiting tables."

"What?"

"That's what Sophia would hire us for. She threw lots of parties and was on committees for various fund-raisers, and she liked to hire us to serve. She said she preferred our brutish self-obsession to the arty-farty self-obsession of unemployed actors."

"How kind of her." She felt him shove up the other leg of her pajamas and stroke her from ankle to knee. She supposed she should stop him, but it was harmless, wasn't it?

"It *was* kind of her. It didn't take long to figure out that Coach Griggs must have given her a list of the guys who were broke. Like the other guys she hired, I had a full-ride football scholarship, but nothing else. Sophia paid us each a couple hundred bucks for a few hours' work, and let us take home as many leftovers as we could carry. We *loved* her for that. Do you have any idea how much a twenty-year-old football player eats? We'd carry off plastic grocery bags sagging with beef tenderloin. Shrimp. Enough cheese and cured meats to make sandwiches for a month." His fingers slowed on her skin as he lost himself in re-membrance. "I can still taste that beef, dumped straight out of the catering pans and into a plastic grocery bag, dribbling juices out of a hole in the bottom all the way home. Blue-red in the middle, rare enough to moo . . ."

"I'm a vegetarian."

He laughed softly. "I guessed you would be."

"What's that supposed to mean?"

"You have 'self-righteous choices' written all over you."

"I am *not* self-righteous," she said, and tried to jerk her legs away from him.

He wrapped his arm round her knees and pulled, dragging her toward him until her butt bumped up against his thigh and her head thumped flat on the cushion of the sofa. "*Shhhh . . .*," he said.

"I will *not* shush! What are you doing?" She felt warm, moist pressure through the thin cotton covering her knees.

"Calming you down."

"Are you *kissing* me?"

"My dear, if you think this is kissing, you have been sadly de-prived of experience." He slid down between her and the back of the couch so that he lay on his side, propped up on one elbow, his body pressed alongside hers. His other arm was across her waist, his heavy hand lying on top of her outside arm and the edge of one breast, gently trapping her.

Flat on her back as she was, he seemed immensely large above her. The warmth and firmness of his body, and the weight of his arm sent a delicious weakness through her. Every breath was filled with his male scent, and she wanted to drown in it. She wanted to be a nameless woman in the dark, giving in to the temptations his body offered. It would feel *so* good. Her heart thumped at the thought of impulsively giving in and doing it, but at the same time a familiar part of herself said, *Get off me, I know you don't like me, I know you're laughing at me.*

"I should go back to my room," she said weakly. "Cat's waiting for her tea."

He stroked the hair back from her face, then traced the shape of her lips with a feather-light touch. He laid his finger against her lips, as if to quiet her. Her eyes had adjusted to the dark and she could see the shape of his features, and the gleam of moonlight in his eyes. He wasn't smiling, or laughing.

You're drunk and horny, and will make fun of me tomorrow, she thought. And yet his finger on her lip held her captive, and made her want to know where it would move next. No guy had ever taken the lead in such an overtly sexual way with her, and she was mesmerized by it.

One of his legs came over hers, nudging its way between them, and he leaned his weight against her, half covering her. She felt his arousal against her hip, and her body seemed to swell and soften in response.

I need to be touched—it's been so long. Just touch me, touch me, please touch me. . . .

His hand trailed down her chin, then to the hollow at the base of her throat. He stroked his fingertips over her collarbone and sternum, stretching the neck of her T-shirt to reach her skin. He pressed his palm flat over her chest, outside her shirt, his hand so wide that he covered part of each breast, then ran his hand down her belly. It came to rest at the gap between her shirt and pajama bottoms, his thumb stroking her bare skin. She felt a flicker of embarrassment about her too-soft belly, but he showed no sign of having noticed.

"How long has it been since you were kissed?" he asked.

"I don't know . . . at least a year, but it was only Cat." The truth spilled out of her of its own volition, a secret she'd revealed to no one until today. He knew about it anyway, so what did it matter what more she said? "She hoped I might be bi, and persuaded me to let her try to find out."

He groaned, pressing himself hard against her. "What did she do?"

Grace saw the scene again, watching it as if she were outside her own body. "She had me take my shirt off."

Declan dropped his face to the crook of her neck, where she could feel his breath. "And then?" His hand moved up under her shirt.

Grace knew the story about her and Cat was turning him on, even as she was puzzled that it would do so; what *was* it with guys and girl-on-girl action? It felt so good to be touched, though, and nothing seemed to matter here in the dark. . . . "Then she unfastened my bra, and had me lie down on her bed. Before I knew what was happening, she kissed me."

"Christ," Declan muttered, and lifted his head to crush his own mouth to hers.

Grace let him, parting her lips when his tongue sought entrance and delved within. He sucked against her, his tongue rubbing hard against her own. His hand slid up toward her breast and she clutched his shoulder with her one free hand, not knowing if she would make him stop or urge him to continue.

A crash of crockery shattered the moment, jolting Grace out of her sexual haze. Cat's voice let loose with a string of curses, and Grace remembered the mugs she'd left on the bottom step of the staircase.

Panic flooded her. She couldn't be found like this! She struggled to get out from under Declan, but he weighed her down, his hand still up her top.

"Let me go!" Grace whispered.

"Grace?" Cat called softly into the darkness. It sounded like she was standing in the doorway to the living room, not ten feet away. "Are you in here?"

Grace froze, not daring to breathe.

Declan's fingers pinched her nipple. She stared, wide-eyed, at him and caught the gleam of light on his grin.

"Grace?" Cat called again.

A lamp clicked on. In its amber glow, Catherine gaped at her.

Frantic in the light of discovery, Grace struggled against Declan and was released, his hand withdrawing from her shirt. Hot with embarrassment, she rolled off the couch and onto the floor on all fours and scrambled to her feet, pulling down her T-shirt.

"God *damn* you," Catherine cursed, glaring at Declan.

"I'm astonished you didn't get further with Grace," Declan said to her, sitting up. "Look how far she was willing to go with me, a stranger she despises."

Grace glared at him, too aghast to speak. Her worst doubts about him were proving true, even as her body still tingled with his touch.

"I was curious how far she'd go," he said, his eyes on Catherine. "I didn't think she'd let me touch so much as her foot, but she *is* full of surprises. A minute or two more, and you'd have seen her getting what she so obviously wants."

The hard words hit Grace in the gut. "I *don't* want that!"

Catherine shot a bitter look at her. "Don't lie to me!"

Her breath caught on a sob of humiliation. She *had* wanted it while Declan's hands were on her and his mouth against hers. She'd wanted it with every cell of her body.

"Good thing she'll be here all summer," Declan said. "We'll have plenty of time to scratch that itch."

Catherine pivoted on her heel and marched from the room. Grace stared after her, then turned to face Declan angrily. *"Why?"*

"Because you let me. Your type always does."

"*My* type?"

"Dumpy women protesting that they don't want to be sexual objects. What you really want is a man with the balls to bend you over a desk and fuck you till you can't see straight. All your feminist crap is a shield you hide behind because you know no guy is ever going to want you enough to do it."

She shook her head, stunned by his blatant chauvinism. "You're wrong. It's not about sex. It's about respect, it's about—"

"Everything's about sex. Grow up and smell the pheromones, Grace. Sexual acceptance and rejection; it's what makes the world go round."

"Not my world."

"Then you're living in fantasyland. Have fun there, alone with your vibrator."

She choked on a sob and fled.

CHAPTER

ℰ 5 ℨ

Grace shivered in the misty air of dawn, her bathrobe inadequate against the chill. The maroon Jaguar and the other cars were all gone, and she wondered which had belonged to whom. The Volvo looked like a piece of forgotten rubbish in the empty courtyard.

Catherine loaded the last of her things into the back of the car and slammed the hatch. "You're crazy to stay," she said. "You know that, don't you? You'll need years of therapy to undo the damage that bitch and that prick are going to do to you."

"He lives in San Francisco. I'm sure he'll hardly ever be here." To Grace's surprise, Catherine hadn't dissolved into more tears and fits of accusatory anger when Grace returned to her room last night. Declan's humiliation of her seemed to have satisfied Cat. Grace had been punished for her sin. Catherine was content with her suffering and happy to take on the role of wise consoler of sorrows.

"That still leaves Sophia to deal with," Catherine said.

"I'm a big girl. I can handle her."

"Not from what I saw. There's a time for retreat, Gracie, and better to do it now and save yourself the wounds. The woman has nearly a century of evil she can work on you; I don't care how smart you are, you're no match."

"I don't need to be her match. I'm going to study her!"

Catherine shook her head. "She'll devour you."

The words were an eerie echo of Declan's. "Yeah, Sophia's warped and horrible," Grace admitted, "but think what it will mean to my thesis to spend the summer here." The idea had come to her in the shower a few hours earlier, as she tried to wash away the humiliation of Declan's touch and figure out why she'd been such an easy target. When she was hurt, intellectual analysis both distracted her and made her feel less vulnerable. Her analysis of the situation on the couch came to the highly scientific conclusion that she was horny and Declan was an insecure asshole who had to prove himself by conquering women. It was biology that had made her give in to him; his square jaw and symmetrical features had undone the primitive areas of her brain, making her want him.

After she'd figured that out, she'd then wondered about Declan and Sophia's relationship, and thus the idea of studying Sophia was born.

"Talk about beauty meeting an unhappily ever after," Grace continued. "Sophia's story can be the centerpiece of my paper. She's an example of every idea I've been developing for the past five years. Where's her happy ending? She's old and surrounded by nasty people, and so bitter she practically creaks with it. She's perfect!"

"She's Satan. Gracie, promise me that the moment you feel you can't handle it here anymore, you'll call me. I'll come get you. You can spend the rest of the summer with me in San Diego, no strings attached."

"Thanks, Cat, but I'll be fine." Just as she was pretending to be fine now, pretending not to be cringing inside at every memory of Declan's hands on her, and her eager, stupid belief that he was turned on by her. He'd probably been retching inside as he stroked her flabby belly.

"Promise me anyway."

Grace sighed. "Okay, I promise. Now get going, so I can go back inside. I'm cold!"

They hugged, Catherine's arms too tight, holding too much unspoken meaning. Grace kissed her cheek and patted her back. "Go on, now."

Catherine released her and opened the car door. "Remember, I'm just a phone call or text away."

"I'll remember." Feeling a stab of guilt for her own cold heart, which wasn't sorry to see Catherine go, she gave Catherine one more hug. "You're a good friend."

Catherine sniffled and looked even sadder. The car door shut and the Volvo coughed to life. Grace waited on the front step, waving until Catherine drove away between the two stone pillars.

Grace took a deep breath and shook her arms and shoulders as if she could shake off the bad juju of the past twenty-four hours.

It's a new day. I can start over. Declan won't ever tell Sophia what he did to me, not if he cares about her good opinion. No one ever has to know.

No one but herself, and it was knowledge she could face only when she dwelled on what a completely screwed-up asshole Declan had to be to prey on her trusting stupidity.

He wasn't here now, though, and she could avoid him if he ever came to Pebble Beach again. Her native optimism bubbled slowly back to the surface, and with a growing sense of new beginnings, she stepped back into the house and closed the door.

Humming to herself, she bounced into the kitchen and

opened the refrigerator. Lali had told her last night to make herself at home in the kitchen, since her mother, Renata, didn't do breakfast.

"A morning person, are you?"

Grace shrieked and dropped a container of yogurt, its white innards splattering on the terra-cotta floor. "Aunt Sophia! I didn't expect anyone to be up so early." Grace grabbed a towel off the counter and swabbed up the yogurt.

"It's grossly unfair that at my age, one tires easily but sleeps hardly at all."

Sophia was sitting in the large breakfast nook at the end of the kitchen, the bay window behind her providing an elegant backdrop of green garden. A plate of toast and a coffee mug sat on the table.

"I'm not always awake so early," Grace said, rinsing the towel in the sink. "I had to see Catherine off."

"I take it by your good mood that you were not sorry to see her go."

Grace shrugged, unwilling to voice anything near the complicated truth.

"You'll both be better for the separation. She can hate *me* now, instead of you."

"So you were doing me a favor," Grace said in disbelief.

"Yes, I do see it that way. Fetch your breakfast and come sit with me. I have something I want to discuss."

God help her, she hoped it wasn't another "favor." A fresh bowl of yogurt and fruit in hand, and a mug of coffee from the pot, Grace slid onto the banquette across from Sophia. Her aunt's hair and makeup were as perfect as if she'd never gone to bed, even though she wore a silk floral robe and Grace could see the collar of apricot silk pajamas. Grace's oversize T-shirt and chenille robe felt ratty in comparison, and she hadn't combed her hair since showering. Even her bowl of yogurt looked unkempt next to Sophia's neat, dry toast.

"I've been thinking about your fascinating thesis on the emotional effects of beauty on women, and it occurred to me that I can help you gain a deeper understanding of it."

"You'll tell me of your own experiences as a beauty, and the troubles it brought? Wonderful! I'd been hoping you might!"

Sophia took a sip of coffee. "That wasn't quite what I had in mind."

"Oh. Er. Ah, I didn't mean to imply that you were obviously miserable, or anything."

"How fortunate for me that the Botox hides so much," she said drily. "No, my thought was that while you are yourself a beautiful young lady, it is a beauty that to most people lies obscured by your slumping posture, your fidgeting, your lack of fashion sense, and your general air of slovenliness. It's obvious that you have neither seen yourself as a beautiful girl, nor have you wished others to see you that way."

Grace's cheeks flamed. "That's not true; of course I want people to think I'm reasonably attractive. It's human nature. What I don't have is a need for people to see me as the prettiest girl in the room, and I don't ever want to be seen as sexy."

"Ohh . . . ," Sophia moaned, and for a moment Grace thought she was going to faint. "Heavens, dear, why ever not?"

"I want people to see *me*—the real me, not just the surface. I don't want to be treated as an object." Declan flashed to mind. "I want them to focus on who I *am*."

"But, darling, who is going to want to get to know a schlumpy girl who walks around with a fish on her T-shirt?"

"You can't be serious."

"Of course I am."

"Well, I think I'm more approachable when I'm dressed

casually. People are afraid to talk to overgroomed women. They think they're self-centered and shallow." Grace couldn't help a glance at Sophia's tailored robe.

"You can be beautiful and well-groomed and still approachable. In fact, you can be the most stunning woman in a room and also be the most beloved, by men and women alike."

"I've never heard anyone say that's the way it works," Grace said drily. Was she delusional? Since when did women fawn on the most beautiful, desirable, talented female in their midst?

"Of course, it takes more than a trip to the hairdresser and a clothes stylist to pull off that kind of charisma. There is a talent to it, and skill, and the courage to put them to use. You *can* make everyone adore you."

Grace shook her head. "Charisma has nothing to do with appearance, and it's not something you can learn."

"How silly of you. Of course it can be learned, just as beauty can be learned. I don't know how you will be able to claim any authority with the young women you hope to reach with your ideas if you yourself have never walked on the other side. They'll look at you and think, 'What does she know? She's fat and doesn't wear makeup, she's single, her clothes are ugly. I don't want to be like her.'"

"And I don't want to be like you!" Grace cried. "I don't want to make people feel bad about how they look, or make them feel stupid."

"I'm being brutally honest with you, I know," Sophia said, laying her hand over Grace's and squeezing. "I'm saying things to you that I wouldn't to any other woman, because I think you can handle it. I think you're smart enough and strong enough to hear what I have to say. You're not going to run crying to your bedroom, thinking I hate you."

That was exactly where Grace's thoughts had been. Sophia's

green eyes were looking at her with such an intensity of caring, though, that she felt herself softening. "Aunt Sophia, I honestly don't believe that happiness comes from being the most beautiful woman in the room. I think it's destructive to a woman's sense of self to strive for such a goal, and to leave her character and intelligence to lie fallow. I'm not going to do that to myself."

"A woman who fully exploits her beauty and sensuality can also develop traits such as kindness and confidence. Which can open doors to her future that would otherwise be closed."

"Those aren't the kinds of doors I want opened."

"But if they *were* the kinds you wanted?" Sophia asked.

"I'll never believe it."

Sophia released her hand and shook her head. "Is that the thinking of a true academic: if it doesn't fit my theory, I'll disregard it?"

"I've already gathered my research—"

"Inadequate research, clearly. Come, I want to show you something." With the help of a silver-headed cane she stood and led the way out of the kitchen, her steps slow but her back straight and her head held elegantly high on her slender neck.

The short journey ended in a denlike room full of books. Sophia inclined her head toward the wall at Grace's back. Grace turned.

Her jaw dropped and the blood washed from her head, leaving her faint.

"You're gathering flies, dear."

Grace popped her mouth shut.

"Have you ever wandered through an art museum, gazing at the faces in the paintings, looking for a face in the past that looked like your own? Some gesture of the hand, a tilt of the head, a hint of expression that you had seen every day in your mirror? And if you did find it, did you want to know who the person was, what her life was like? Was she similar to you, or dissimilar? What would she say to you across time, if she could speak?"

"That's you, isn't it?"

Sophia nodded.

"It's almost my face," Grace said, stunned. "But I could never look like that. I would never *try* to look like that!"

"Why not?"

Grace shook her head. "It's not who I am. It's you."

"Darling, it was only part of me," Sophia laughed. "I assure you, I did not spend every hour of my waking life seducing men. It was a role I played, when it suited."

"I don't believe you."

Sophia looked at her in surprise. "Don't you?"

Grace shook her head. "You're still the same now as you were in that painting. I saw how Declan and Dr. Andrew were looking at you; you have them wrapped around your little finger."

Sophia's face softened. "Such dear fellows. It's not every young man who would willingly spend time with a woman old enough to be his grandmother."

"I don't think it matters if they're dear or not, or young or not; I think you collect men the way other women collect china figurines."

"I'm not sure if you mean that as a compliment."

"Neither am I," Grace said.

Sophia laughed. "Grace Sophia, you are not as innocent as you look!"

Grace felt a smile tugging at the corners of her mouth. "I'm not sure if you mean *that* as a compliment."

"I do. Knowledge is always worth more than innocence. Or ignorance."

"On that, at least, we agree." Grace looked up again at the

painting that could have been of her, if she'd been someone else entirely on the inside. Or was the woman in the painting so fundamentally different from herself? Grace put her weight on one foot, relaxed her mouth, and lowered her lids to a sultry level, trying to imagine Dr. Andrew looking into her eyes and willingly twisting himself around her little finger.

A movement caught the corner of her eye. She turned and saw herself in a Venetian mirror. She looked like a drunk chipmunk.

Who was she kidding? Her face was a little like Sophia's, but she would never be the cynosure of all eyes that her great-aunt had been and still was. She didn't even want that type of attention. All it was good for was attracting men like Declan. To try to be like Sophia was to go against everything she stood for. "I don't want to look like that," she said, almost to herself.

"*Tsk.* And here I thought we were being honest with each other."

"I don't! All anyone would see would be my body. Guys would think about trying to get me into bed instead of listening to what I said."

"Darling, you have it backward. Men listen to what you have to say *only* if they want to get you into bed. It's a fundamental law of nature."

"Not the men I want to know."

"Darling, all men."

"Men today are different. They've been raised to see women as their equals."

Sophia laughed. "Child, you're no more going to change men's primary interest in sex by preaching respect, than you'll get them to love peace by giving boys dolls instead of toy guns."

"Well, whatever the case, I'm not going to change who I am to suit their basest desires. There's no advantage to it. All I'd do would be to lose my self-respect." She'd had a reminder of that truth less than eight hours ago.

"How sure are you of that?"

"Completely!"

Sophia sat down on the couch and gestured to the easy chair across from her. Grace took a seat. "I can see I'm not going to persuade you with words alone," Sophia said. "If you are anything of a scientist, though, you'll be open to new evidence, and be willing to change your theories if they do not hold up."

"Of course."

"Then let's try an experiment."

"What kind of experiment?" Grace asked, wary. Every conversation with Sophia led to a trap, and this one seemed no different. Her aunt was too good at laying the bait, though, for her to walk away with her curiosity unsatisfied.

"A deeply entertaining experiment for us both, I hope. Over the next few months I will transform you into the type of charismatic, seductive bombshell you so despise, and at the end of the summer you will decide whether or not your theory of beauty bringing misery still holds, or whether your world has opened up in ways you never thought possible."

"All that sounds like is my agreeing to be brainwashed for three months," Grace grumbled, even as a little devil on her shoulder started whispering persuasions in her ear. It *would* be invaluable information, given to her freely by an old pro, just as she'd told Cat she wanted. She'd thought that *Sophia* would be the subject of her study, though, not herself. She'd thought she would be the clever, distant observer, safe behind her notebook.

"You can't lose," Sophia said. "Whether you change your mind or not, think of all the insights you will have gained into what a woman goes through to be beautiful and adored! You'll understand her sacrifices and her devotion to her craft. You'll experience for yourself the addictive pleasure of being admired. Think of the perspective it will give to your paper!"

"Would you tell me about your own life, as part of the deal?"

"Where it's pertinent and won't bore you to tears, certainly." Sophia smiled wickedly. "But I won't share a single anecdote of abuse and abandonment if you don't agree to the deal."

Grace chewed her lip. "I've struggled my whole life to put more importance on who I am than what I look like."

"Are your convictions so weak that they could be undone by three months under my tutelage?"

That was what she feared, irrational as it sounded. Look at the damage Sophia had done with a single comment about her needing a bra. Buying a training bra hadn't been the end of it; Grace had spent the next five years obsessed with not letting her breasts be noticed by guys. She'd developed young and dramatically, though, and her efforts to slide under the boobdar of teen boys had been futile. Other girls had handled the lecherous looks with rolled eyes and raised middle fingers, but Grace had always been timid, and had slumped her shoulders as if she could make her breasts recede back into her chest.

"I'll sweeten the deal for you," Sophia said. "If you put yourself in my hands for three months, at the end of it—whether you've changed your mind or not—I'll give you twenty thousand dollars on top of your salary as my companion."

"You can't be serious," Grace gasped. That would be enough to buy a car! Or to pay her rent for nearly two years! She could take a trip abroad! She could pay off part of her student loans! She could—

"In return," Sophia said, breaking into her mental spending orgy, "you have to follow my directions and make an honest effort. No going through the motions and calling it good enough. No begging off because of embarrassment or fear. No protesting that it's too hard or too stupid or too degrading."

"*Would* it be degrading?"

"Of course not. Not by the standards of normal people, anyway."

Grace's better judgment told her it was too good to be true. The temptation before her was so great, though, that she knew she was in danger of giving in. *Twenty thousand dollars!* the devil on her shoulder whispered. And then there were the research benefits, too.

And beyond even those temptations, there was the hidden part of her—hidden ever since she was a child and her mother had declared a ban on Disney princesses in the house—that wanted to know what it felt like to be beautiful and sexy, and to have men so obsessed with her that they would give their lives in exchange for her slightest smile of favor. That hidden part of her wanted heads to turn when she came into a room, and every man to imagine what it would be like to sleep with her.

She looked up at the portrait over the fire. *Could* she look like that? Part of her desperately wanted to find out.

Grace shoved the treacherous thoughts aside and tried to think critically. "What do you get out of this?"

"The satisfaction of proving myself right." Sophia rubbed her hip. "Distraction from this would not be unappreciated, either."

"That's all?"

Sophia's eyes went to the painting, and her voice was wistful. "There's vanity on my part, I won't deny that." She met Grace's eyes and smiled. "I want to see my younger self live again."

"I'm not you."

"Ah, child. At this age, illusion will suffice."

Grace looked at her aunt and saw a soft yearning in her eyes, and then a twinge of pain crossed her features, her hand pressing against her hip. Sophia smiled, her lips trembling. She looked fragile and alone. Feeling a surge of pity, Grace leaned forward and stretched out her hand. "You have a deal."

Sophia's brows rose in surprise, and she took Grace's hand. "There's one more condition, though: you must keep this a secret from everyone. *Everyone.* If you tell a soul before the summer's over, then no twenty thousand."

"Is there a reason?"

"Call it a whim on my part."

Grace shrugged. She'd be too embarrassed to admit to this deal, anyhow. Good God, if her mother or Professor Joansdatter ever heard about it— She broke out in a sweat at the thought. "Mum's the word."

CHAPTER

ε 6 Ȝ

Research Notes

June 14

Subject, Sophia Fenwick, is an eighty-five-year-old single (widowed, married unknown number of times) Caucasian female. Formerly a B actress, with claims to a bit part in South Pacific (subject insists she was up for Mitzi Gaynor's role), she now resides in a mansion in Pebble Beach, California, and appears to be extremely wealthy. The source of her money is presumably from former husband(s). No children. Lives alone with staff members. Has a bad hip, but otherwise seems healthy, and has maintained an attractive appearance. Plastic surgery the most likely explanation for present eerie beauty.

Sophia exhibits signs of inconsistent thinking. S. believes that sex appeal in the human female is determined by the female's core beliefs about her sexiness, not by her physical appearance. While this theory holds a certain feminist appeal, vis-à-vis inner confidence determining one's attractiveness, it is nonetheless in direct contradiction to S.'s own habits of dress and grooming (and plastic surgery?), and her frequent vitriolic judgments upon the physical appearance of other females. These judgments may be a defensive gesture. S. appears highly competitive and status conscious, and may be threatened by the presence of Author (me), who is young and may represent a past that S. cannot regain.

Sophia is employing classic abusive manipulation techniques in an attempt to break Author down in order to rebuild Author in her own image, akin to a boot camp drill sergeant training "maggots" to be soldiers. S.'s abuses include telling Author that vegetarians are a pain in the ass, that feminists hate being women, that capri pants should never be worn by anyone more than one hundred pounds; and that Author's (admittedly well-worn) undergarments are a particularly unsavory form of birth control, a sin against femininity, would frighten bears, and should be staked, burned, and buried, preferably in an unmarked grave.

Sophia also directed her minion Darlene to steal and destroy orthopedic sandals prescribed by Author's podiatrist. S. refused to compensate Author for cost of sandals, and is clearly unrepentant; S. seems unable to see her actions as excessively controlling. Sociopathic tendencies suspected.

June 15

Lessons today consisted of screenings of several film noirs with femmes fatales: The Maltese Falcon; The Big Sleep; Gilda; and Niagara. Author was asked to meditate upon what made each femme fatale sexy. Author responded that the f.f.s seemed mentally unstable and emotionally immature, and that men who liked that type of woman deserved what they got.

Author notes consumption of Scotch by Sophia in response to frustration with Author. Author's suggestion of yoga as a stress-reduction alternative was met with unwarranted outpouring of inappropriate language.

June 16

Day was devoted to Sophia's extensive collection of art history books and discussion of beauty, charisma, and sex appeal of various naked subjects of varying weight, coloring, and facial features. S. contends that the artist painting each woman saw beauty where others might see none, and by virtue of putting the woman in a painting, both convinced her she was beautiful, and also convinced the viewer. S. uses this as proof that beauty is not based upon physical reality, but upon attitudes and expectations. If you behave as if you are beautiful, others will believe you.

Author pointed out that many models were prostitutes in real life.

Sophia's arguments beginning to lack energy; responded to prostitute comment with weak sigh. Author feels Author may finally be getting through to S., and changing her mind.

Or perhaps Sophia's enthusiasm for bombshell lessons is waning.

Either way, S.'s Scotch consumption notably on the rise.

CHAPTER
ع 7 ૭

"Grace, come in here. I have a surprise for you," Sophia called from the Louis Quatorze living room.

Grace froze like a burglar in the night, in midstep across the checkerboard floor of the foyer, her hands full of purloined chocolate chocolate-chip banana cookies fresh from Renata's oven. Sophia hadn't put her on a diet, but Grace knew her aunt's sharp eyes observed every crumb that passed her lips.

"Grace?"

In desperation Grace eyeballed a potted palm as a cookie stash, but rejected its stems and soil—cookie spoilage danger!—in favor of caching the goods under her T-shirt, in the small of her back. She stuffed the hem of her shirt into her jeans, making a neat little pouch above her waistband. As long as she didn't turn her back, Sophia would never see the warm, soft lumps of sweet heaven.

With the cookies making gentle heating pads over her kidneys, Grace sidled nonchalantly into the living room. "What's up?"

Sophia sat perched on the seat of an easy chair, dressed in a white silk blouse and navy, high-waisted pants that Katharine Hepburn would have loved, her hair neatly held back in a tortoiseshell clip at the nape of her neck. A large cardboard box was open on the coffee table in front of her.

"I've decided you need something more lively and hands-on than books," Sophia said, looking pleased with herself. "Something to distract you from thinking too much."

Grace's heart soared, one crazy, impossible thought suddenly filling her mind. What other "lively" thing could be in a big cardboard box other than: "A puppy? You got me a puppy!" she cried, overjoyed. Any moment now, a furry muzzle and black eyes would pop up over the edge of the box.

"Why in heaven's name would I buy you a puppy?"

"No puppy?" Grace said, her smile dying. A small spark of hope flared back to life. "I don't suppose it's a kitten?"

Sophia's lips thinned. "Women who want to marry should not be allowed to own cats."

The comment surprised a laugh out of Grace. "You *can't* have a logical argument for that."

"All a cat is is a surrogate lover. Instead of fawning over an animal that cares more about a can of Fancy Feast than about her, a woman should be out looking for a real man to take care of her."

Too caught between disbelief and horror to speak for several seconds, Grace put her hand to her forehead and shook her head, gaping at her aunt. "Where do I even *begin*?" she finally said.

Sophia flicked negligent fingers at her. "Let's skip your part. It's too predictable. 'Women can take care of themselves, blah blah,' yes, we've heard it all before. The part of the equation your kind never wants to see is that women need men just as much as they need us. Owning a pet diverts attention from seeking and securing that primary human relationship. A lot of men dislike cats, and I'm certain it's because men sense the competition for a woman's affection."

"For God's sake, who'd even *want* a man who felt threatened by a cat?"

Ignoring her, Sophia went on philosophically, "Of course, it never helps the cat's case when it craps in a man's shoes while he takes the mistress to bed." She shrugged. "But that's neither here nor there, and nothing to do with what I've ordered for you. Come see."

Wary, Grace inched forward. With trepidation she peered over the edge of the box and was confused to see a colorful array of tissue paper, lace, and silk. "PJs and underwear?" she asked. No one had chosen her underwear for her since she was fourteen.

"Darling, please. Children wear PJs and underwear. Women wear *lingerie.*"

Grace picked a peach silk tank top out of its tissue paper wrapping, and her confusion turned to delight. She had always secretly yearned for silk pajamas. She went through the box, eager to find the other half of the set. "Did they forget to send the bottoms?"

Sophia reached in and hooked a scrap of silk by her finger, raising it up for Grace. "Here."

Grace blinked at the G-string, with its tiny triangle of fabric and its strip of satin elastic butt floss, and felt her delight fade. She should have known Sophia wouldn't buy her anything she'd want to wear. "I can't wear that."

"It's in your size."

"You know what I mean. I'd look ridiculous."

"You'll only look ridiculous if that's how you feel."

Grace poked a finger into her thigh. "How I *feel* won't change the shape of these, or the size of my butt." She went back to the box, her skepticism increasing with every item she pulled out of its tissue paper.

Garter belt. Black and red push-up bra. White lace negligée that would conceal nothing bigger than a freckle. More G-strings, and panties made of stretch lace.

The lavender satin item in the bottom of the box pushed her over the edge. It was a corset. A goddamned *corset,* with black lace trim. Grace lifted the offending item and its matching panties out of the box and glared at her aunt. "Exactly how far back in time do you intend to push women's liberation?"

Sophia beamed. "Isn't it beautiful? The Victorians understood a thing or two about female sexual power. They say that men would faint at the sight of a woman's ankle."

Grace rolled her eyes. "Only you could see sexual power in the oppression of Victorian women."

"Why else do you think the men were so obsessed with oppressing them? They were terrified of the strength of their own desires. Give a woman an hourglass figure and then put a 'do not touch' sign on her, and a man can think of doing nothing else."

"While the poor woman struggles to breathe, and has her organs displaced by a medieval torture device."

"There's an elastic panel in the back of this one, so you'll be quite comfortable wearing it under your clothes."

Grace laughed in disbelief. "Do you have a hoop skirt for me, too?"

"I'm not putting you in costume, darling. I'm simply asking you to wear lingerie that says something other than 'abandon all hope, ye who enter here.' You must dress as if you believe yourself a woman of sexual substance, who invites the admiration of men."

"And a corset and G-string are supposed to do that for me?"

"You cannot achieve a sex-vixen mind-set while wearing granny panties."

Grace groaned and sank down onto the sofa. The lingerie spread over the coffee table represented everything she had spent her life trying not to be. To dress in such froth would be to say her value was determined solely by the sexual desire of men.

"No," she murmured.

"What was that, darling?" Sophia said, examining a transparent pink chiffon robe with marabou trim.

Grace held her hand palm out at the lingerie, as if to stop it from existing. "I don't want it."

Danger glinted in Sophia's green eyes. She set down the robe. "And why not?"

"It's not who I am."

"We have already established that for this summer, you will be other than you have always been. God knows we have a lot of work ahead of us; do not tell me you balk at a mere upgrade to your lingerie."

"It's not *mere* to me. You keep talking about sexiness coming from within, and all bodies being beautiful, yet you try to dress me in a corset that changes my shape."

"It's not your shape I'm trying to change, but your perception of it."

Grace jumped off the couch and grabbed at the lavender G-string panties. "And these are supposed to make me feel better about my body *how*? Can you imagine what these will look like on me, with my big butt exposed like a full moon?"

Sophia's eyes widened and then she sighed with resignation. "Good afternoon, Andrew."

Horror slowly frosted Grace's skin, and for one chilled moment she felt she might faint.

Behind her, Andrew cleared his throat. "H-hello, Sophia. Er—Grace."

Grace squeaked and tried to throw the panties into the box. They tangled in her fingers and fell to the floor at her feet, where they lay sprawled and tawdry.

"Er, let me get that for you," Andrew said, coming round her and bending down. He was wearing a white doctor's coat and, on his head, an old-fashioned reflector.

Startled out of her paralysis, Grace said, "No, no, I'll get it," and bent down quickly. She got her hand on the panties just as

Andrew did, their fingers meeting on the satin. Their eyes met, and Andrew's face turned scarlet.

"Er, yes, okay," he murmured.

She felt the desperation of the misunderstood and wanted to correct the impression she must have just given him, but what to say?

"Grace," Sophia broke in.

Grace felt a spurt of gratitude. *Thank God, Sophia will save me from myself.* "Yes?"

"There's a smear of brown at the back of your T-shirt. You've also left a brown stain on my sofa. Why, pray?"

Grace gasped and slapped her hand to her back, finding the squashed cookies. She twisted her face in miserable apology as she turned to Sophia. "It's cookies. The chocolate must have soaked through when I sat down. I'm so sorry; I'll scrub it off the sofa."

"But why on earth do you have cookies tucked into your shirt?" Andrew asked in bewilderment.

Sophia raised her own brow in question.

"I, uh—wanted my hands free?"

"Grace," Andrew said, stiff and professionally concerned. "I think you and I should have a private word."

"What? Why?"

He didn't answer, though, so she followed him out into the foyer with the dragging feet of a child knowing she was in trouble, but not knowing exactly how bad it was going to be. She tried to postpone his words by asking, "Where did you find that thing you're wearing on your head? A prop shop?"

Flustered out of his clinical seriousness, Andrew put his hand to the reflector, his face showing his surprise to discover it there. "Sophia bought it. From eBay, I think."

"Do you actually use it?"

"No."

"So it's just to humor her, like the costumes she makes the rest of her staff wear. You don't feel silly in it?"

He cleared his throat, his lips tightening again. "I do. A little. If you must know."

"Then why do you wear it?"

He rubbed his hand over his face. "Because it's easier than *not* wearing it."

"Ah." The reflector looked silly, undignified. A man who had gone through medical school and a residency should have the strength to say no to a patient who wanted him to dress up as a caricature of his own profession.

Maybe Sophia made Declan wear a green visor and ink guards on his wrists when he talked money with her, too. Or maybe coattails, cane, and a top hat like the millionaire in Monopoly. And a bushy white mustache. Grace giggled, on the edge of hysteria.

Andrew evidently took her giggle personally, and grew stern again. "Grace, I want you to be honest with me."

Trepidation smothered her smile. She nodded, wary, and tried not to let the hysterical giggles escape.

"How long have you been a food hoarder?"

She gaped at him. "A what?"

"Food. Hoarder."

"I'm not!"

He put his hands on her shoulders and turned her round, then tugged up her shirt. The cookies fell out onto the marble floor with a *splat, splat*.

"I just didn't want Sophia to see them!" Grace said.

"Why not?"

Grace snorted. "Why do you think? She—" Grace suddenly stopped, her tongue tripping over the knowledge that she could not say *one word* about the bet between her and Sophia, and

Sophia's efforts to transform her into a bombshell. She couldn't say that she knew gorging on cookies didn't fit Sophia's ideas of how a bombshell behaved.

"You're hiding food," Andrew said.

Grace chafed under the accusation, but she couldn't exactly deny it, what with the evidence lying on the floor. "Just cookies." She pursed her lips. "And maybe a Snickers bar now and then."

"You're a binge eater, aren't you? You have the puffy, bloated look of someone who has a carbohydrate addiction."

Deeply affronted, Grace drew herself up. "I beg your pardon!"

"You're damaging your metabolism, and I hate to think of what your liver must look like."

"What's wrong with my liver?!"

"It's probably fatty. You're on the road to becoming a diabetic."

"It was a couple of freakin' cookies!"

"The simple carbohydrates, the sugar, the binge eating—you're killing yourself."

"I don't have an eating disorder!"

He looked at her with deep medical compassion. "Look at the evidence and face the truth, Grace. Accepting that you have an addiction is the first step to healing it."

His misguided compassion was too much, on top of everything else. Devastated, she cried out, "So what if I do?" and burst into tears.

"Good, Grace! Acceptance is *good*!"

"Screw you," she wailed, and ran up the stairs to the safety of her room.

CHAPTER
8

Research Notes

June 18
Author in deep mental funk. Is liver fatty? Is love of a good cookie a sign of carb addiction? But what then of equal, if not greater, love of bacon? Bacon ≠ carb.

June 19
Author admits to self that real cause of funk is sense of being hopelessly unattractive to males. Dr. Andrew thinks she's bloated, and obviously finds Author physically unappealing. Declan finds Author both physically and psychologically unappealing. Not that his opinion matters, the scum-sucking son of a carp . . .

Bombshell lessons obviously a waste of time. Author either incapable of learning, or Sophia's premise of being able to teach sex appeal is erroneous.

June 20
Sophia's frustration with Author's lack of progress and "poor attitude" is expressing itself in a surprising decline in personal tidiness. Lock of hair escaped control of clip, and food stain was

noted on blouse. More alarming, S. only shrugged when food stain pointed out.

Sophia has declared Author's core beliefs about sexiness of self to be inadequate to the job of creating external sex appeal, and beyond remediation. ("Beyond God and the devil," exact words.)

Lessons aborted midday.

Scotch decanter is empty.

June 21

S. has formulated a new plan for education of Author. Author must now "fake it till she makes it"; i.e., mimic the sexy until she truly becomes sexy. Focus of training will now be on external appearance, with Author's interior self left to languish.

Sophia contends that once Author looks sexy on the outside and experiences success re: capturing the attention of men, Author will gain confidence and become sexy on the inside. This is directly opposed to S.'s initial thesis of the inner woman determining the outer woman.

Author is pleased to note that this is in keeping with Author's original beliefs re: pursuit of beauty leading to an empty soul.

(Ha!)

June 23

Author being put on strict weight-loss diet.

Author would like a glass of Scotch.

June 24

Author has suffered the mental and physical horrors of a bikini wax. Great holy monkey balls, the pain.

June 26

Sophia's external sex appeal lesson focusing on posture and gait:

Heeled shoes must be worn at all times, up to and even including the sexual act. Author suspects that resultant painful foot deformities may partially explain S.'s foul temper. (Author freshly mourning theft of orthopedic sandals.)

In order to create the desired hip sway while walking, feet must be placed directly in front of each other as if walking on a balance beam. S. has installed such a beam on the floor of her exercise room for the purpose of training Author, which has proven an ineffective teaching method when coupled with five-inch platform heels. Author's ankles strained, toes blistered, arches aching.

S. has compared Author's gait to that of Bigfoot, with hunched shoulders and head jutting forward as if chewing berries off a bush. S. employs her cane to whack Author in appropriate body locations to improve gait: head up, shoulders back, hips forward.

Author is exhibiting signs of Pavlovian fear response to presence of cane, including tic under one eye.

June 28

Author's mental health status is showing signs of decline, including obsessive thoughts of violence toward Sophia and contemplation of theft of Valium from S.'s medicine cabinet to medicate self. Both are early indications that the pursuit of sex appeal leads to mental illness and drug addiction in women.

CHAPTER

9

"Come on! Faster! Faster! Faster! Hup, hup, hup!"

Grace gulped in air, her thigh muscles burning, her lungs raw, the blood pounding in her head. *I'm going to have a stroke, oh God, I'm going to die right here on these freakin' stairs.* Below her the waves of the Pacific washed against the shore of the cove, their rushing sound lost in the louder rushing of her breath. The wooden staircase bolted to the cliff face had become her personal torture rack as she climbed it for the third time.

"You're almost here! Hup, hup, hup!"

Grace glared at the overlord above her: a personal trainer with a blond ponytail and an infuriatingly perky disposition. Grace had been under Cyndee's thumb for only three weeks, since late June when Sophia had changed training tactics, but it felt like she'd descended into an eternal hell. It was PE class all over again, only this time the teacher was smaller, younger, cuter, and deeply concerned with the flabbiness of Grace's upper arms and buttocks.

Her legs so weak she could barely feel them, Grace sank to her knees and crawled the last few steps to the top, collapsing on the ground at Cyndee's feet.

"Good job, Grace! Way to go! Okay, let's do a cool-down walk through the gardens and we'll call it a morning. Don't forget to hydrate!"

Grace rolled onto her back and opened her mouth. "Just pour it in."

Instead, Cyndee reached down and grabbed Grace's hand, her wiry strength dragging Grace upright. "Come on! We don't want you to stiffen up!"

Too exhausted to curse, Grace let herself be dragged upright. She took a swig from the proffered water bottle, blinked stinging sweat from her eyes, and trudged after Cyndee down the garden path. Being transformed into a bombshell bore a depressing resemblance to fatty-weight-loss camp. Not only was she subjected to Cyndee's death marches but a nutritionist also had taken up temporary residence specifically to feed Grace, his ascetic presence in the kitchen infuriating Renata and destroying any interest Grace had ever had in healthy food. There was only so much tofu and broccoli a girl could eat, and she did not and never would consider five raw almonds a sufficient midday snack.

She *had* lost twelve pounds in the past three weeks, but was convinced that at least a third of that weight had come from brain matter. She felt light-headed and stupid most of the day.

The sweat was beginning to dry in her hair and the salt to crystallize on her face by the time they finished the mile-long twisting loop of path across the headland, and it was with the happy trot of a horse returning to its stable that she approached the stretch of grass below the terrace. After ten minutes of stretching exercises, she'd be done for the day. She'd have a blissful hour to herself before Sophia began her afternoon lessons. At the thought of her reprieve, her mood began to improve, and she felt almost cheerful.

She was sitting on the ground with her legs parted wide, trying to touch her right toes, when Declan appeared like an evil spirit conjured from the bushes. Her cheerful mood, fragile to begin with from hunger and exhaustion, plummeted.

He looked fresh and relaxed in a pale blue T-shirt, khakis, and deck shoes. The thin shirt hinted at the square, sculpted pectoral muscles of his chest, and where the shirt met the waistband it lay flat and smooth, with no hint of love handles or a beer belly. Grace noted with a faint sense of despair that his waist size was probably smaller than her own.

"I was surprised to hear you'd hung around," he said, standing over her. "I didn't think our company was to your liking."

Grace glared from under her salty brows.

"Hi!" Cyndee said, bouncing over to him, her ponytail swinging. "I'm Cyndee! Grace's trainer!"

"Hi!" Declan said back. "I'm Declan! I'm single!"

Grace ignored them; she would not sink to his level.

She reached for her left toes. Her pale leg looked like an unformed log against the emerald grass. From the corner of her eye she could see Cyndee's toned and tanned legs, each no bigger than Grace's upper arm.

Cyndee giggled and poked Declan in the gut. "It doesn't look like *you* need a trainer."

"I can see a reason or two I might want one. Could you pencil me in for tonight?"

Cyndee's giggles rose an octave. "I *might* be able to find some time for you, but you'd better be ready to work hard."

Declan took out his phone and programmed in Cyndee's number. "Do you like seafood?"

"Hee-hee!"

"I'll take that as a yes."

Cyndee bounced around and spied Grace. "Okay, Grace, good job! Hit the shower!"

Grace lumbered to her feet, feeling like the sediment at the bottom of Cyndee's bottle of bubbly.

"Grace," Declan said, "after you've cleaned up, why don't I

show you a bit of the area? We could stop and have lunch somewhere while we're out."

"Lunch?" How on earth could he possibly think she'd want to
have lunch with him? "No, thank you."

"No?"

A tempting black bean burger with soy bacon (or maybe real
bacon? She could be forgiven real bacon, couldn't she, under such
trying circumstances?), avocado, and a heaping side of fries appeared in Grace's imagination, rich in salty deliciousness. She'd
almost be willing to endure Declan for an hour if it meant wolf-
ing down that puppy. She mentally scooped a big blob of ketchup
onto a fry and bit it. *Ohhhh . . .*

Cyndee was bouncing in the corner of her eye, lithe and full
of energy, her clothes betraying no unwelcome bulge. Cyndee
drank wheat grass and eschewed sugar, wheat products, and po-
tatoes. Grace swallowed her saliva, thought of twenty thousand
dollars, and shook her head. "Thanks, but no. I've got stuff I need
to do."

"Surely nothing that can't wait a few hours?"

"Sophia needs me this afternoon."

Cyndee sucked her front teeth and smiled with closed lips,
eyes going back and forth between them, the hope plain on her
face that Declan's attention would return to her.

Declan was not yet ready to oblige. "I've already received
Sophia's permission to steal you away from your duties, whatever
they are."

She wasn't about to enlighten him. "I appreciate the offer,
really, but today's not a good day. Some other time, perhaps," she
lied. "Why don't you take Cyndee to lunch?"

Cyndee grinned.

"Because I asked *you*."

Cyndee's grin lost a few watts.

He was determined, Grace had to give him that. He must have enjoyed making a fool of her that night on the couch and be eager for another chance; or maybe he didn't realize how deeply he'd affected her. She wouldn't be surprised if he was that callous. "Look, it's very nice of you to try to entertain me, but it's not necessary. Really. Thanks for the offer, but no." Together the group started walking back to the house.

Declan's jaw worked. He obviously wasn't used to hearing a rejection. "You'd make your aunt happy if you came out to lunch."

"Oh, I doubt it," Grace said lightly, then lifted her arm and poked a finger at her underarm flab. "I think she'd rather see me losing some of this academic weight. I don't want to embarrass her by being a porker."

She was rewarded by a look of distress on Declan's face. "Good God, you're not a porker. Did she call you one?"

Grace realized she was on dangerous ground, and couldn't give Declan a real explanation about why she had a trainer and needed to lose weight. "Sophia mentioned being concerned about my health. In modern euphemism, that means I'm a porker," she said cheerily, as if it didn't bother her in the least. "Have you noticed how delighted people are to have health as an excuse to chide other people for lugging around a few extra pounds? It gives them a coded way to say, 'I think you're fat and unattractive.'"

"But fat is a very important health issue!" Cyndee cried. "It's not about appearance!"

"She's putting you on, Cyndee," Declan said. "Don't listen to her, she doesn't mean it."

"Think what you want," Grace said, and then wagged a finger at Declan. "But when the day comes that a girlfriend says she's worried about your getting cirrhosis, it'll be because she thinks you're obnoxious when you drink, not because she cares about your health."

Declan scowled.

Delighted by his reaction, Grace laughed. "Someone *has* told you that!"

They reached the terrace and Grace trudged up the stone steps, her legs protesting each movement, her butt protesting that Declan, a few steps behind, was in too good a spot to watch it jiggle. She resisted the urge to pull down the hem of her shorts.

"I'm not giving up yet," Declan said behind her.

"But you will sooner or later," she said brightly. She waved good-bye over her shoulder and went into the house, headed for the sanctuary of her room, hoping with every step that he'd stop following her. Playing Miss Cheerful had taken the last reserves of her energy.

Halfway up the main stairs she realized that he hadn't followed, and an inexplicable disappointment made her turn and look back at the empty staircase. No doubt he was still out on the terrace, his arm round Cyndee's slender waist, letting her pant and squirm and lick his face like an eager puppy.

So be it. He was a horrible man. Besides, she had Dr. Andrew to think about. Aunt Sophia had an appointment with him the following morning, and Grace's heart thumped a little more strongly at the thought of Andrew noticing the weight she'd lost.

She pushed open the door to her room, and was startled by a wild flutter of color. A confusion of blues, greens, corals, and yellows resolved itself into Aunt Sophia, Darlene, and a few dozen dresses, tops, skirts, and shoe boxes scattered over the bed, the furniture, and hanging on a rolling clothes rack where gossamer hems and dangling sashes floated in the breeze from the open windows. Grace gaped at the feminine chaos, her gaze flitting from sea green chiffon to orange floral print to black satin. There was not a single item that looked like something she had ever worn, and they were all . . . *beautiful*!

"Quickly, darling, into the shower with you, and be sure to shave your legs and under your arms," Sophia said from her perch on a Louis Quatorze chair, a garment of teal blue silk spilling over her legs. "We don't have much time to get you ready for your outing with Declan."

Grace barely heard, her eyes still greedily taking in the wondrous clothing. So many pretty, pretty things. She'd never worn pretty things; she hadn't had the money, or the places to wear them. "I'm not going out with Declan."

Darlene looked up from the box of shoes she was unpacking, wadded paper in hand.

Sophia blinked. "Didn't he invite you?"

"Yeah, but I said I didn't want to go."

"Nonsense! Into the shower!"

Grace shook her head, her wide eyes fixed on the fabric flood, a haunting sense of guilt creeping over her at her lusting reaction to the *Vogue*-worthy collection. Shopping for trendy, sexy, expensive dresses had never been a politically correct activity in her home, landing somewhere between reading *Cosmopolitan* and learning to pole dance on the list of Things Serious Women Do Not Do. "You were going to teach me how to walk up and down stairs today."

Sophia waved away the protest. "That can wait. How you could possibly think descending stairs more important than lunch out with a handsome young man, I cannot fathom."

Grace barely heard her. She went to the rack and ran her fingertips over the sea green chiffon, feeling the forbidden desire tremble through her. A hangnail caught in the fabric, pulling a thread and causing a pucker. She winced and tried to pull it out flat. "You didn't buy all these for me, did you?"

"No, of course not."

"Oh, that's good," she said, disappointed.

"They're on loan from shops in Carmel. We'll only keep the ones that look good on you."

She brightened. "And that I like?"

"Your taste is not to be trusted."

Grace turned to her. "It's my body being clothed."

"While you're in my employ, your body belongs to me," Sophia said, meeting her eyes with a solid gaze that had "twenty thousand dollars" written across it. "Darlene, please go see that Declan waits for my niece. Keep him entertained."

"I think he's being entertained quite well by Cyndee," Grace said as Darlene clumped from the room.

Sophia sniffed. "Cyndee and her type are inconsequential. They'll never capture the type of men we're after."

"I'm not after anyone. That wasn't part of the deal."

"I didn't say you had to keep them. But learning to be charismatic without men on whom to practice is like learning to ride a bicycle without a bike."

"So that's why Declan asked me out—you put him up to it! Does he know he's your guinea pig?"

"As far as he knows, all I want is for him to show you around and rescue you from my tiresome company." Sophia smiled angelically. "What you can make him do beyond that is your first test."

Grace felt a flutter in her stomach. "I don't like him."

"I don't see how that matters."

"Aunt Sophia, you don't understand. I *really* don't like him," Grace said, her voice cracking, and to her mortification, tears welled in her eyes. Goddammit, he wasn't supposed to upset her like this!

Sophia's gaze rested on her for a long moment, assessing. "He did something to upset you, didn't he? Something beyond being rude at tea."

Grace sniffled and rubbed her nose with the back of her hand. "I didn't want to say anything to you. It happened that first night I was here."

"Do you want to tell me what happened?"

She shook her head.

Sophia raised an eyebrow and waited.

Grace moaned in defeat, and gave a short, bare-bones account of what had happened. "So you can see why I don't want to spend the afternoon with him or, God forbid, *flirt* with him!"

"On the contrary. It makes him perfect for your practice."

"But, Aunt Sophia!"

"If you don't care whether he likes you, you can work on seducing him without fear of failure. If he doesn't fall for you, what do you care? The hunter is not personally offended when the prey eludes her. She simply adjusts her tracking skills until she's successful."

"I don't want to be successful with him."

"Grace, darling. You aren't thinking this through. What do you do to the prey at the end of a hunt?"

"I don't know. Kill it and mount its head on your wall?"

Sophia smiled sweetly.

A bubble of surprised laughter popped in Grace's throat. "You mean I could take my revenge."

"He'll be a challenge. You'll have to have him tightly caught before you deliver the death blow."

An image of a lovesick Declan down on one knee, proclaiming his adoration of her, filled Grace's mind. *My, you are full of surprises,* she would say. *I was wondering how far you'd go with a woman you once called dumpy.* His face would fall, his heart crumpling like tinfoil as for the first time in his life he had his heart broken and was made to feel a fool.

Why are you doing this to me? he'd ask.

Because you let me, she'd say.

And because he was a rotten bastard who deserved to have his heart trod upon. Grace had never been one to seek retribution for wrongs done to her, trying instead to take the moral high road, but it was luscious to imagine having the power to humiliate Declan. If she was honest with herself, hadn't she only developed her "it's better to rise above it" philosophy because she was too cowardly to take action against her enemies?

Not only did Declan deserve such treatment, he would benefit from it. He'd learn empathy, a trait crucial to developing a strong, loving relationship with a woman. Grace didn't believe that anyone was pure evil. Declan was callous because he hadn't ever experienced the pain of being rejected by someone he wanted. She would be doing him—and any future women he dated—a great favor by squishing his heart.

Grace's delight faded at a suspicious thought. "Declan is your friend. Why would you want him hurt?"

"Blood's thicker than water, Grace. He hurt you, which is as good as hurting me."

Grace narrowed her eyes and shook her head. "I don't think that's it. No . . . you don't think I'll succeed! You don't think I'll ever have the power to hurt him!"

Sophia shrugged. "The man's a player. More talented women than you have tried and failed to capture his heart."

Grace propped one hand on her hip. "I thought native talent had nothing to do with it. You said you could teach me how to be the woman no man could resist. *No* man."

Sophia sighed. "Players are different. It would require too much of you."

"How much?"

"Everything."

"You mean . . . ," Grace trailed off, her stomach sinking.

"He won't fall completely for someone he can never touch. He will be intrigued by you, he will pursue you and perhaps even become obsessed with you—which is good, and necessary—but he won't lose himself entirely without the bonding that comes with physical contact and with sex. He will eventually—not too soon, but *eventually*—need that, and the burst of hormones that comes with sexual release. Without that, he'll never believe himself wholeheartedly in love; but even *with* sex, love is no guarantee. He is as likely to lose interest in you after sex as to bond with you." Sophia watched her dismayed reaction, then nodded. "So you see why it's much better that you use him for harmless practice. To sleep with a man you dislike, in the faint hope of exacting revenge . . . it's too much, Grace. You couldn't do it, and I wouldn't want you to."

Grace felt a welter of emotions: doubt, anger, revulsion, fear, and under it all sneaking sexual arousal. She tried to smother it and focus on the possibility of revenge. It had never occurred to her that she could hurt Declan as badly, or even worse, than he had hurt her. She could humiliate him. How would that feel, to rule over him in such a way?

She'd even be willing to concede that Aunt Sophia was right about the powers of bombshellitude, if she could use it to pierce the rhino hide of a man like Declan.

"If I *did* get Declan obsessed with me," Grace said, "and he fell for me? What if I could do that, with or without sex?"

"My dear," Sophia said drily, "if you can make Declan O'Brien fall in love with you, I'll turn that twenty thousand dollars into fifty."

CHAPTER
10

$\mathcal{D}$eclan shut off his smart phone and stood looking out at the ocean, wondering what else he could do to fill the time waiting for Grace. He'd already returned phone calls, replied to e-mails, and checked up on the progress of his development project with the architecture firm and his contacts in the county, but if he didn't find more busywork to do, he risked dwelling on the last time he'd seen Grace, and what an utter ass he'd been.

Cyndee had scampered off to wherever she'd come from, leaving him with faint interest in their date tonight. The sex that followed would be athletic and enthusiastic, but he didn't want to spend the whole night with her; the woman couldn't sit still or be quiet to save her life. How had such noise ever evolved in the human female? He'd have thought they'd all been eaten by lions on the savannah before Homo sapiens left Africa.

He blew out a breath. It had been stupid to ask out Cyndee the human pogo stick. He didn't know what had come over him: Grace had looked at him with eyes that declared him a chauvinist pig, and the next thing he knew he was doing his best to prove her right. It was as if he unconsciously wanted her to hate him even more than she already did.

On the night of Grace's arrival, he'd had a little too much to drink and decided to spend the night; one of the guest rooms was his whenever he was in town. He'd made the mistake of sitting down on the couch in the living room, though, and before he knew it he was zonked out, waking only when Grace began her midnight serenade.

He didn't know what had motivated him to all that followed. There were Sophia's instructions to behave as normal—i.e., as a cad—but he'd gone beyond that. He'd wanted to chase Grace away from the house entirely, hoping she'd leave in the morning with her volatile friend.

Once he'd started touching Grace, though, all that mattered was the warm, soft female who was slowly giving herself to him. All cats were gray in the dark, and this one had been in heat. Her flesh beneath his touch had been deeply, darkly inviting, filling him with the animal urge to conquer and consume. At that moment, he *had* to have her. Rational thought had ceased.

It hadn't returned when Catherine crashed into the crockery; it hadn't returned when she stood in the doorway calling Grace's name. It was only when the light came on that his brain reengaged.

He wished it hadn't. Interrupted passion, embarrassment, Sophia's instructions, the hateful imagined image of Grace and Dr. Andrew in marital bliss, they all came together and made him behave in a way that now brought an unfamiliar twinge of shame.

He thought he was a nice guy under the hound exterior. Not yet ready to settle down, but never the type of asshole who ended up on DontDateHimGirl.com, either. A good guy who'd never intentionally hurt someone innocent.

Now, every time he looked at Grace he would see the ugly truth reflected in her eyes. Given the right situation, he could be a dick.

It was exactly how Sophia wanted him to behave, but he was having a hard time feeling good about it. It was so much more fun to be a womanizer when it came naturally, without conscious thought. Self-awareness was a bitch.

To please Sophia he would take Grace out today, and he'd be as rude and crude as Grace no doubt expected of him, but he wasn't going to touch her again. A guy had to be able to look at himself in the mirror.

Deep in thought, he didn't realize Grace was approaching until she appeared in the corner of his eye. With a start he looked down at her, his vision falling smack into as lush a mound of breasts as had ever graced the cover of a men's magazine. They welled up from the V-neck of a green dress that wrapped round her body and tied at the side, hugging a small waist and full hips that belonged on Kim Kardashian or Marilyn Monroe. He was used to California gym addicts with their sinewy arms and boys' hips, and in comparison, Grace's voluptuous feminine display was shocking, almost pornographic. There were so many wild curves flowing this way and that, he didn't know where to look, or even if he *should* look.

"Christ, what happened to you?" he blurted. Had her eyes been that bright a green before? And—was that makeup she was wearing? Her hair was up in a high ponytail, leaving the smooth column of her neck bare.

"I took a shower."

"You must have damn good soap."

"Positively transformative," she said and put on a big pair of sunglasses, the better—he suspected—to hide her true thoughts. "I'm looking forward to this very much," she said robotically. "It's very kind of you to show me around."

"What did Sophia have to do, bribe you?"

Grace jerked guiltily, then rubbed her arm. "Mosquito," she offered in explanation. Her mouth twisted as if tasting something unpleasant, and then curved into a smile. Her voice dropped and she purred up at him with seeming sincerity, "Will you forgive me for my unappreciative behavior earlier? I was too worn out by my workout to give proper thought to how wonderful it would be to be shown around. This is supposed to be one of the most beautiful parts of California, and you were so kind to offer to introduce me to it. Please forgive me."

"Er . . . ," he said in confusion. He was too surprised to make sense of what was happening. *She* was apologizing to *him*?

Grace laid her fingers on his arm, the contact startling him. "Say you forgive me?"

"Did Sophia slip you some of her pain meds?"

He was rewarded by the tightening of her lips. The hint of her real emotion made him feel on more solid ground: she wasn't entirely the baaing lamb of sweetness she pretended.

"Pain meds?" she said. "What nonsense. Of course not. I've just realized that you've been a perfect gentleman, and that you deserve to be treated as one."

He grunted, which seemed the only polite response to such a pile of rubbish. He was curious, though, about what she was up to. Maybe this outing would prove entertaining after all. He gestured to the terrace stairs. "Shall we?"

Grace walked beside him down the stairs and around the side of the house. He kept glancing down at her, expecting to catch her making obscene gestures at him. Her Stepford wife change of tone was a mask for some purpose, he was sure of it.

His 1956 Jaguar convertible hunkered in a shady corner of the courtyard, waiting to be set free upon the road. They reached the passenger door at the same time, both their hands reaching for the handle, landing upon it together. Grace's hand tightened on the latch, and Declan expected her to make a feminist remark about not being so weak that she couldn't open her own door.

Instead, her grip loosened and fell away. He opened the door and she slid into her seat, and smiled up at him again. "Thank you."

Smiling up at him like that—she was really quite lovely. Did she know? He grunted in response to her, and went round to his side and got in.

"What a beautiful car! Did you find it in such perfect condition, or did you restore it?"

"I restored it," he said. "But I'm sure you don't care about cars."

Her mouth twitched, as if her first impulse was to agree, but then it formed itself into a lipsticked smile once again. "I don't care about modern cars, but *this* is something special. I noticed it the first day I got here, and wondered who owned it."

He didn't believe her for a moment. He grunted yet again—he was devolving into an ape in her unexpectedly polite company—and started the engine. His ears noted the velvet purr that said the carburetors were still in perfect balance. The timing might be a hair too advanced, though; he might want to back it off a bit.

"Where did you find it? There can't be many like this around." Grace ran her fingertips slowly over the polished wood of the dash, and he imagined her doing the same to him. "It's gorgeous. Tell me all about it. Is this wood original?"

Her compliments warmed him. He was proud of his handiwork and he loved the car, so if she was trying to soften him up for a nefarious purpose, she had chosen her method well. He put the car in gear and drove down the driveway, biting back the volumes of detail ready to spill forth about the car. He had touched every bolt, belt, and piston and could happily go on about it for hours to a fellow enthusiast. But Grace was *not* an enthusiast, and she was feigning interest. "I didn't figure you for a car person."

Her lips formed an O of innocence. "But I've never been in a car like this. It feels so *different* from anything else. Can you blame me for being intrigued?"

He smiled despite himself.

He glanced over at her just as they drove over a small bump, making her breasts bounce. His cock stirred, and in a desperate attempt to focus his mind elsewhere he told her about the car: the old barn full of disused vehicles, the eccentric owner, the damage done by rats, chickens, possums, moisture. Encouraged by her ahs and nods and prodding questions, he yammered on for fifteen miles, until the tight turns of Highway One with its sheer drop-offs into the Pacific Ocean gave him a more demanding distraction from her breasts. As full of jiggling delight as those breasts were, they weren't worth driving off a cliff for.

Almost, but not quite.

Grace listened to the car talk with half an ear, most of Declan's story unintelligible to her with its talk of the differential, valves, and manifolds. She'd enjoyed the bit about the rats nesting in the seat stuffing, but there were no romantic tales of former owners or *Topper*esque ghosts to turn the car into more than a beautiful hunk of metal for her. When not focused on the corset presently cutting off the circulation below her waist, her mind wandered to the views of water and man.

More interesting than the car itself was the light in Declan's eyes as he talked about it. With his eyes shining behind his sunglasses and his posture tense with enthusiasm, one hand leaving the wheel to gesture excitedly, it was easy to forget for a moment that she loathed him. He was gorgeous, a hunky man-god full of joy, and he obviously loved the Jaguar with a pure, artless passion.

Had he ever felt that way about a woman?

A wash of doubt hit her. Even with Sophia's help, it was crazy to think *she* could be the one to finally break his impervious heart. Falling in love couldn't be forced. People had tried to control the hearts of others for centuries and never succeeded.

What were her real chances of success? In Sophia's presence, anything seemed possible. Alone out here with Declan, though . . .

She remembered the feel of his arousal against her thigh, that night on the couch. He hadn't faked *that*. So it was possible he was attracted to her, at least as much as he was attracted to any woman.

Grace also had confidence in her ability to learn. If she could learn calculus and to play the piano, she could learn to seduce a man—body and soul. How hard could it be? If your average gold-digging bimbo could do it, surely she could, too, especially when being taught by a master like Sophia.

No goal was worth attaining if it came too easily.

The car conversation with Declan had flagged, which Sophia had warned would happen. "Don't fill silences with chatter," she'd warned. "Men don't want to hear it. Find something to ask him about that truly interests you—about himself, his work, the sports he plays, or his opinion or knowledge of the world. If you can't think of anything to ask, make eye contact and smile, and tell him what a marvelous time you're having.

"The most important part of today's lesson," Sophia had gone on, "is that when you are with a man, he feels he is responsible for everything that happens, from the weather to the traffic to your happiness. Each of your smiles and frowns will be taken personally, even if you're smiling because you saw a pretty dress in a shop window. He's the one who took you by the window, so he'll take credit for the smile. The converse is that everything bad must be ignored by you. If you get in a car accident, praise him for his quick thinking that kept it from being worse. If you get stung by a bee, say the sting is to help you remember such a lovely afternoon."

"Isn't that kind of transparent?" Grace had asked.

Sophia laughed. "Darling. Men see what they want to see, and they all want to believe they are gods in the eyes of women."

Grace looked over at Declan, and when he glanced at her she smiled. "It's a beautiful day."

He nodded.

"It's *glorious!*" she cried, flinging her hands into the air.

"It's not *that* exciting," he grumbled.

"Are you kidding?" she demanded, beginning to believe it as she said it. "This is everyone's dream of California—driving down Highway One in a convertible, the sun shining, a handsome guy at the wheel. What more could I ask?"

A self-satisfied smile pulled at the corner of his mouth, a dimple pressing into his cheek. "It *is* a nice day for a drive."

It worked! Sophia was right, he was mentally taking credit for the weather, the road, everything. Sophia was a genius!

Her self-confidence high, Grace set a mini goal for herself: by the end of this outing, she'd get Declan to kiss her. Not a peck-on-the-cheek kiss, either, but a real full-contact tongue thruster.

She grinned. She'd have him dancing for treats by the time she was done with him.

The road noise meant conversation was on a semi-shouted level, so Grace was content to let Declan play tour guide, pointing out the occasional landmark. The more she smiled and nodded and asked innocuous questions designed for him to display his knowledge of the area, the more relaxed he seemed to become, so that by the time they looped back through farmland, toward Monterey, he was driving with his elbow on the door and an easy grin on his lips.

Grace had started to enjoy herself as well, and not just in see-ing how well she could control Declan's mood. He was a good guide, telling entertaining anecdotes and reciting snippets of history about the places they passed. She was surprised that he almost came across as . . . charming.

Perish the thought!

Eventually, though, Grace's empty stomach began to complain that they'd been driving for at least forty minutes, and her jolly mood began to fade. She was *hungry,* as only a half-starved dieter postworkout could be. She hoped Declan remembered that lunch had been part of his offer.

Grace surreptitiously wedged a finger into the top of her lavender corset, trying to relieve some of the binding pressure. "Comfortable," her ass, although it did make her feel strangely sexy to have her waist pinched in and to know what a naughty pair of panties she wore. It just didn't seem right that a girl could be squished to the point of numbness by her overconstructed underwear but still have enough space in her stomach to feel hungry. At least they were headed west, which meant back toward civilization. Lunch couldn't be far behind.

Just as her mouth began to water at the thought of a basket of warm, soft sourdough bread smeared with butter, Declan turned off the main route onto a side road.

"There's something I want to show you," he said.

"Great!" Grace said faintly. They left vineyards behind and traveled up into grassy hills cut through by ravines thick with pine.

They passed a few houses, and fields fenced with barbed wire holding the occasional drowsy cow or horse. Declan slowed the car to a crawl as the road deteriorated, and without the sixty-mile-per-hour breeze Grace began to feel the heat of the sun on her head and shoulders. Sweat popped out between skin and corset, and she suddenly wished she had that big bottle of water Cyndee kept trying to force down her throat.

At last he pulled off to the side of the road and parked near an opening in a fence. The engine died and Declan got out. "Are you up for a short hike?" he asked, coming around to her side and opening her door.

Grace put her feet in their high-heeled sandals on the rough ground. "Sure!" she lied, and resigned herself to dusty feet and ruined shoes, and lunch being far away. She followed him into the field, eyes on the ground, stepping carefully in the long golden grass that still held touches of springtime green.

Were there rattlesnakes in this part of the country? Ticks? Ground-dwelling wasps or yellow jackets? She and the outdoors usually got on fine as cordial acquaintances, but she felt vulnerable, wobbling precariously in her open-toed shoes. When a bird burst from the grass nearby, she jumped and nearly lost her balance, grabbing Declan's arm for support and emitting what she had to admit was a squeal.

Note for further research: which came first, the helpless damsel or the ridiculous shoes? She could devise an entire study around personality changes in women depending upon their footwear for the day.

"Are you okay?" Declan asked.

"Yes, sorry," she said, letting go of his arm. "Lost my balance for a moment." She remembered Sophia's advice and, smiling, added, "Thanks for catching me."

He took her hand and put it back in the crook of his arm. "Just a little bit farther, I promise."

"No worries," she said, but couldn't think of anything both positive and believable to add. She was too hot and hungry to be clever.

As they entered an area of flattened grass, he picked a broken wooden stake with a fluorescent pink streamer from the ground.

"What the—?" he muttered, then looked out over the field around them, which dropped away down a long, gradual slope to the valley below. "Stay here a minute, will you?" he asked, and jogged off.

Standing motionless and alone, Grace finally became aware of the countryside around her. The vineyards and farms through which they'd driven stretched across the rolling valley and up the lower slopes of hills, their man-made regularity blending easily into the softness of nature. Sounds enfolded her in quiet layers: the sough of the faint breeze over the grass, crickets chirping, the scratching of a bird that landed on the flattened grass and poked for food; the distant, fading rumble of a tractor. It was a beautiful, peaceful place, and she wished she were in a better mood to appreciate it.

Declan was halfway down the slope, picking another broken stake out of the grass. He tossed it aside and took out his cell phone.

Grace could feel sweat trickling down her temple and between her breasts and prickling on her upper lip. Her hands were getting the tight, overstuffed-sausage feeling that always came with heat. Hunger, thirst, the bright light, and her high ponytail conspired to threaten her with a monster headache, and in hopes of defeating at least one of them she reached up and pulled the elastic from her hair, letting the red waves fall around her shoulders. Her scalp thanked her even as her nape protested the warmth.

She found a safe-looking patch of flattened grass and sat down, unbuckling the torturous shoes and setting them aside. Ticks and snakes be damned, her poor suffering body couldn't take it anymore.

She stretched her legs in front of her and leaned back on her hands, the relaxed posture giving her a bit of space in her corset.

A breeze swept over her, cooling the moisture on her face, and she closed her eyes. If she sat very still, maybe she wouldn't melt.

Declan's voice carried to her, a deep, irritated murmur as he talked to someone on the phone. A few minutes later she heard him approaching, but didn't open her eyes until he sat beside her on the grass. "So what's going on?" she asked.

"Bored kids, I hope," he said. He was sitting with his knees up, his arms resting atop them. "All the survey stakes have been pulled up and scattered."

"Scattering stakes doesn't sound very entertaining, even for bored kids. What is this place?"

"It's the future home of a hundred and twenty middle-income families, if I can pull it together, and if wrongheaded environmentalists don't muck it up."

"A housing development, here?" she asked, appalled. "But it's so beautiful! Why would you destroy it?"

"People need homes."

"Let them live closer to town! Why erase an open space like this?" Aunt Sophia's voice was in the back of her head, scolding her for her negative tone, but she couldn't hold back the words.

"It's relatively cheap land."

"So you'll make a bigger profit, at the expense of the environment?" she cried.

"No . . . ," he said with exaggerated slowness, as if speaking to a dim-witted child. "Because middle-income families cannot afford homes built on expensive land. The people who work in the Monterey area can't afford to live there."

She shook her head. "There has to be a better solution."

"I welcome you to try to find it. In the meantime, I trust you won't stick your nose into business you don't understand."

She made a noise of disgust. "So why did you bring me here, anyway? You had to have guessed what I would think."

"I thought you might enjoy the view," he said flatly.

"Oh." He'd been trying to be nice and, she realized belatedly, he had been showing her a part of his life. She swallowed further argument, though the taste was bitter, and tried to think flattering thoughts. "It *is* a lovely view. I wouldn't mind having a house that looked out on it myself."

He slanted an assessing look at her. "It's not going to be a bunch of tract homes, you know. If all the funding and approval come through, we're going to build a sustainable community with shared common spaces and vegetable gardens. There will be gray-water recapture, solar-heated water, we're investigating innovative building materials like straw bales . . . all things that will bite into profit, but will result in a model community that could be emulated throughout the country."

"So why are environmentalists on your case, when it's such a green project?" she asked.

"Because they're zealots who think it's a sin to build a house!"

Grace murmured noncommittally, suspecting there was more to it than that. However green the development, it would still mean that this quiet hillside would be covered in a crusty scab of houses. "Well, whatever the case, I'm sure you're more than a match for them."

"Your friend Dr. Andrew is one of them."

"Really?" she squeaked, perking up, then catching herself. The last thing she wanted was for Declan to sense her interest in Dr. Andrew. "But he's not my friend. I've only seen him once since the day I arrived, and he was in serious doctor mode, costume and all."

Declan chuckled and shook his head. "Sophia."

"What does she make *you* wear?"

"I don't do costumes."

"Maybe a pin-striped suit and a pocket watch?"

"I don't make a fool of myself to curry favor."

"That's hardly fair; pleasing someone isn't the same as currying their favor. There's such a thing as kindness."

"Either way, the ass gets kissed. I'm surprised Andrew hasn't been hanging around more."

"Does he usually?" she asked, playing with a blade of grass, afraid to meet his eyes.

"Only when he wants something."

"Then I guess there's nothing he wants."

"You don't think he might be interested in you?"

"No, of course not!" She felt a blush blooming on her cheeks. After their last encounter, it would be the furthest thing from his mind.

"You underestimate your appeal."

She raised her eyes, surprised by the compliment.

"Although . . . ," he said, looking her up and down, "I'm not sure that this spruced-up version of yourself will be to his taste."

She looked down at her dress. "What's wrong with it?"

"You'll intimidate him. His type doesn't do well with overt sexuality. It scares them."

"What nonsense. Besides, this is *not* a sexy dress. It's perfectly decent."

"Not on you it isn't," he drawled.

Her blush deepened. "At any rate, I'd think that a medical doctor would be at home with the human body and sex. It's a perfectly normal biological function."

Declan laughed. "Just because he knows how to give you a pelvic exam doesn't mean he'd have a clue as to how to give you an orgasm. You can't learn it from a textbook."

"So you're the expert on that?"

"Damn right."

"Riiiight."

"Hey, a hundred satisfied customers can't be wrong."

"The type of women you sleep with, they're all probably a bunch of fakers."

His grin was devilish. "Want to find out for yourself?"

"No," she sniffed.

He leaned close, his mouth near her ear. "Try me," he whispered, sending shivers down her neck.

"You're disgusting," she said, heart thumping. "Never."

"The lady doth protest too much."

"The lady's stomach turns."

He tsked and sat back, a devilish grin on his lips. "And here we were having such a nice outing. I knew it was too good to last."

"Not on *my* account," she said. "Seriously, do you behave this way all the time with women? Because if you do, it's beyond me how anyone ever lets you score."

He shrugged, untroubled. "A lot of them seem to like it. Be honest. Even you like a bit of caddish come-on, a bit of naughty innuendo."

"It makes my skin crawl."

"I'd be more convinced if you said you were indifferent," he said.

"You're sicker than I thought if you prefer loathing to indifference."

"Ah, but loathing means you're affected. And that you're appalled at your own reactions. You're attracted despite yourself." He leaned close again, his torso almost, but not quite, touching her own. He took his sunglasses off, then slid hers down her nose. Electric turquoise blue gazed intently into her eyes.

"What are you doing?" she gasped, trying and utterly failing to sound severe. Her heart was thumping.

"Looking."

"At what?"

"Not *at* what. *For.*"

"*For* what, then?" she asked.

"Hatred."

She gave him her hardest look. "See it yet?"

"Nope." He leaned back.

Grace slid her sunglasses back up, her hands shaking. "I hide it well."

"Nah. You're too attracted to me to hate me, that's all."

She shook her head in disbelief. "Unbelievable."

"How long's it been since you've been laid?"

"Excuse me?"

He put his fingertips to his lips, raised his brows, and in a Queen Victoria accent said, "Oh my, oh dear, we musn't speak of such things!"

"It's not prudish to refuse to answer such a rude question. You're . . . you're . . . being *vulgar.*"

"I'm a man. What did you expect?"

"A bit of gentlemanliness."

"'Gentlemanliness.' Haven't heard that one for a while. Sure you wouldn't rather have sex?"

Grace rubbed the spot between her eyebrows, feeling the strain of keeping up her end of this conversation. "I'd rather have lunch."

"Hunger is a sublimated desire for sex."

She groaned in frustration. "Or maybe I'm *hungry.*"

"Okay, I'll ask something a little less intrusive. When was the last time you had an orgasm?"

She gaped at him.

"I assume you've had one, at least once?" he asked. "Maybe you gave it to yourself. I can't see you letting a guy do it."

"*Why* do you insist on tormenting me?" she wailed.

"So you think talking about sex is equal to torture. Interesting."

"I do like talking about it—with the right person." She gave him a pointed look.

"I don't mean talking about the politics of it. I mean talking about the nuts and bolts. The physical reality. You and your type are all talk, no action." He added almost as an afterthought, "Worse yet, it's boring talk."

"Oh, for God's sake, what type of juvenile manipulation technique is *that* supposed to be?" she said. "Now you think I'm going to unfasten my dress and get all melty for you, just to 'prove' that I'm not a sexually frozen, intellectualizing feminist?"

The corner of his mouth twitched in a shamed-dog grin. "I was hoping."

He'd just been egging her on this whole time? She laughed. "Keep right *on* hoping."

They sat in silence, and gradually the chirping of the crickets and the gentle breeze soothed away Grace's annoyance. The most troubling part of the whole conversation—if she'd admit it to herself—was that talking about sex brought sex to the forefront of her mind, and what the mind thought, the body readied itself for. Declan was a horndog who didn't belong in her life, and yet . . . and yet, her body *had* become "melty" at the thought that maybe, just maybe, he might touch her.

How pathetic.

"You know . . . ," Declan said into the quiet, "I could give you an orgasm without laying a single finger on you."

"We're back to that topic, are we?"

"Bet your precious Dr. Andrew couldn't do that to you."

She stared at him for a long moment. "What is wrong with you? I mean, really? Were you weaned too early? Were you traumatized by walking in on your parents having sex? What?"

"Not a single point of contact, my body to yours."

Grace snorted. "Your conceit knows no bounds," she said, even as she squirmed a little, her curiosity sparked. "How?"

"I won't tell you unless you agree to let me do it."

"You know I won't."

"On the contrary," he said.

His look of smug certainty made her want to smack him. "Why on earth would you think I'd go for it?"

"It's win-win for you. If I can't do it, you get to laugh at me. If I can, you . . . well, you get an orgasm."

"With you watching."

"I've got to get *some* benefit."

"And if you failed, you'd blame me," she pointed out. "You'd use it as proof that I'm what you think I am, a joyless prude. Sounds lose-lose to me."

"Aren't you at least curious?"

He wanted to make a fool out of her again. It could be his only motivation. "Why would you even suggest such a stunt to me?" she asked.

"The truth? Thinking of you doing it turns me on."

She blinked, surprised. Absurdly, insanely, she was flattered, and a little aroused herself. "So where your penis leads, you follow."

"You say that like it's bad."

She shook her head. "I can honestly say I've never met anyone like you. I'll give you that, Declan. You are a unique piece of work."

"Glad to hear it. My offer is sincere, by the way. I *could* give you an orgasm without touching you."

She felt tingling over her skin, and for a moment she didn't doubt him. She looked him in the face, trying to gauge what was going on in his head. Maybe he had some sort of personality disorder, or an Asperger's-like social disability that made him unaware of how far over the line he'd gone.

Or he was joking.

She narrowed her eyes behind her shades. No, not joking. *Bluffing.* He didn't expect her to take the offer, and when she refused, he'd have fodder for 101 new insults and accusations. No way he could do what he said. And he knew it.

It was time to turn the tables.

Grace put back on her mask of sweetness and curiosity. "So you truly can do that, give a woman an orgasm with just mind power or your voice or something? Since I *am* so prone to intellectualizing sex, it sounds like something worthy of study. I'd like to see if you really can do it."

His face went still. "You're saying yes?"

Ha! She knew he'd been bluffing. "Give me your best shot," she dared. With all this blather about following his penis and being so freewheeling about sex, she was beginning to suspect that *he* was the one who was all talk, no action. No way on earth could he have predicted she'd take him up on his offer.

"You'd have to play along. I can't do it if you're fighting me."

She could sense him trying to buy time. He was desperately seeking a way out of his own trap.

"You'll do it, really?"

She felt mirth bubbling up inside, and forced it down. He looked so stunned! "I *said* yes."

He looked intently at her for several long seconds. "You swear," he finally said, "you'll do whatever I say."

She felt a quiver of unease. That intent look of his, could he really be considering— No, no way. "What the hell. I'm on vacation," she said blithely, and crossed her arms over her chest and waited, her lips pursed and eyes open wide in obvious expectation of the nothing that was to come. "Go for it."

"You could at least act like you were turned on by the idea," he grumbled.

Grace smothered her smile of victory. Score one for Team Grace. "That's *your* job, isn't it? Turning me on? Of course, if you know you can't . . ."

"Oh, I can."

"There's not *too* much dishonor in a forfeit . . ."

He stared at her for another endless moment, then spoke. "Lie back."

Grace flinched. "Wha—?"

"You said you'd obey me. Lie back."

"I don't like the word 'obey.'"

"Call it 'collaboration' if that pleases you more."

"Does that please *you*?" she said, buying time as her stomach fluttered. What was going on here? He was supposed to back down.

"To know that you so badly want me to bring you pleasure that you're willing to help?" His voice dropped. "Oh yes, that pleases me."

"That's not what—"

"*Shhhh*," he whispered, and held his index finger a hairbreadth above her lips. "Allow me the fantasy. And lie back."

Confusing thoughts crowded her head. He couldn't mean to try it. And he couldn't mean he really *was* turned on by the thought of watching her reach a climax. Most confusing of all, why was her body tingling, enjoying the shock of what he'd said he'd do?

Don't fall for his games, Grace, she warned herself. *Make* him *fall for yours.* Sophia had warned her that she'd need to engage his sexual side if she was going to hook him. This was part of the hunt.

"Don't let me touch you," he said, leaning so close to her that she was forced to lower herself onto her elbows. He kept coming, forcing her to lie back in the grass, and propped his hands on either side of her head, holding himself above her. His turquoise eyes were dark with emotion, his face strangely serious. She caught the flicker of his gaze over her face, as if he was searching for some clue of what she was thinking, and she felt a sudden certainty that he'd never done this before.

He doesn't know if it's going to work.

A smile curved on Grace's lips. A deep feminine instinct told her to go ahead. She sensed that all her power lay inside that flicker of uncertainty.

"Take off your sunglasses," he said.

Grace did as he bid.

Holding her gaze, Declan lowered his mouth toward hers, stopping so close that she could feel the heat of his lips above her own. He hovered there for a moment, then moved over her cheek, her temple, tracing in the air above her skin the path that his lips would have taken upon her skin. Grace held herself motionless, tense with the possibility that at any moment he would break through that invisible wall and make contact.

"Close your eyes," he said.

She obeyed, feeling at once more vulnerable but also more intensely aware of the moist warmth of his breath upon her skin. He moved his mouth over her ear and gently breathed, then trailed the gossamer touch of air down the side of her neck, dwelling at the base, creating a pool of heat.

"Lower the top of your dress," he murmured against her skin.

Her eyes popped open. "No!"

He raised his head. "You said you'd play along."

"I didn't think I'd have to undress!"

"I didn't hear that as a condition. Do you forfeit, then?"

She bit her lip, hesitating.

He laughed softly and started to ease away from her. "I knew it. You lose."

Anger flared inside her. He knew it, eh? "Who said I'd let you off the hook?" She sat up and untied her dress at the waist, enjoying the look of shock on his face. When the knot came free she hesitated again, caught for a moment on the reality of baring herself. "Are you sure no one else will see?" she asked, though it was his own eyes that concerned her.

"There's no one here but us. For the moment, anyway."

Still she hesitated. To be bare breasted in the open in a field with a man she did not trust . . . "You first," she said.

"Me?"

"Strip. I'll do whatever you tell me to, but only if I'm not the only one exposed."

"Fair enough."

Thirty seconds later, he was tossing his boxers aside. He sat beside her, uninhibited, seemingly indifferent to the evidence of his excitement. Grace couldn't help staring at it, then forced her gaze away, following a trail of hair to his navel, then up to his broad chest where it spread into a wide pelt coating the muscularity of his upper body.

"Too hairy for you?" he asked, a laugh in his voice.

Grace flushed. "No, I just . . . I, uh," she fumbled.

"Lower the top of your dress," he said softly. "And take off your bra."

She teetered for a long moment on the edge of forfeit, the idea of doing what he said—both disrobing, and whatever came after—having too much against it to let her continue. She felt like she had when as a girl she'd come to her turn to use a rope swing into a lake. She'd dragged the end of the knotted rope with her up the ladder nailed to the side of a tree, but when she turned around and saw the vast distance between where she was and the water, she'd frozen, images of all that could go wrong flooding her head.

"You don't have to, Gracie," her brother had said. He was next in line; half a dozen kids waited behind him, dripping in their wet bathing suits, their eyes on her.

She hadn't said anything. She'd looked back at the lake and known that she either did it now or lived with the knowledge that she'd wimped out. Do it or not. Something inside her had disengaged from the fear, and a strange, disembodied calm had come over her. She gripped the rope and swung.

The same thing happened now. Feeling as if she existed outside herself, in a world without fear, she opened her dress, revealing the corset beneath.

She heard Declan draw in a quick breath, and gathered the courage to look at his face. His eyes were upon her body with the same intensity that she knew her own had had on him. She unhooked the front of the corset and opened it.

She had good breasts, she at least knew that. They were full but high, and cantilevered off her chest with no visible means of support. She had a small rib cage that made the breasts themselves look even larger than they were.

"Good God, those are natural, aren't they?" Declan breathed.

"Every inch. And *you* don't get to touch them."

"Then you do it for me."

Her eyes widened. "What?"

"Touch them."

Feeling awkward, the protective safety of dissociation threatening to break, she placed a hand on her shoulder and started to slide it downward.

"Yes, like that! Slowly, slowly, down, down . . ." His voice went hoarse, his gaze fixing on her body as if nothing else in the world existed.

Grace followed his commands like a marionette pulled by strings composed of words. She'd never touched herself in front

of someone before, but her awkwardness fell away under his fas-
cination and she started getting aroused by *his* arousal. Her own
hand became more sensual in its touch, lingering and fondling.

"Lie back."

She met his eyes as she did as he bid, reading the excitement
there.

"Close your eyes," he commanded. And then he directed her,
move by move, in how to touch herself.

She knew where he'd eventually send her hands. When the
command finally came and she slid her hands down over her
waist, her belly, her upper thighs, and began to pull up the hem
of her slip to reveal the indecent panties, she opened her eyes to
watch Declan's reaction. Sunlight blinded her to all but the tense
shadow of his body rising up beside her, a dark satyr naked with
her in a field. She closed her eyes again, her mind filled with half-
dreamed images of Greek myth, gods and maidens, satyrs and
minotaurs, bacchanalian frenzies of naked flesh and wild, open
spaces.

Grace felt herself approaching her peak, and in her mind images tumbled over one another of male joining female, of men
and gods and mixtures of both pressing into women's flesh; into
her own flesh, as she became each maiden pinned and plundered
upon the grass. In a desperate moment, she reached out blindly
and grasped Declan's arousal. He groaned, and she gasped and
arched, her muscles going rigid with pleasure.

And then the waves receded, washing away, taking with them
the fantasy images that had filled her mind. She let go of Declan
and brought her hands up to her chest, resting them idly there as
she came back into herself, feeling almost as if she'd been elsewhere and was just now settling back into her body.

Reality returned with the prickling of the ground against
her skin and the chirping of the crickets. She sat up, blinking,

and pulled her garments back into order, and as she did she met Declan's eyes. He hadn't moved: he was still nude, still erect, still gazing at her with unsatisfied intensity.

A shy smile touched her lips as she covered her breasts. "You weren't bluffing. I'm not sure your methods were entirely fair, and technically I did it to myself, but if anyone asked, I think I'd have to say you did what you said you could."

"Thanks," he said hoarsely, still making no move to dress.

She glanced at his sex, so obviously primed and ready, and in need of relief. He was probably hoping she'd offer her hands or lips. That hadn't been part of their deal, though, and her sated desire made it easy to shove aside the feminine guilt of receiving without giving in return. A small, wicked, shameful pleasure at her power over him and her first taste of revenge licked at her heart.

It was only when she reached for her shoes that the understanding apparently dawned on Declan that there would be no tit for tat, no reciprocal sexual attention. In a rush of movement he began to dress, so that by the time Grace was standing on shod feet, he was clothed beside her.

Grace remembered Sophia's words of advice about compliments. She'd wandered far off the lesson plan today, and it was time to return. "Thank you very much for that lovely interlude," she said, taking Declan's arm as they started back toward the car. She tried to keep the wickedness out of her voice, drowning it with honeyed sincerity. "I've never experienced anything quite like it, and will remember this day for a long time."

"So will I," he said curtly. He was walking stiffly, his pants tight across his crotch.

Her inner vixen purred with cruel delight. Perhaps even more compliments were in order. "Every time I hear crickets I'll think of today. Won't you, too, every time you *come* here? You probably won't be able to help thinking of your victory and gloating over it, every time you come. Do you come often?"

He slanted a dark look at her. "Excuse me?"

She blinked in innocence. "Do you come often? To this field. The construction site."

"Often enough."

She squeezed his arm. "Good. I'd like to think that you'd be reminded of this day every time you come, even though I *was* the loser."

He scowled. "Are you messing with me?"

"Hmm?"

"Nothing," he growled.

They reached the car and got in. Grace resecured her hair in its ponytail, and was about to put on her sunglasses when she suddenly put her hand to her mouth in alarm and gasped.

"What?" Declan asked.

"I'm so sorry, I've just realized—we left things a little, er, *unbalanced,* didn't we? I mean, you never got to . . ."

He looked at her, wariness and a flicker of hope in his eyes.

Grace blinked at him. "If it's not too late, I mean, if the mood hasn't been killed . . ."

The hope flamed. "Yes?"

"Maybe I could do my part to help you . . ."

His lids lowered seductively. "You mean . . . ?"

"Yes! It seems only fair. I could, well . . ." She saw the expectation in his eyes, the rekindling flames of lust, and it was like the scent of blood to the hunter. Her long-term plan to slowly win his heart and then crush it fell to the side, victim of this unexpected opportunity to inflict a wound. Her eyes wide with innocence, she took aim. "I'd be happy to tell you how to . . ." She faltered, the harsh *go fuck yourself* waiting in the back of her throat.

She couldn't say it, couldn't pull the trigger on the crude words. "I could tell you how to *do* yourself."

There was a long moment of silence, and then his face darkened. "You *are* messing with me."

Grace feared that she'd pushed him too far, and knew her thoughts were showing on her face. *Think of something harmless, something innocent! Something that will make you look ditzy and frothy!* Out of her disturbed mental depths sprang an image of *My Little Pony*. Ponies! With strawberry-scented manes. Ponies dancing and singing and having their hair combed. She felt her face relaxing into the innocent happiness of a three-year-old. "I enjoyed what you did for me. Why shouldn't I want to reciprocate?"

He started the engine. "It's kind of you, but I'll pass, thanks."

Ponies! This one has bubblegum hair! "Are you sure? I really wouldn't mind. You see, I've never watched a guy jerk off before."

He gave her a look, warning her that she was on thin ice.

Grace put on her sunglasses and smiled.

CHAPTER
11

Declan didn't talk to Grace during the drive to the restaurant, his mind spinning round his unsatisfied desire and the ludicrous notion that she had all but told him to go fuck himself.

She hadn't really meant her words that way, though, had she? He kept glancing over at her, checking for signs that she knew she'd scored a point off him. All he saw was serenity, however, and a few times he thought he heard her singing under her breath, a bouncy, childish, vaguely familiar song about little ponies.

He was capable only of impersonal civilities until after they'd pulled into the gravel parking lot of a small, rustic restaurant with a view of the ocean. He opened Grace's car door for her and kept up the polite facade as they went inside and were led to a table. He followed her through the restaurant, unable to keep his eyes off her full buttocks as she swayed ahead of him, and felt his hackles rise as he saw the eyes of several other men in the restaurant, both young and old, swivel to ogle Grace and her Marilyn Monroe curves. He shot them all dark looks.

When they ordered, Grace asked for the halibut. Declan scowled, and as soon as the waitress was gone said, "I thought you were a vegetarian."

"I am," she said, and laid her napkin in her nap. Her back was straight, her posture perfect. He'd have thought she was as prim and proper as a virgin princess, if not for her ridiculously voluptuous breasts and the image burned into his brain of her lying in the sunlight pleasuring herself through her split-crotch panties. Split-crotch panties and a corset, for God's sake! How the hell was he supposed to have expected *that*?

"Halibut are animals," he pointed out, quite reasonably, he thought.

"But not farmed."

"It's okay to kill a wild animal, but not a domestic one?"

"It's the industrial farming practices I protest," she said, beginning to look annoyed.

"Then eat free-range."

"Why do you care what I eat?"

He laughed. "I don't. I just don't like it when people say they're something that they're not."

She took a sip of water and smiled sweetly. "I'm flattered that you'd rather listen to me spell out all the details of my food choices than be satisfied with a single, imprecise word like 'vegetarian.' You must really want to know all about me." She blinked innocently. "Shall I list every animal and animal product I will and will not eat, and give you the reasons why? It should make for a good lunchtime conversation; thank you for suggesting it!"

He narrowed his eyes, examining her face for telltale clues. A small twitch at the corner of her mouth betrayed her. "Goddammit, you're messing with me again! Did Sophia teach you to do that?"

"*Again?* When was the first time?"

He leaned forward over the table and was pleased to see her eyes widen in alarm. "Not half an hour ago, as you very well know. You're a cock tease, Grace Cavanaugh."

She leaned toward him until their faces were only inches apart. To an outsider they must have looked like lovers sharing sweet nothings. Her expression remained pure, her voice sweetly high. "Can you swear to me, Declan O'Brien, that you have never in your life—no, make that never in the past year!—had a sexual encounter with a woman where you came but she didn't?"

"I always reciprocate."

"*Always?* Really! Well, you *are* an unusual man, aren't you? So there was never a time that you rolled over and went to sleep, figuring she'd had plenty of foreplay and hey, women are different, they can be happy even without an orgasm?"

"I've never heard any complaints," he said, an unwelcome note of defensiveness in his tone, embarrassing to his own ear.

"That's because you were asleep." Grace tapped the tip of his nose with her index finger, like the fairy godmother chiding Little Bunny Foo Foo. "She was probably lying beside you while you snored, fantasizing about another man as she finished herself off."

His twinge of embarrassment was his clue that she'd hit upon a truth. Of course it never happened the first few times he had sex with a woman, but yeah, once they were more comfortable with each other, once he no longer felt he had to impress and win her, he did occasionally slack off a bit and pretend not to see that flicker of disappointment in his partner's face. It was so sweet to slide into sleep afterward; what guy wanted to sit up and go back to work on a woman, especially when it could take another half hour to get her off?

"Pussy tease," Grace whispered naughtily, making it sound like an invitation.

He sat back and crossed his arms over his chest. "Even if that might have happened once or twice—if!—that doesn't make it right that you left me hanging."

She sat back, too. "So I'm to do as you say and not as you do?" The exaggerated innocence was gone from her face, replaced by a knowing wickedness that unsettled him. Where was the fumbling, uncertain Grace Cavanaugh he expected, or even the boringly righteous one?

"Those were past relationships," he said. "Nothing to do with this one, between me and you."

"Declan," she drawled. "We do not have a relationship."

"There's sure as hell *something* going on," he muttered.

"And even if we did have one, if I were you I would think twice about asking me to treat *you* as you have treated me."

And there she had him. His behavior that first night was neither forgiven nor forgotten, nor should it be. He retired from the discussion in defeat.

Grace moved the conversation on to innocuous topics and he gladly followed. Somehow she'd turned the tables on him, and he felt like a fourteen-year-old boy in the presence of a dangerous femme fatale.

What the hell was going on?

CHAPTER

12

"He didn't touch you *at all*?" Sophia demanded, putting down her dinner fork.

"Nope. I took his arm a couple of times, but Declan didn't lay a finger on me during our outing." Grace speared a snow pea on her fork and nibbled it, trying to make it last. She had only eight of them on her plate. She'd counted. She was regretting her dietary restraint at lunch. Temporary sexual satisfaction and a purring sense of what she could only call vindicated bombshellitude had made her willing to forgo the bacon burger and fries she'd dreamed of.

The afternoon had left disturbing images in her mind. Ever since she'd parted from Declan several hours ago, she'd been having intrusive, arousing thoughts of him.

"How very odd," Sophia mused. "Declan is usually such a physical man. Did it seem that he *wanted* to touch you?"

"There was a point at which I strongly suspected he did, yes," Grace said drily, "but he didn't give in to it." There was no way she was going to tell her aunt that Declan had sat naked next to her and watched her masturbate in a field. She was having some trouble believing it herself. "Then at lunch I got a bit argumentative with him, and that seemed to kill any remaining attraction he felt."

When did she ever lose herself in her own desires like she had in the field? She was always in control of herself during sex, always mute, a part of herself distant and observing, aware of the awkwardness of sex and how she wasn't living up to the enthusiastic acrobatics and full-throated moans and cries of pleasure that were the standard for a liberated woman. Only repressed women were silent and still, right? But somehow, alone with Declan in that open field, she had disengaged from her self-consciousness. Her higher brain had shut off and the lower animal had taken over.

She must have looked ridiculous, her pale flabby body lying on the ground in the corset, all arched and contorted as she petted herself. But Declan hadn't seemed to think so . . .

"Grace, Grace, Grace," Sophia said, and sighed. "How are you going to crush Declan if you can't keep better rein on your emotions? Arguing with him to what end? Winning a battle of words is not going to win you his heart."

"Am I supposed to play dumb and agree with everything he says?"

"When you show your intelligence, then yes, it must appear to be in support of his position. He won't like you if you make him feel like an idiot."

"I would think an intelligent man would enjoy a spirited debate."

"Men have to fight for status and resources all day. If you were his business partner, sure, go ahead, argue with him. But as the woman he goes to for relief from the rigors of the world, no. He won't see it as a welcome challenge; he's more likely to feel a need to soothe his ego with a softer woman."

Grace curled her lip. "So I'm just supposed to be a big downy pillow for his tender ego to fall on at the end of the day?"

"And what do *you* want, Grace? A man who constantly

questions your choices and thoughts, or one you know will always support you?"

"A true loving partner can and should do both. You can't automatically expect support from a spouse if you're being an idiot. The days of Tammy Wynette and 'Stand by Your Man' are over, and good riddance. You can't coddle someone, protecting them from reality as if they were a child. If they're making a mistake, they should be told—and first and foremost by their partner!"

An expression of delicate pain flitted over Sophia's face, her gaze briefly rising heavenward. "So when the world is against you because you made a mistake, your husband should be first in line to tell you you're a fool?"

Grace tucked in her chin. "I should hope he'd be gentler about it than that. But yes, he should tell me if I'm wrong."

"Like a parent corrects a child?"

"No, *not* like a parent correcting a child. Like two equal adults trying to help each other."

"By criticizing."

"No! You're deliberately misunderstanding me!" Grace cried.

A smile played on Sophia's lips. "Do you love me at this moment more than ever?"

"No!"

"And whose fault is that?"

"Yours! Obviously!"

Sophia chuckled and took a sip of wine, her eyes dancing with merriment. "And still you think that arguments strengthen your relationships with other people."

Grace opened her mouth to protest, then scowled and shut it.

"And where is Declan this evening?"

"Out with Cyndee." Grace played with her precious vegetables, starting to feel uncomfortable. There hadn't been anything worth arguing about with Declan during lunch. She'd been feeling powerful and had deliberately antagonized him, and enjoyed each verbal stab she'd landed. There'd been nothing kind about her actions, quite the opposite.

Sophia gazed at her, silent and sage as an owl.

"Well, what are you supposed to do, then, if someone you care about is being an idiot?" Grace finally asked.

"There's your start, right there."

"Where?"

"In a questioning mind, being willing to accept that you do not already have all the answers. Really, Grace, for a supposedly open-minded, liberal woman, you have a remarkably rigid, judgmental viewpoint."

Judgmental? Rigid? Me? Was that how people saw her? Sophia's accusation shot an arrow into the core of who she'd always thought she was. Her lower lip trembled.

"Darling, don't look so downhearted!" Sophia chided gently. "It's a small flaw and common as daisies. It even has its advantages; it keeps a person from flitting off after flaky notions. You don't want to be blown by the wind, this way and that, do you?"

Grace shook her head, and sniffed back the incipient tears. She *was* judgmental, wasn't she?

"You're a brilliant, gorgeous, warmhearted woman, and best of all, you care about learning and growing."

Aunt Sophia thought she was brilliant? The ache in Grace's heart eased slightly.

Sophia reached across the table and put her hand on Grace's, squeezing it in gentle reassurance. "If you *do* sometimes feel that you want to be more flexible, I'm sure you'll find a way to do it. There's nothing a woman like you can't do, when you put your mind to it."

"Thanks, Aunt Sophia. It means a lot to me to hear you say that."

Sophia's eyes crinkled. "So how do you feel about your mean old aunt now?"

Grace smiled. "Very fond."

"Exactly," Sophia said with smug satisfaction, and sat back.

It took Grace a moment to put the pieces together, and then she choked on her shock. "You——! You just played me, didn't you?"

"I meant every word."

"But——!"

"But?" Sophia echoed innocently.

"Ooooh!"

"It's all part of what I've been trying to teach you, Grace. A large part of charisma is in making other people feel that, in your eyes, they matter. They are worthy of attention. You care about who they are, what they say, how they feel, what they think. To do that, you must be open to and respectful of ways of being that are different than your own. You must *listen* to people. Not argue with them. Argument means I'm right, you're wrong. Listening means I think your perspective matters and can teach me something. And what you can learn is how to get what you want from that person . . . or how to destroy them."

Grace stared at her aunt in horrified awe. "You're evil."

"Powerful women usually *are* called nasty names. Ball breaker. Witch. Tartar. Castrating bitch. Why not add 'evil' to the list?"

Grace pointed an accusing finger at her aunt. "Don't try to pull that 'put-upon feminist' stuff with me. You're a master manipulator."

"Which just means I'm old and I'm wise. All social interaction is a game of manipulation, Grace. One way or another, we're all trying to get what we need at the least cost to ourselves."

She was starting to feel queasy. "Is that what all these lessons in being a bombshell are really about?"

"I said that from the start. But maybe you weren't listening."

Grace slowly shook her head. "I'd thought it was just about being sexy."

Sophia gave the sigh of the weary. "I feel like Anne Sullivan, having finally succeeded in getting Helen Keller to recognize the word 'water.' Hallelujah! We begin to progress."

Grace didn't know if she wanted to progress. Spike-heeled shoes and low-cut dresses suddenly seemed harmless compared to the mind-set Sophia was trying to teach her.

"How are you going to approach Declan the next time you see him?" Sophia asked.

Grace grimaced, the day's events somehow seeming an even worse reflection on her character after this talk with Sophia. She *had* manipulated him, and gotten what she wanted. She'd been mean. She'd been selfish. She'd been argumentative and judgmental. "Declan seems to bring out the worst in me. Maybe I should practice flirting with someone else for a bit."

"Like whom?"

"Someone who doesn't make me so angry. Maybe . . . Dr. Andrew?" Grace peeked up from under her eyebrows and found Sophia's green eyes resting on her. Grace shrugged a shoulder. "He seems nice." And maybe she could be herself with him, and have him like her.

"Indeed, he is nice. Nice enough that I think the two of you might make a very good match."

Grace's mouth dropped open. "You do?"

"Yes. It was obvious the day you arrived that there was an affinity between the two of you."

A rush of relief went through Grace. "Then I can practice my lessons on him, instead of Declan!" Andrew, who seemed in tune with who she had always been, not Declan, who made her act in ways so unfamiliar, both good and bad. Mostly bad.

"What of your plans for revenge?" Sophia asked. "Are you giving up so soon? I was serious about the fifty thousand dollars if you get Declan to fall in love with you."

Grace choked on a bite of snow pea. "You were?"

"It would be good for him to have his heart broken. And what better final exam for all my teachings?"

"I . . . I don't think I'm up to conquering Declan quite yet." The viciousness of the plot was finally becoming real to Grace, and she wasn't sure she could ever go through with it, especially not for money. At the same time, part of her was afraid that she *might* have the stomach for it. What if she truly succeeded, and then enjoyed stomping all over Declan's heart? *Gah!* It would make her no better than Sophia. "I can't seem to control my tongue around him. I obviously need more practice."

Sophia pursed her lips, considering. "He really did hurt you that first night, didn't he?"

Grace blinked in surprise and nodded.

"You feel vulnerable with him. You strike out because you're afraid of him."

Grace hunched her shoulders. Yes, she was afraid of him. Afraid, too, of the twisted, unruly emotions he roused in her.

"Dear, that's all the more reason to continue trying to win him over. You can't go through life striking out at people who hurt or scare you. All that does is show them that you're weak. It tells them that they've wounded you, and a strong woman never shows her wounds unless it serves a purpose."

"But how am I supposed to control the fear? I can't help how I feel when I'm with him."

"You put on fresh lipstick and you smile and you charm him. You make him believe that it will take more than a few mistakes on his part to hurt a woman like you. You remember that you are Grace Sophia Cavanaugh, a beautiful, intelligent woman, and his opinion and feelings about you are of no consequence. You charm him not because you care what he thinks about you but because it's the most effective way to disarm an enemy."

"Won't that just make him think he can treat me badly and get away with it?"

"No. He'll relax and let down his guard. If he's unpleasant to you, it's because he's scared, too."

"Of *what*? What could he possibly be afraid of?"

"That, my dear, is for you to find out."

"But how am I going to develop a relationship with Dr. Andrew if he sees me with Declan?"

"I think pursuing both at once could work out very well. Andrew has a tendency toward passivity where women are concerned; he loves from afar. If you give him plenty of encouragement, he'll be spurred to compete with Declan for your affections. But don't make it *too* easy for him; every man needs to believe that he's the hunter. He'll be proud as a lion when you eventually dump Declan in his favor."

Grace tilted her head, looking at her aunt with a now-familiar mix of awe and disbelief. "You've worked this all out already. You enjoy moving us around like chess pieces, don't you?"

Sophia smiled serenely. "It's better than watching Animal Planet all day."

CHAPTER

13

"I had a really nice time," Cyndee said, leaning against the jamb of her open apartment door, her key ring jingling as she swung it back and forth on a finger. "Dinner was really good. I liked it a lot."

"I'm glad you enjoyed the meal," Declan said, his gaze skimming over for the hundredth time the body so clearly on offer, hoping he would see something to rouse his appetite. She wore a cheap, clingy red cocktail dress that showed off every toned inch of her superbly fit physique. There were hollows between her neck and collarbone, shadows where her ribs connected to her sternum, and her upper arms were no bigger around than a cucumber. He'd happily slept with many women who looked the same, although he'd never quite overcome the fear that if he held one of them too hard she'd snap in half.

Grace looked pillowy and soft, as if her body would bounce back from any grabbing or bumping, and there was plenty to grab and bump. She was a hot fudge sundae to Cyndee's tiny scoop of lemon sorbet.

Cyndee wet her lips. "I promised you a workout. Do you think you're up to it?"

He'd been hungry for sex since Grace walked up beside him in her green dress, and his balls were well past indigo. All evening he'd tried to convince himself that a few hours of mattress work with Cyndee would cure what ailed him, but now that sex was his for the taking, he didn't want it.

At least, not with Cyndee.

Grace had brought him to this point—*twice,* if he counted the night on the couch—so Grace should be the one to provide relief.

"I'm sorry," he said to Cyndee, "but I don't think it would be ethical. It might create a conflict of interest for you."

Cyndee's pert little nose wrinkled in confusion. "Huh?"

"Grace is your client, but she's also a friend of mine. If things didn't work out between me and you, it could cause problems between you and Grace. I wouldn't want to endanger your working relationship with a client."

Cyndee rolled her eyes and heaved an exaggerated sigh. "For God's sake, Declan, if you don't want to have sex, all you had to do was say so. Go wank yourself, will ya?" She flounced into her apartment and slammed the door in his face.

Declan blinked in surprise as the dead bolt engaged with an audible click. What *was* it with women telling him to go fuck himself today?

Happy to be free, he jogged back to his car and drove toward Sophia's house, where he'd be spending the night. It was only eleven o'clock; Grace might still be up. She was probably lying across her bed on her stomach, reading a dreary feminist manifesto, and wearing nothing but underpants and a T-shirt.

His balls ached at the thought.

He'd left her feeling badly used, even though it had been his own fatheaded idea to claim he could give her an orgasm without touching her. It had been a bluff, meant only to rile her; he'd never imagined she'd call him on it. He'd never done anything with another woman like what he'd done with Grace out in that field, and he knew he'd never forget the sight of her touching herself in obedience to his every word. She'd been as uninhibited as a wild creature, seeking her release under the blue of the open sky. When she'd wrapped her hand around him, he'd felt a shock of pleasure that almost sent him over the edge.

Then she'd climaxed, her hand had dropped away, and she had lain for several long moments enjoying the aftermath of her own pleasure. She'd sat up and covered herself, ignoring the rock-hard bit of anatomy she'd grabbed in her moment of need.

From a strictly rational point of view, he had nothing to complain about. Emotionally and physically, however, he suspected he'd been had.

He came to the turnoff for Sophia's driveway and slowed, then changed his mind and roared past, heading south for Highway One and a long drive to clear his head.

Going up to Grace's room in the hopes of her saying "Why, yes, I'd love you to take me, would you prefer the bed or the chair?" was obviously not going to work. She was playing games with him, and winning.

He wouldn't approach her until he'd figured out her playbook, and how to rewrite it in his favor. By the time this game was over, Grace Cavanaugh would be begging him to score on her. It would be touchdown, Declan O'Brien.

Assuming that he could figure out *how*.

Grace peered out a hallway window for the eighth time, checking the courtyard below for Declan's car. It was past midnight and he still wasn't back from his date with Cyndee. All she could picture was the two of them noisily boinking each other, Cyndee bouncing on top of him and squeaking like a chew toy, her ponytail swinging.

She made a fretting sound and forced herself to return to her room, swearing that she wouldn't check again. It was undignified. Besides, she didn't care about Declan and Cyndee.

Andrew was her focus now. Declan could go share STDs with however many women he wanted.

Really. She meant it.

She returned to her desk, where she'd been typing up her latest research notes.

Where was she?

Ah, yes.

Author continuing to show clear signs of mental disintegration. Feeling lust for man Author despises is contrary to Author's self-identity as a woman who puts the inner person above the outer shell. Acting further on that lust may critically rupture Author's sense of self. Despised male must be avoided at all costs.

New question: Has Author's recent focus upon appearance created a greater value in her eyes in the physical appearance of others? Author's judgments of others may become progressively shallower as more time and energy is spent trying to be attractive. The importance of anything is dependent upon the attention one pays to it. This could explain Author's attraction to the despised male. His sexually attractive appearance has taken on disproportionate importance in Author's mind because Author has been forced to obsess about appearances.

Alternative theories for Author's attraction to Declan:

Chronic physical hunger displaced into appetite for sex, any sex, with anyone.

Pheromones. Despised male's man musk had been noted upon initial meeting on stairway.

Anger/fear transformed into false sense of sexual tension.

Reverse psychology—Author attracted because trying hard not to be. Bad boy/good girl dichotomy creating artificial sense of excitement.

Grace sat back and read over her theories. They looked sound and relieved her of the fear that she might actually *like* Declan. She'd have to pay close attention to her emotions and physical state to ensure that something innocuous like hunger did not lead her into bed with the man.

She should probably have a baggie of almonds handy at all times: snacking as prophylaxis.

After the long, disturbing dinner talk with Sophia, the two of them had retired to her den, where Sophia had given her a new set of lessons to use in pursuit of Dr. Andrew. They were subtle, intended to reach his subconscious, and seemed free of negative potential. She read back over what she'd written.

Lessons for use on Dr. Andrew

Mirroring:

Every high school psychology student has learned that mirroring behaviors indicate that one person is in tune with another: for example, when you pick up your glass, the person across the table does the same. Sophia says that clumsy flirts try to fake this response, intentionally mirroring their target so exactly that they are quickly detected. The key to successful mirroring is to delay the response by a few seconds and to alter it. Instead of picking up the water glass as soon as the other person does so, the skilled seductress will count three beats and then swirl the contents of her wineglass.

Author's practice of this technique with S. has confirmed that the concentration required to delay and alter the mirroring taxes one's mental resources to such a degree that simultaneous intelligent conversation is impossible. Author suspects this is S.'s goal.

New question: Given that physical behavior can create emotional/psychological conditions (i.e., smiling on purpose has been shown to improve mood), does intentionally mirroring a person with whom one is not naturally in sync create a feeling of bonding? By behaving as if you like someone, do you in fact begin to like him better? (Another theory as to why Author is attracted to the despised male!)

Touching:

Sophia advises touching own hair, lips, and sternum while conversing with Andrew. He will read this as a sign that Author is attracted to him, and his attention will be drawn to all areas touched. This is supposed to be performed with such subtlety that no conscious note is made of self-touching actions. Overt displays of this sort can be read as signs of mental unbalance: drunkenness, desperation, easy virtue, social clumsiness.

Author has firsthand reason to doubt the veracity of this theory. Author believes that, given proper circumstances (i.e., the woman is attractive enough that the man would be willing to have sex with her—this is not a high bar to surmount; even Agnes Gooch got laid), the more self-touching the better. Declan may be an anomaly, however, easily stimulated to sexual excitement. One wonders about his childhood.

Sophia also advises frequent light touching of Andrew on the hand or arm. This will let him know it's okay to touch Author in return. No mention made of what grabbing Andrew's dick would let him know, although Author suspects the meaning is clear.

Why didn't Declan ignore his "I can make you come without touching you" and go ahead and touch Author? Why didn't he even ask, when he so clearly wanted to do it? Obviously, proving himself right was of greater importance than physical gratification. This fits with Author's earlier experience of him as arrogant pig. Conclusion must be that he has an abnormal disconnect between heart, body, and mind.

Note: Must find a copy of the American Psychological Association's Diagnostic and Statistical Manual of Mental Disorders and determine whether Declan meets the criteria for personality disorder. Despised male may also be a psychopath. This might also explain Author's incomprehensible attraction, as psychopaths are known to be preternaturally charming when they wish to be.

Grace chewed her lip. That last bit seemed a little harsh. She shrugged, then closed the file. She stored her files on the University of Washington's server, just in case someone got snoopy with her laptop. The only other person with access to it was her advisor, Dr. Joansdatter, but she never opened files unless Grace asked her to, to review her work.

Grace opened her e-mail and found the draft of a letter to her mother.

> *To answer your question about how the dissertation writing is going, well, Sophia has been giving me a lot to think about, and I'm wondering how to work it into my thesis. I'm still trying to get her to open up about her past, but she keeps changing the subject. She says she's more interested in the present, and only fools and the nearly dead dwell on times and people long gone.*
>
> *I know that Sophia was always considered the black sheep (black ewe?) of the family, and that Grandma hated her. Did she ever give you a hint as to why (beyond the obvious flaws of Sophia's character)? I know your relationship with Grandma was strained, but I just wondered if before she died she softened up a bit and shared more about her sister.*
>
> *I like Sophia more than I thought I would. I think there's a heart under all the venom, and whether she's being kind or cruel, she's never boring.*
>
> *No mention yet of when she's actually going to get her hip replaced, by the way.*
>
> *Much love to you and Dad,*
> *Grace*

She sent the e-mail, then, with a sigh, forced herself to respond to the latest "What's the evil bitch up to now?" message from Cat.

Cat,

Don't worry so much! I wouldn't want Sophia for an enemy, but fortunately she seems to like me, and in her own perverse way she wants to help me. I've been taking copious notes on her, and really think my summer here is going to add a valuable dimension both to my dissertation and to my thinking as I move forward in the field of Women's Studies. Sophia is making me look at things in a whole new way, and that's always important. I think when we're in an academic environment we run the risk of our viewpoints becoming too narrow and inflexible, and too divorced from concrete reality. We get wrapped up in our theories and see people only through that filter. We forget what a variety of ways there are of being in the world—or worse yet, we never get to see those ways of being at all.

I guess that's true of anyone living their life, academic or not. But I have realized that I was too emotionally invested in being right where Sophia was concerned, and wasn't having as open a mind as I should have. Which isn't to say I'm unaware of how treacherous dealing with her can be or how warped some of her ideas are. Don't worry, I haven't drunk the Kool-Aid! Sophia's a genius in her own way, though, and it would be a waste not to learn what I could from her.

We'll have lots to talk about when the summer's over. You'll probably be appalled by what I've learned, but don't worry, I haven't been transformed into an evil mini-Sophia.

Not quite yet, anyway.

Ha-ha, just kidding!

Love,

Grace

CHAPTER 14

"And then Brooke told Chandler that I was hanging out with Brandon, so now he thinks I like *him* instead of *him,* and I don't know what to do." Lali threw up her hands, then dropped them onto Andrew's arm and looked imploringly into his eyes. "What do you think, Dr. Andrew? Should I tell him how I feel?"

"Er . . ." Andrew cast a helpless look at Grace, who shrugged. They were walking down the path onto the beach in Carmel, joining dozens of others who'd gathered for a volunteer beach cleanup. It had been Lali's idea to go, and she'd swept Grace and Andrew along in her wake, for which Grace was grateful; her own halting attempts to speak to Andrew had resulted in foot-shuffling awkwardness on both their parts. All Sophia's advice the night before on how to handle him had fled from Grace's mind, chased away by the embarrassment of their last meeting and the knowledge that he thought she looked bloated.

Her confidence was further lowered by remembering his comment on the day she'd arrived, about how it wasn't the beauty of the face across the dinner table that mattered. It no longer seemed quite so sweet. If a guy liked you, you should seem pretty in his eyes, even if you were a bit out of shape and liked the occasional chocolate chocolate-chip banana cookie.

Lali shook Andrew's arm. "You're a guy. What do you think? Would he like that or be turned off?"

"I . . . uh, tell which one what?"

Lali rolled her eyes and turned to Grace. "*Men!* They act like we speak in tongues. Ooh! There's Kristie. If I don't see you later, don't wait for me! I'll get a ride with Kristie." She dashed off across the sand to her friend, leaving the two of them alone.

Grace and Andrew headed toward the tables where the organizers were handing out trash bags and directing the volunteers. Grace glanced shyly up at Andrew, hoping to catch his eye or at least exchange a smile, but his attention was elsewhere and he seemed oblivious to her presence. Or maybe he, too, was just too shy to look at her.

But then Andrew's face lit up with recognition and was transformed from coolly distant to warm and vivacious. "George!" he called as they approached one of the tables, behind which stood a skeletal, wildly bearded man in an old T-shirt declaring LIFE'S A BEACH, AND MOST DUMB SUCKERS ARE CRAPPING THEIRS UP!

"Dr. Andrew," George answered, and pumped his hand in enthusiastic greeting. "Good to see you out here!"

"Just doing my part," Andrew said as Grace smiled by his side, waiting to be introduced. The thin man had squirrelly eyes, open a little too wide, so that the whites showed at the top of his irises. *Was he on drugs?*

"Excellent, excellent," George said, handing Andrew two bags. "See you at Thursday's meeting?"

"Wouldn't miss it!" Andrew moved away from the table, leaving Grace standing there, still expecting to be introduced. George's eyes skimmed over her, then looked past her at the next volunteer coming up for a bag.

Grace felt a small stab of hurt. Was she invisible today?

"Who was that?" Grace asked as she caught up to Andrew and they moved out of earshot. "He acted like I didn't exist."

"Don't take it personally. He's probably hungry."

Grace felt a stab of shame and looked back over her shoulder at the man, whose skeletal frame and ragged clothes now made sense. A homeless man was volunteering to help save the environment, and here she'd been silently calling him Squirrel Eyes. "You mean, like homeless hungry?"

"No, I mean he hasn't had his midday nutritional allotment."

Grace swung her gaze back to Andrew. "What?"

"His midday—"

"Oh, lunch!" she laughed, and suddenly remembering Sophia's advice to touch him, gave him a nudge with her elbow. "You had me for a moment."

"I guess you could call it lunch. He follows CRON."

"Is that a guru?" Grace asked, lurching through the soft sand. She could already feel sweat starting to break out. She was wearing a big straw hat, an apricot cotton sundress, and pale green Havaianas flip-flops. She grabbed Andrew's arm to stop him as she slipped out of the flip-flops and bent to pick them up. When she glanced up at him this time, still bent over, she was rewarded by his gaze on her chest.

Ha! He wasn't so impervious to her after all!

"It's an acronym: Calorie Restriction with Optimal Nutrition."

"Oh, a diet. No wonder he's grumpy." They resumed their walk toward the south end of the beach, Grace walking a little closer to him so that their arms occasionally brushed. Apparently her question had distracted him from the allure of her feminine self, though.

"CRON isn't a diet, it's a lifestyle," Andrew said, becoming animated. "Calorie restriction is the only proven way to slow the aging process. You cut down on your food intake by about forty percent—while maintaining maximum nutrition—for the rest of your life."

"How perfectly horrible."

"You think cancer, heart disease, and death aren't horrible? CRON might give you a long life free of all those things."

"I'd throw myself off a cliff if I was never going to be able to eat pizza again, and I mean pizza on a fairly regular basis," she said teasingly.

He met her eyes. "When you're seventy-five, you might think a little differently about whether or not you should have eaten those pizzas."

Grace bit the insides of her cheeks, clamping down on the urge to argue, and forcefully shoving aside the thought that Dr. Andrew was a wack job on the topic of food. *Open mind, Grace, open mind . . .* She made herself smile and entwined her arm in his, and felt his surprise at the contact. "You seem to know a lot about it," she purred. "Is George a patient of yours?"

"I met him at a CRON meeting."

"You're one of them?" she squeaked before she could control herself.

"There's some sound science to back it up, although of course no one is sure yet if it'll work the same way in humans as in animals."

"But how could it possibly be good for you? I'd feel awful if I ate so little. I wouldn't have any energy or be able to think."

"Not at all! You get great energy doing CRON, and until you try it, you don't realize how much the processed crap that makes up the standard American diet is fogging your brain. About the only complaint people make is of a loss of libido."

Grace stared at him in shock. "No libido?"

"The body doesn't want to reproduce when its calorie intake is low."

"So you—er, I mean people who do CRON, they don't have sex?"

"I don't mean *that*."

"Phew! Long life is one thing, but long life with no food and no sex . . . What's the point?"

He stiffened. "To be perfectly honest, CRONies do think much less about sex than those who eat a standard diet. But that's good, and I should think you'd approve. Isn't civil discourse between men and women much easier if there isn't a constant subtext of sex? Isn't it much easier for them to be friends and coworkers?"

"You're right, of course," she said, even as she felt a stab of disappointment. She wanted to be friends with Andrew, but she also wanted him to ogle her, at least a little. She wanted him to have a sexual thought or two with her in the starring role.

An image of yesterday afternoon in the field with Declan made her stomach flutter. That had been *so* naughty, and nothing about the day had been about building a stable friendship.

But Declan was bad. Andrew, and his ideas, were good. She squeezed his arm and leaned a little more against him, looking up at him with as open an expression as she could muster. "Tell me more about CRON. I'm very interested."

He happily obliged, just as Declan had in talking about his car. Gesturing with his free hand he said, "It's pretty exciting, isn't it, the idea of living to be a hundred and twenty, or even longer. It's conceivable that you could extend your life so far that with the medical advances of the next fifty years, you could live past two hundred! Can you imagine?"

Sadly, Grace could. "At one pizza a week for fifty-two weeks in a year, for two hundred years, that would be more than ten thousand pizzas a girl wouldn't eat. Probably not much bacon, either," she added faintly.

Andrew put his hand over hers on his arm and stopped walking, looking down at her with eyes moist with emotion. "Your body is a beautiful temple designed by God, Grace. You should not spoil it with poisonous foods."

She gazed back, feeling the warmth of his regard. He thought her body was a beautiful temple . . . but he also thought she was vandalizing it with her eating habits.

"You don't truly want to put destructive garbage like pizza in it, do you?" he said.

Yes, she did, she very much did. She would slather her temple with tomato sauce and melted cheese, given half the chance. But she stuck to Sophia's advice, and said, "I'm a vegetarian already." She shuddered, suddenly overcome by a *lust* for freshly cooked bacon—crispy, fried, rich with salty, fatty goodness. Bacon still warm from the pan, with a thin rind of maple-cured deliciousness on the edges. Her mouth watered. *Bacon, bacon, oh, how I love you, bacon . . .*

"That's good! Grace, that's so good." He beamed at her as if she were a child in need of praise for using the potty.

She felt patronized, and a shard of orneriness made her modify what she'd said. "Well, flexitarian, to be precise. Declan accused me of hypocrisy for calling myself a vegetarian when I still eat fish and dairy."

Andrew looked appalled. "There can be a lot of mercury in fish, you know. And dairy . . . Grace, no, really, you need to switch to soy or almond milk."

"Maybe you can help me become a better eater," she said, and batted her eyes at him even as she wanted to cry inside. Good-bye, ice cream; good-bye, cheese; so long, butter and all the marvelous things to be made with it. She was already on starvation rations thanks to the sadistic nutritionist, and it was pushing her over the edge. She couldn't think straight half the time, and her moods were going wonky. She sat around fantasizing about food when she should be writing her dissertation. There was no way she could face a whole lifetime of restricted calories.

"I'd *love* the chance to help you, Grace! You'll see, this will be the best thing that's ever happened to you." He patted her hand where it rested on his arm.

Instead of being thrilled, she felt slightly depressed.

She forgot about Andrew's hand on top of hers as she imagined a bacon and butter sandwich: She'd use white bread, sprinkle sugar on the butter, lay on four or five strips of bacon, then squish it all nearly flat, until the bread was as thin as a flour tortilla. *Mmm*.

Maybe Andrew could eventually be persuaded to eat proper food like that. And then his libido would fire up, and—

"I really don't see why Declan should care whether you're a flexitarian or a vegetarian," Andrew said.

The mention of Declan's name shook Grace free from her mental food orgy. So there *was* competition between the two men. Excellent. "Neither do I. He wouldn't recognize anything as food unless it had four hooves and a brand on its butt."

"He *is* a bit of a Neanderthal, isn't he?" Andrew asked, glancing at her from the corner of his eye as if to gauge her reaction.

"I didn't know men like him still existed," she drawled, thinking of how good Declan had looked naked. "I thought they'd all gone the way of the woolly mammoth. Still, I suppose there are women who find that type of raw masculinity appealing," Grace said, hoping to tap into that sense of competition. They were now a couple hundred yards past the last of the volunteers. "This looks like a good spot to go to work, don't you think?"

"I've never understood why women are attracted to that sort," Andrew complained, bending down to pick up a plastic bottle. "Don't they know what a lousy husband he'd be?"

"Oh, I suppose every woman has *some* vulnerability to his type."

"But not you, surely?"

"No, of course not," she soothed, picking up a chunk of Styrofoam for her bag. "I can appreciate him as a physical specimen, but that's as far as it goes. I, of course, could never be interested in a man without a graduate degree."

"But—" Andrew started, then seemed to swallow his own words.

"What?" Grace asked innocently.

"Declan does have an MBA," he admitted.

"Does he?" Grace said in false surprise. She took on a musing stance. "Hmm. So there's a brain with the brawn."

"But that's not the type of degree you were talking about. It might as well be a glorified accounting degree. You're more interested in ideas. You're an intellectual and want someone you can talk to."

She smiled warmly at him. "Yes. You understand me perfectly."

He visibly relaxed.

"Besides, it's not like Declan would see anything here to his taste," she said, and touched her hand to the neckline of her dress, letting it linger there atop the mound of one full breast. The breeze off the ocean had raised her nipples into pebbles beneath the apricot fabric, and she saw Andrew's gaze linger on the small peaks. Maybe he wasn't quite so low on libido after all. "So I'm perfectly safe from a sexual caveman like him."

"Perfectly," Andrew said weakly.

They wandered through the shoreline greenery, picking up bits of flotsam and jetsam: more Styrofoam, shoes, scraps of floats and ropes, ancient aluminum cans bleached by salt and sun, and random pieces of plastic. The ocean was calm, the waves making a gentle *shoosh shoosh* upon the shore. It wasn't bad for a first date, Grace decided. They had a pretty setting, a nontaxing task to fill the silences, and the pleasure of sand on bare feet. It was worlds calmer than her outing with Declan had been.

And that's a good thing, she told herself.

"Why does Sophia like Declan so much?" Grace asked some minutes later, her mind having failed to move off the topic of the despised male.

"She feels possessive of her projects."

"Projects?"

"Without her, he probably would have ended up selling cars after college," Andrew said.

"Yeah?"

"He had a full-ride football scholarship. He was hoping to go pro, but his junior year he blew out his knee and, with it, all his chances. Sophia redirected him toward business and helped get him into Wharton. He probably wouldn't have his MBA or have gotten into such a good firm on Wall Street without her, and he sure wouldn't have been so successful in San Francisco and around here if not for her connections. Half of his clients are friends of hers."

Grace felt a prick of disappointment. She'd thought Declan was a self-motivated achiever, not a product of someone else's patronage. "That was generous of Sophia to help him like that."

"Sophia can be very motherly, and like a mother, generous to a fault."

"You think she was wrong to help him?"

"I don't think it's ever wrong to help someone who needs it," he said primly.

"But?"

"But I've never been happy to see charm rewarded over merit." He laughed self-consciously and gave her a rueful smile. "Maybe that's left over from watching the popular kids in high school get away with almost anything. You'd think I'd have grown out of that type of petty jealousy by now."

She smiled in return, warming to his admission of such a familiar weakness. *This* was why she'd been attracted to Andrew from the beginning; setting aside the food weirdness, he was just like her. "Did we go to the same school? I know exactly what you mean."

"Weren't you popular?"

"Geek, through and through," she said happily. She didn't need to pretend otherwise with Andrew. God, what a relief.

"No one would guess it now," he said, his eyes taking a detour over her figure.

She chuckled. Those twelve pounds seemed to have made a difference in how he saw her. He *was* ogling her, which just went to show that guys were guys, geek or jock. "Thanks, I think. I liked being a nerdy girl, though."

"Why?"

"A theory I had. I thought that smart kids were too busy following intellectual pursuits to spend time and energy developing their social skills. The social butterflies, on the other hand, weren't intellectual enough to be absorbed in the world of the mind. I thought I'd rather be intellectual and a little awkward than popular and vapid."

"Is that where your thesis idea came from?"

"Kind of, yeah," she said, even as she felt a faint discomfort. The assumptions her dissertation was based on were beginning to sound the faintest bit silly to her now. Not that she didn't think there *was* truth to her hypothesis, but maybe not the all-sweeping truth she'd once thought.

"So you think you can persuade popular girls to give more attention to their minds than to whether or not to get breast implants."

"You think it's hopeless."

"As hopeless as turning one of us geeks into a sex symbol," he said, smiling.

She smiled back, thinking of Sophia's lessons. "I don't know. . . . When we put our minds to something, is there anything we nerds can't do?"

"But we wouldn't ever pursue such ends. You wouldn't want rewards for having a pretty face, would you?"

"I know I *should* say no, but I've been trying to be more honest with myself lately." She touched his arm and leaned close. "Wouldn't you like to live on the 'other side' for a bit, to see what it's like? To experience what it's like to be one of the beautiful people?"

"I already know what it's like, just from observation," he said. "Self-obsessed. Entitled. Ignorant. Like Declan."

Grace drew back. He sounded exactly like she had a few weeks ago. She should be cheering him on, but she wasn't. *Why not?* "You really don't like Declan, do you?"

"I'm sorry," Andrew said, grimacing. "I shouldn't let my dislike show so clearly. I know you spent the day with him yesterday." He slanted her a glance.

"To please Sophia. It was nice to be shown around. I haven't had anyone to explore the area with," she said, tossing him a broad hint.

"The area is about as safe as safe gets. You shouldn't have any qualms about exploring it on your own."

She rolled her eyes under the shield of her hat brim. Maybe geeks *did* need to devote some time to learning social skills. "Declan took me to the site of his development, up in the hills. It was very pretty out there, and I doubt I would have found such a place on my own."

Andrew straightened up with a faded Budweiser can in his hand, his face darkening. "That development! If his type has its way, the entire county will be slathered in housing developments and private golf courses, and the only green you'll ever see will be the containment swales for the runoff water. Destroying open land like that is a sin."

"He says they're going to be environmentally friendly houses."

"The only truly green house is the one that isn't built! Once land like that is developed, it's gone forever. There's plenty of space in towns that could be made into high-density housing, although it would probably be better not to encourage population growth at all. The Monterey Peninsula is in a delicate balance between man and nature as it is, with at least seventy of its plant and animal species threatened. The Smith's blue butterflies are disappearing, and so is the Monterey pine. The Monterey pine, for God's sake!"

Grace looked up the beach to the multimillion-dollar houses lining the shore. She'd read that Carmel used to be a bohemian art colony, but when she and Declan had driven through, all she'd seen were luxury cars and faux fantasy cottages that only the super rich could afford. She was beginning to see Declan's point about there being nowhere for normal people to live. She didn't know enough about it, though, to say whether Andrew's high density or Declan's green village made more sense.

Debating the issue wasn't going to win her any points with Andrew, anyway, if Sophia was to be believed. Better to pretend to agree. "It *will* be sad to see houses there. It was a magical spot, so quiet except for the crickets; I've never heard so many in the middle of the day. The sound of them weaves a sort of spell."

He moved down the dunes and she followed. "Monterey was once thought to have its own unique cricket."

"Oh?"

"No specimens survive, just a drawing by Ed Ricketts."

"Who?"

"Ed Ricketts. 'Doc.' Haven't you read any of the Steinbeck stories set around here? *Cannery Row,* or *Sweet Thursday*?"

"Yeah, of course."

"Ricketts was the inspiration for the Doc character. He and Steinbeck were friends."

"It was a real guy?"

"He was a marine biologist. But in his papers he left a drawing of a cricket with unusual markings that he'd labeled *Gryllus steinbecki*: the Steinbeck cricket. No one ever found a real one, and no one knows if they truly existed, or if he created it and named it after Steinbeck as a joke."

"Wouldn't that be something if there were Steinbeck crickets in that field of Declan's?" Grace said, laughing.

"If there are, they won't last long." He shook his bag of trash. "Looks like we've done our share, doesn't it? Shall we call it a day?"

Grace's lips parted. This was it? They were done? No sitting on the sand and talking, nudging up closer and closer to each other, taking advantage of the solitude and lovely surroundings, waiting for the sun to set? "Uh, sure, okay."

He trudged off and she hurried to follow.

"Do you want to have lunch before we head back to the house?" she asked his back.

"Lunch?" He stopped long enough for her to catch up.

"If you don't have anything on your schedule. Maybe you have an appointment or something."

He glanced at his watch. "No, I have time. I guess I could eat."

"I'd like that very much." She blinked up at him. What was Sophia thinking, saying that she needed to be subtle with Andrew? He needed hitting over the head.

"I know a place that serves CRON-friendly food."

Oh Lord. "Wonderful!"

Grace wrapped her hand around his arm again, taking possession. She might not get fed a decent meal today, but before they parted company she was going to squeeze a kiss out of him. If a girl couldn't have bacon, at least she could have action.

CHAPTER

15

"If you got your hip replaced, you could join me down on the rocks and I would teach you how to fish," Ernesto said to Sophia.

"I know how to fish. I choose not to."

"Then you could sit and admire me while I fish. I could be happy with that." Lali's grandfather smiled warmly, the skin creasing around his dark eyes. With his shock of white hair there was something of Spencer Tracy to him, Declan thought; or perhaps it was the idea of *The Old Man and the Sea* that drew the parallel.

The three of them were sitting on the terrace, sipping iced tea and enjoying the gentle breezes.

Sophia said, "I'm too old and too wise to spend my day sitting on a cold, hard rock admiring an average man."

"I know you are, *querida*. That is why you will sit and admire me, a man far above average."

A vixenish smile curled on Sophia's lips. "The sight of you, while splendid, is not so inspiring that it will hurry me to the operating table for a new hip. I need a greater inducement than to be allowed to watch you fish."

"*Cielito*, there is so much more a new hip will allow." The look he gave Sophia was so smolderingly intimate that Declan quietly excused himself and left them to their flirtation. A glance over his shoulder as he went down the terrace stairs into the garden told him that they hadn't noticed his departure.

He'd known there had been a flirtation between Ernesto and Sophia for many years, despite Ernesto being fifteen years Sophia's junior. He also knew of at least half a dozen other ongoing flirtations Sophia had with men in the area. Collecting them seemed to be a hobby of hers, an afternoon in their adoring company better than any rejuvenating spa treatment. Of them all, Ernesto was the only one who could get under Sophia's skin with his teasing. He didn't have the awe of her that the others did, and Declan suspected Sophia liked him all the better for that.

Declan had spent the morning meeting with the head of the construction company that would be building the housing development, but as they pored over the blueprints, Declan's mind had wandered again and again to Grace.

A small voice protested that he should stop this game they seemed to be playing with each other. There was no upside to pursuing a sexual relationship with her. It wasn't worth the grief she was causing him, and the rift it could cause in his relationship with Sophia.

His competitive instincts had been roused, however, and after a brief battle with reason as he drove on Highway One last night, he had accepted that he wasn't going to be able to let it go. And really, he owed her a good time after being such an asshole that first night.

He came around a curve in the garden path and saw Andrew and Grace sitting on a stone bench with a view out over the ocean, their backs to him.

As he watched, Grace put her hand on Andrew's thigh and turned to face him. Without thinking, Declan stepped to the side to conceal himself behind a large bush. He peered through the leaves at the couple, a stab of dark emotion piercing him.

Grace leaned toward Andrew, her face upturned for a kiss. Andrew shied away.

Declan chortled. The goddamned weenie was scared.

Grace lifted her hands to Andrew's face and framed it. Andrew's body stiffened, and Declan grinned in anticipation of what Andrew might do next. Bolt? Push Grace away?

Declan didn't believe that Grace and Andrew could engage in a major makeout session. It was against the laws of nature.

Grace slowly pulled Andrew's face toward hers and gently kissed him on the lips. She kissed him a second time, then a third, caressingly, her lips brushing across his. Andrew relaxed, his arms coming around Grace's waist.

Declan's stomach dropped, and a furious feeling of wrongness overwhelmed him. He was on the verge of rushing forward to break them apart, when Andrew's enthusiasm took a sudden lunge forward. He squeezed Grace, his mouth opening wide to cover her lips and half her chin. While Grace made muffled noises of protest he pressed her back on the bench, crushing the straw hat beside her and apparently crushing Grace as well.

"Ow, ow, ow!" she cried, pulling free of his slobbering mouth and pushing at his shoulder.

Andrew jumped off her like a dog scolded off a couch, and with as little care; his hand used her breast for leverage, earning a furious curse from Grace as she cradled the injured mound.

"Sorry! Sorry!" Andrew said, his long limbs full of fluttering anxiety. He reached up and smoothed his hair.

Grace sat up slowly, her own hair mussed. "It's okay. Don't worry."

"I should go." He clasped his hands together.

"No, it's okay," Grace said. "My fault."

Declan snorted from behind his bush.

"I need to go anyway. So, er . . . it was a nice day. 'Bye!"

Andrew dashed down the path in the opposite direction from where Declan hid.

"See you on Thursday?" Grace called after him but received no reply. Her shoulders slumped and she leaned forward, resting her elbows on her knees. She picked up the hem of her dress and wiped her chin, then dropped it and hung her head.

Declan stepped back onto the path and went to her. She raised her head at the sound of his approach and looked back over her shoulder.

"Oh, it's you."

He was taken aback to see that she was on the verge of tears. He sat down next to her, noting the sheen of tears in her eyes and the redness of her nose. "Are you all right?" he asked softly.

"Dandy," she said, sitting up straight and sniffling. "Were you spying?"

"Yes."

She chuckled wetly. "No evasion, just *yes*?"

"Yes." With a feather-light touch he brushed the hair back from her face. He was used to seeing her defiant, angry, self-righteous, indignant, surprised, annoyed, impassioned. Never like this, wounded and vulnerable. Unhappy. It distressed him.

"You must have thought that scene was pretty funny."

"Not really." He dropped his hand to her back, to the bare skin between her shoulder blades, and drew soothing circles with his fingertips. He needed to know what had doused the fire in his Grace. "I could tell it was a lousy kiss, but surely not worth crying over?"

She gurgled a sad laugh. "No. It's not that."

He flattened his palm on her back and rubbed. "Then what?"

Grace smiled sadly and shook her head. She couldn't tell Declan that what depressed her was the sudden conviction that however different she might look on the outside, she would never be anything but a geek, and geeks married geeks. Someday she'd find herself married to a man like Andrew: smart, conscientious, cute in his way, passionate when encouraged, but always awkward and shy, waiting for her to take the lead, needing guidance in how to please her physically.

It wasn't necessarily bad; it did encourage her to be proactive where she might otherwise be passive, and she would unquestionably be married to a peer rather than to a man who thought he was her master. But . . .

But it suddenly seemed that life wasn't going to be very exciting if she had to rely on herself for all the seduction and adventure. And she didn't consider exploring the wonders of CRON at a meeting next Thursday to be an adventure. She could have that much fun alone for a week with a six-pack of Slim-Fast shakes, thank you very much.

If she had to be the one in charge in a relationship, then when would she get swept off her feet by passion? When would she be surprised? When would she feel taken care of? Equality was what she'd always wanted—and was *still* what she wanted—but she was starting to realize it wasn't going to come without a price.

And the price was swept-off-her-feet passion.

She shook her head. She'd never been a sexually passionate person. Maybe it was time to give up the dream that someday she would be, if only she met the right man. She was sure that she and Andrew could eventually build a satisfactory sexual relationship, and that was really all anyone could ask for, wasn't it? Everyone knew that passion faded. What mattered was friendship.

"You're being awfully nice," Grace said as Declan's hand moved down her back. "I would have thought you'd be cackling with glee, poking fun at our bumbling."

"Pretending to be thoughtful and caring is my way of lulling you into a false sense of security. My focus is entirely on getting you into bed."

She laughed, even as goose bumps rose on her skin and a muscle deep inside her contracted. How could *he* have this effect on her? Life wasn't fair. "I would have thought you'd had enough sex with Cyndee last night to hold you."

"You would think that, wouldn't you?"

"You *did* sleep with her, didn't you?"

"I'm sorry to say there was a conflict of interest." He nudged her to straddle the bench, facing away from him. She obeyed, and he put both hands to work on her shoulders, his touch neither too hard nor too soft.

"Whose conflict with which interest?" Grace asked as she relaxed into the massage, feeling strangely safe in his hands even as her body tingled. The fumbling with Andrew was quickly fading from her mind.

"Mine with hers. Or hers with mine. It doesn't matter, does it?"

It did matter, but she wouldn't let him know that. "Poor Declan. You're not having any luck, are you?"

His hands moved down her bare arms and she felt him lean close, his breath warm beside her ear. A shiver went up her nape. "It's all part of my plan, as is this innocent back rub. All the cheesy pickup manuals for men tell them to touch a woman to get past her defenses."

Grace's spine went rigid, reminded so suddenly of the exact same lesson that Sophia had taught her. She pulled away from him and stood. "You're not going to get past *my* defenses."

He crossed his ankle over his knee and held it there, the picture of nonchalance. "I'd prefer it if you didn't feel the need for defenses with me at all."

"And where would *that* leave me?"

He smile was slow and delicious. "In my bed, where I would make you very, very happy, I promise you."

The offer went through Grace like a caress. She bristled against it, fearing its effect on her. "Does being this cocky usually work on women?"

"No. They think it reeks of lounge lizard."

His answer surprised a laugh out of her. "Then why would it work on me?"

"Because I already know you want to sleep with me."

"I do not!"

"Your pride makes it difficult for you to admit it to me, I know."

"You're insane," she spluttered.

"We're both curious. We're both horny as hell. So why not go ahead and do it?"

"Sex should mean more than that."

"Sex *can* mean more than that. But it doesn't have to. There's plenty of joy to be had in the purely physical. Say the word, and we'll do it."

"I will *never* say it."

His grin turning devilish.

"That sounds like another challenge."

She showed her teeth in a wicked smile of superiority. "And we know how that turned out last time."

"If memory serves, I did what I said I could do."

"Yet you still lost," Grace pointed out.

"I wouldn't say that. But if it's what you believe, then why not take me on again?"

She laughed at the absurdity of it. "Go ahead. Give me your best shot."

He shook his head. "Come to my room tonight."

"I won't do that. It would be like a lamb walking to its own slaughter.

"Afraid you'll give in?"

Yes! "No. Come to my room instead," she said without thinking, "and I'll prove you wrong."

"You need the security of being on your own turf?"

"No, of course not."

"Then come to my room, anytime after eleven."

"I—" she started.

"I'll be waiting for you." He slid off the bench and sauntered back toward the house.

Grace snorted and put her hands on her hips.

"Anytime after eleven," he called back. "I'll be waiting."

Cocky bastard. There was no way she was going to his room. Was there?

"*Damn*," she said under her breath. It was going to be a very long night.

CHAPTER
ℰ 16 ℱ

Grace came to the end of a Tchaikovsky barcarolle and checked the time: 10:55. She dug through the sheet music in the piano bench and found a familiar piece by Brahms. She sat again and started playing.

She wasn't going to go to Declan's room—crazy to even consider it!—but she couldn't stop herself from checking the clock at the end of every piece of music. She hoped Declan could hear her playing; it was a clear message that she was having nothing to do with his little game.

Although he *had* cheered her up. She'd forgotten all about CRON meetings and clumsy kisses until nearly an hour later, when Sophia asked her how her outing had gone.

What could she say? It had gone well, as far as meeting her goals were concerned. And she had since persuaded herself that she couldn't fault Andrew for being an inadequate lover, when she knew that she herself lacked skill in that area. She'd been known to unthinkingly crawl across a boyfriend's groin before, placing her knee in exactly the wrong spot, and she'd been scolded for not showing more enthusiasm during love-making. She didn't want to think of what a poor blow job she gave.

She shouldn't expect more of Andrew than she was capable

of herself. She'd never seen any study to suggest that men automatically knew more than women about sex. To believe they did
was to indulge in cultural stereotypes and double standards about
male and female sexual behavior.

And yet . . .

Declan knew how to touch her. Declan wouldn't hoist himself off her with a hand planted on her breast. He might even be
able to wring from her those cries of ecstasy that so far remained
unvoiced in her sexual life.

Then again, Declan was not a potential long-term partner,
like Andrew. If only she could take the best of both of them, she'd
have herself the perfect man.

She finished the Brahms: 11:10. Time for another rendition of
"Makin' Whoopee." Ha!

She played the piano for another half hour, expecting at any
moment that Declan would appear and make a taunting comment. She'd have a snappy comeback, they'd verbally joust a bit,
then he'd end the debate by kissing her and dragging her under
the piano for some violent lovemaking.

Eleven forty-five. No Declan.

Grace sighed and shut the piano, feeling bereft and vaguely
frustrated. If he was waiting in his room, he'd probably fallen
asleep by now. She was the only one suffering, and it was her own
fault.

She'd go to her room and prepare for bed, and not let herself wonder if he would come to her. She trudged slowly up the
marble stairs, then paused at the top and looked down the hallway
to the wing where Declan slept. Dimmed sconces lit the way,
creating an inviting path to sexual ruin. Her heart thumped at the
thought of following that corridor and opening the door to his
room. He'd be naked under a sheet, drowsy, but so happy to see
her . . .

She hesitated, the desires of her body seducing her mind into thinking it would be okay, why not? You'll enjoy it. It's just bodies having fun with each other. Harmless and natural.

She forced herself to turn away and head to her room. She couldn't give him the satisfaction of seeing her appear at his door. With a sigh of self-congratulatory relief, she opened her door.

"Hello, Grace," Declan said.

Grace squeaked in surprise. Declan was lying naked on her bed, his back propped up on pillows, the covers folded down to the foot as if to clear the way for serious mattress action. Several candelabrum were near the bed, casting a golden, adoring glow over Declan's worthy body. Music played softly on the radio.

"Wh-what are you doing?" Grace demanded.

"Nothing, yet." He grinned, his teeth Cheshire cat bright.

Grace hurriedly closed the door. "You're supposed to be in your room."

"My mistake," he said cheerily.

"Your mistake, my ass."

"I'll trade you my mistake for your ass. It *is* what I came here for."

She scowled. "That's not funny."

He patted the mattress beside him. "Take off your clothes and come get comfortable."

"Are you drunk?"

"Only on the thought of what we're going to do," he said with a cheesy grin. "I've been thinking about it since this afternoon."

"You go back to your room!"

Declan slid off the bed and walked slowly toward her, sending a wave of sensual panic up her body: she wanted him to stop but also wanted—desperately!—him to keep on coming and do with her what he would.

He stopped toe-to-toe with her and planted his palms on the door to either side of her head, trapping her. She looked into his eyes, her senses filled with his nearness, his warmth, his scent, and most of all the sheer mass of him, so much larger and stronger than herself. A primitive part of her soul silently moaned in pleasure.

Declan slowly lowered his mouth to hers. She watched, wide-eyed, as his face came closer and closer, her whole body tense and poised for flight or fight. His clean, faint masculine scent came off him with the heat of his body, the broadness of his chest and shoulders blocking out the rest of the world. She could feel her heart pounding in her chest and tingling heat flying through her like a flock of startled sparrows.

Declan's lips met hers, a gentle swoop of a kiss that brushed the surface of her lips and then floated free. She closed her eyes and he kissed her again, and she turned her head to follow his lips as they left her, as if begging him not to leave.

Declan's lips landed a third time, and stayed. His lips moved on hers, nipping, pulling, sucking, sliding. Bit by bit he deepened the kiss, breaking down her sham of a resistance until she found herself kissing him back, her head straining forward for deeper, harder contact. She parted her lips and his tongue plunged inside, teasing hers with strokes of wet friction.

Her hands rose to Declan's waist, then slid down to grasp his buttocks, pulling him toward her and feeling his hard erection against her.

Declan's arms came down, wrapping around her and pulling her away from the wall. Breaking the kiss for only the necessary moment, Declan raised the hem of her knit shirt and jerked it off over her head. In another moment he'd undone her bra and tossed it aside. Grace felt a moment's alarm, but then his mouth was on hers again, his arms around her, pulling her torso against his. She was lost in her physical reaction to him, her brain shut off.

She didn't even know he was unzipping her skirt until it fell at her feet, leaving her clad only in her underpants. He maneuvered her slowly toward the bed until they bumped up against it. The mattress touching her warned Grace of what would come next, and a sliver of pride stabbed through her sensual bliss. She wouldn't let herself be had so easily.

She broke the kiss, pressing her palms against his chest to create some separation. She met his eyes. "I don't want this."

His gaze was fierce with sexual tension. "Won't you say it now?"

This was Declan, not some fantasy male who existed only in her imagination, and she would have to see him in the morning. She shook her head.

"Why won't you admit it?"

"Because I'm stronger than you, and I want you to know it. If I ask you to sleep with me, then you win."

His jaw tightened, but her words seemed only to stoke the fire in his eyes. "You *will* ask me. You'll demand it."

"You're wrong."

"Am I?"

She nodded slowly, a delicious frisson running through her body. She knew the challenge she was throwing before him, and how hard it would drive him to seduce her. She *wanted* him to win but didn't believe he could. He'd have to overcome every ounce of her self-consciousness, and that was more than any man could ever do.

Declan turned her around and held her in an embrace, her back to his chest. His lips close to her ear, he whispered, "Do you want to prove I'm wrong?" His hand slid slowly down her belly and into her panties.

Grace closed her eyes and leaned back against him, her knees going weak. "I can prove it," she answered.

He tugged her underpants down until they fell free, the silky fabric pooling on her feet.

Declan's hands rose up her body to cup her breasts, as his lips found the tender spot at the base of her neck and kissed and teased, his tongue and teeth nipping and rubbing, sending shivers of electric delight over her skin.

He put one knee on the bed to ease her onto it with him, turning her and pressing her back until she lay face-up beneath him. He slid his hands down her arms to her wrists, then raised them above her head, pinning them to the mattress as he kissed her again.

He broke the kiss and raised his head, grinning wickedly at her.

She wondered why until he released her wrists and she became aware of what he'd done.

She was tied to the bed. She craned her neck, trying to see above her head. "Declan, what—"

"I can't have you touching yourself this time. The only relief you'll get is from me, when you beg for it."

"You planned this!" she protested. By craning her head she could just see the padded handcuffs and the tether to which they were affixed. It had all been hidden under the pillows.

"I warned you I'd been thinking about this all day."

She tugged against the restraints, but they held firm. A shiver went over her, of fear or excitement she wasn't sure. No one had ever tied her up before. "You're scaring me," she said, not sure if it was true.

He stroked the hair back from her face and looked into her eyes. "I won't hurt you or go against your wishes. You know that."

She did know that, for *almost* certain. Truth was, though, she didn't really know *what* he was capable of, did she? She hadn't predicted he would tie her up.

"I won't hurt you, but I'll torment you." He smiled, slow and lazy, and traced his fingertips over one breast, circling in on her nipple and gently squeezing it like a ripe berry. "Just remember that it's always in your power to put an end to your suffering. You only need a single word."

"What word?"

"Yes."

A rush of panic and desire went through her.

"Now where shall I start?" he said, playing with her nipple. "Here? Or maybe you'd rather feel my tongue somewhere else?" His fingers trailed down her body to the juncture of her thighs, and then his hand grazed over her hip.

"Perhaps I should begin where I left off this afternoon, with a massage." He reached down over the side of the bed, then returned with a small bottle of massage oil. He poured some into his palm and rubbed his hands together, then laid them on her sternum. "I'm going to enjoy this," he said.

Grace shivered in anticipation, both scared and thrilled. Oh God, he was really going to touch her!

Declan glided his oiled hands over her breasts, releasing the delicate scent of almonds. She watched his face, its expression one of intent absorption as his warm, strong palms slid over her flesh, like a sculptor working in clay. His gaze flicked up to hers, his eyes dark except for the gleam of reflected candlelight.

Embarrassed, Grace closed her eyes and turned her face, tucking it against her arm. Having her eyes closed, though, was almost worse—physical sensations seemed twice as strong without visual distraction. She buried her face deeper into her arm and tried not to enjoy his touch too much. He *wouldn't* make her say yes!

Declan moved from her chest to her arms and hands, her

torso, her legs and feet. He turned her over to do her back and her buttocks, and even to dig his fingers into the base of her skull, tempting her to release all her tension. For several minutes she forgot herself, and time lost meaning as she floated free of the world, forgetting why and where and with whom she was. Even embarrassment disappeared under the soothing, sensual touch of his hands.

He turned her onto her back again, then raised her knees and then spread them apart, making them fall to the sides like an open flower.

Grace's eyes went wide, all the relaxation jolted out of her. "What are you doing?" she cried, as she tried to close her legs. His hands held them open, making her feel even more exposed and vulnerable.

"If I told you, it wouldn't be a surprise."

"I don't *want* surprises."

His gaze searched hers, then he slowly released her knees.

She felt an almost overwhelming urge to close them, but his eyes on her were a challenge, asking if she had the courage to leave herself open to him, to play this game they had dared each other to. Her pride gave her strength, and she let her legs lay open in invitation. She would make herself obey, and let him do as he wished.

Declan gave his satyr's grin, then grabbed a pillow and put it under her head. "I want you to be able to watch me," he said, and then lay down beside her, his head toward her feet, his body partially propped up on the mattress by an elbow between her legs.

Again he massaged her with the almond oil, working his free hand over her abdomen, her hips, her inner thighs. There was no relaxation for her this time, only a slow building of anticipation and impatience as she waited for his touch to turn from massage to sexual caress. She wanted to groan at him, *Get to it!*

When he lifted his hand away, Grace made a tiny whimper of disappointment, and then clamped her lips shut at the betraying sound.

His gaze locked with hers, and he lowered his hand to touch her. She turned her head and closed her eyes, feeling the heat of a blush.

Grace's nerve endings felt as if they weren't just waiting for his touch, but reaching for it.

He took her to the very edge of release, and then . . . stopped.

She shifted and tried to bite back the small noise of impatience that threatened to slip from her throat.

After several seconds he touched her again, and she inched toward the edge of bliss, her body straining, and then . . . he stopped.

She moaned softly in frustration. Enough of this teasing!

His next touch was quick and light, as sudden and fleeting as a hummingbird. Her body jerked, her eyes flying open. He was still watching her, his face deadly serious. She turned her face to her shoulder, eyes shut once more, and vowed not to open them again.

"Remember that I have the advantage of seeing how you touched yourself. And I'm determined to show you that I could do it even better."

She began to arch her back in pleasure, then caught herself and forced herself to remain still. In this contest she could hold the advantage only if he didn't know what she was feeling.

But, oh . . . it felt so good!

His pressure increased, his touch giving her what she wanted much too slowly. She wanted to beg him to go faster, and had to clench her jaw against the words.

Just as her frustration was verging on anger, he suddenly shifted gears and changed to a fast, flicking touch that tore a soft cry from her throat.

She could feel herself approaching the crest of her passion; she was rising swiftly toward it, carried by his touch. She pressed her hips toward him. She wanted him inside her right now, all of him, leaving no space in her for thought or emotion, just raw physical passion.

Her legs tensed, her body straining toward its goal. She was only a few heartbeats away from satisfaction, and with that knowledge a rush of triumph went through her: he'd said he would make her ask him for sex, but she hadn't. She'd won! She would reach her peak, and then all danger of giving in to him would be gone, her passion spent!

Just one more moment . . .

He lifted his hand away.

Her eyes flew open and she whimpered in protest. *"Declan."*

The barest whisper of a smile breathed across his lips. "You don't really think I'll let you off so easily, do you?"

She stared at him dully, her mind foggy with lust, until she felt his touch on her inner thigh, lightly feathering along her skin exactly as he had done ten minutes earlier. As if he was going back to the beginning, to start all over.

"No . . . ," she said softly, shaking her head.

"All you have to do is say yes," Declan said, "and you can have what you want."

"And if I don't say it?"

"We have hours ahead of us. I can bring you to the brink and leave you there a hundred times, until your body is burned by its own desires. If you go to that point, you won't be able to come at all." He touched her lightly, and she closed her eyes and moaned. "Don't do that to yourself just to spite me."

"It's not spite," Grace gasped. "It's to prove that not every woman wants you."

"I don't care what other women want, only what *you* want." He lifted his hand away.

Grace's body cried out in protest, but she forced herself to smile. She licked her dry lips. "Do your best. I'll never want you inside me."

"You already do. The only question is how long it will take for you to admit it."

"Eternity."

"Then you leave me no choice, and I'll show you no mercy."

She didn't want mercy. All she wanted was for him to touch her again, and he did. Over and over again he brought her up to the brink and abandoned her, her hips writhing with desire she could not control. The only mastery she had was of her tongue, and she held it silent.

Even that became almost too much. She started to second-guess herself, to silently argue that this was only a game, he already knew she wanted him, why not say it and get what they both wanted?

With each round of slowly intensifying touch, it took less and less time for her to reach the brink, but always he stopped just short of sending her over. How did he *do* that? How did he know just when to stop? She started to watch herself, seeking the clues she gave away to let him know when she was about to climax. If she could send the wrong message, even for as little as a few seconds, she could throw herself over the brink before he knew what was happening.

She sensed her whole body tensing as she neared the crest, her legs stiffening, the movements of her hips more frantic as she silently screamed, "Don't stop! Don't stop! I'm almost there!" And of course he stopped and started over.

The next round, she was ready for him. As the arousal built and she felt herself approaching the edge, she forced her body to remain at its level of tension, forced herself to pretend less passion than she felt.

Yes, she silently whispered to herself as his touch increased in intensity.

Yes, just a little more. She felt a strange dissociation from her body as she held control, faking relaxation when she wanted to grind herself against him.

Just a little more . . .

And then it came: one touch too many. Her body froze on the cusp, and then tumbled downward in pulsating waves of release. Her whole body tightened, her back arching, her thighs clamping together over his hand, her own hands gripping the bonds above her head.

"*Got* it," she sighed in triumph and relief.

She felt Declan remove his hands from her, and opened her eyes.

"Goddammit! You tricked me!"

A smile curled her lips. "Some of us play the game better than others."

His eyes narrowed. "No one said the game was over."

She smirked. "You're the short stack of chips at this poker table, buck-o."

"A naked woman still in handcuffs should think twice about taunting the man who put her there."

Her glee died. "What do you mean by that? It's over, Declan. Just admit it."

He grabbed a pillow off the floor and coaxed her to raise her hips, sliding it beneath them. "Have you never heard of multiple orgasms?"

"Sure, but I never—"

Her words were cut short by what he did next.

"It's not going to work," she said weakly, even as he patiently began to coax the first shimmers of desire from her and she melted into the bed, her limbs going limp. "It *can't* work, can it?" she asked in wonder as she felt a tingling pleasure begin to spread through her loins.

He built her passion slowly this time, with no cycles of arousal and abandonment. He switched pace and pressure, keeping her guessing, never letting her get bored.

Grace wanted it to go on forever; she wanted to reach her second relief; she wanted to feel him inside her. She wanted all of it, but mostly she wanted him to keep doing exactly what he was doing.

"Say yes, Grace."

She imagined him coming over her, his strong body between her thighs, his manhood pushing deep within her. Below, his tongue echoed her imaginings.

For the second time, her body reached its relief, her muscles tensing as her body fell into waves of contracting pleasure.

"No! Goddammit, *no!*" Declan howled. He punched the mattress in frustration.

Grace chuckled deep in her throat, and stretched languorously. "Thank you, Declan. What does that make the score? Two—zip?"

Declan rolled off the bed and stalked round the room, running his hands through his hair in aggravation, his cock erect and woefully unsatisfied. Grace was too sated to do more than lie there smiling.

"You're all out of tricks, aren't you?" Grace said in mock sympathy. "Poor thing."

Declan glared at her, his eyes wild. He muttered something unintelligible beneath his breath.

"Would you please take off the cuffs? My arms are going stiff," she said softly.

He sighed and unlocked the cuffs. Then he pulled the sheet over Grace and crawled in behind her. He pulled her into his arms, spooning her from behind.

"I guess that was something to write home about," Grace whispered drowsily.

Declan closed his eyes, pressed his face into her hair, and pulled her more tightly against himself, his arm between her breasts, his body protectively cupping the warm softness of hers. She was much smaller than he was, but her curves gave her enough solidity that he didn't fear crushing her. There was something deeply comforting about holding her.

He wasn't a man to analyze sex—far from it—but he dimly recognized that something important and unexpected had happened here tonight. Grace had challenged him in a way he had never experienced, and had held her own against all he could throw at her. It wasn't just sexual, either; it had been a mental and emotional game they had played with each other.

All this, from Grace. *Grace!* The insecure Women's Studies student in a fish T-shirt!

She wasn't who he'd thought she was. She was a vixen, full of tricks and temptations, and motives he couldn't fathom. She was like . . . *like a young Sophia.*

His eyes opened, his body stiffening. His long-standing wish to meet a younger version of Sophia had come true. People always said to be careful what you wished for—now he understood why.

Grace was a young Sophia but scarier; she was a sex monster who came across as a virgin. And she loathed him. She hid it, but there were moments when he'd catch the anger in her eyes and know that he might never be forgiven for how he'd treated her the first night.

A sick sense came to him that he had burned a bridge he would come to regret. He may have lost the woman of his dreams.

He buried his nose in Grace's hair, inhaling the damp, earthy remnants of passion. She had set her sights on the passionless Andrew Pritchard. Andrew would never be able to meet her needs, but Grace thought she wanted him, for whatever reason.

Jealousy burned like acid.

So why the hell was Grace playing sexual games with him? She must have reasons of her own, of which he had not a clue. He had thought he was in control of their relationship, but he suspected now that Grace had used his self-assurance against him and was holding the reins all along.

"What the hell are you up to?" he whispered into her hair.

There was no answering murmur. His redheaded vixen was sound asleep.

CHAPTER

17

"Your aunt still hasn't had her surgery?" Cat asked over the phone.

"No," Grace said, sitting on her bed. It was late Saturday morning, and beyond the French doors the sky and ocean were a wash of brilliant blue. The cheerful sunlight was at odds with her cloudy mood. "Andrew pesters her about it at least once a week, but she always manages to turn the conversation in some direction that flusters him and he forgets to pursue the issue until the next time he's here."

"That seems kind of weird, doesn't it? I mean, I thought the whole purpose of having you there all summer was so she could have help while she recovered."

"What can I say? She does what she wants."

"And she has plenty of hired help already," Cat said slowly. "She has to have had an ulterior motive for inviting you to stay."

"I think she just likes having people around."

"Are Andrew and Declan spending a lot of time there?"

"Declan hasn't been here for over two weeks," Grace said, affecting nonchalance.

The morning after their sexual contest she'd woken up alone in her bed. Declan hadn't just left her room; he'd left the house and the town. Sophia told her later that morning that he'd gone back to San Francisco.

Grace had felt a slight disappointment, barely enough to dim her glow of victory and sexual satisfaction. He had retreated in defeat, unwilling to face the woman who had bested him! Or maybe he was afraid that if he stayed, Sophia would sense that the two of them had been intimate. He couldn't know Sophia would be more amused than distressed.

That first morning after, just thinking Declan's name made her whole body tingle. The attention he had lavished on her and his determination to make her feel pleasure no matter the consequence to himself had gone a long way toward breaching the walls she'd built against him. His adoration of her body had felt like an adoration of her, the woman inside. When she'd briefly stirred from sleep to find herself held warm and secure in his arms, she'd assumed he must like her, maybe even love her a little. And she'd allowed herself to feel a frisson of the same, her blood humming with the excitement of new hopes.

But as the hours turned into days without a word from Declan, Grace's euphoria had drained away. She'd thought she'd won the battle in her bedroom, but she'd lost. She'd let him fool her into thinking he cared, *again*. How could she have been so stupid?

Her burgeoning romantic hopes were replaced by darker emotions.

Violent emotions.

Blood-tinged, incoherent, howling animal emotions.

Emotions that needed an ax for full expression, one of those old medieval axes they used for chopping off heads. After she chopped off his head, she'd disembowel him and leave his innards on the rocks for the seagulls to eat.

"Declan's not around," Grace told Cat now, "but Andrew is here a lot, and he's got me going to this CRON group he's part of."

"A what group?"

Grace explained the theory of calorie restriction and longevity. The members of the CRON group struck her as fanatical, obsessed with eating only the peels of apples and charting the nutritional value of every microgram of food they put in their mouths. Several had histories of eating disorders, although they all claimed to be taking charge of their health through CRON.

But the biggest downside was that what Andrew had explained about libido was apparently true. Testosterone dropped. Several members of the group had been celibate for more than a year, and not just because they were nut jobs who couldn't find a date.

"Are you actually doing this calorie-restriction thing?" Cat asked incredulously. "You, who never met a Ben and Jerry's flavor that couldn't be improved with hot-fudge sauce?"

"Shocking, huh?" Grace said, feeling a prick of annoyance. Why should it be such a surprise that she might give up ice cream, at least for a summer? Was she such a glutton that it seemed impossible? "You're not going to believe this, but in the two months I've been here I've lost thirty pounds."

"Grace!"

"It's great, isn't it?"

"*Grace!* That's almost four pounds a week. That's not healthy," Catherine scolded.

"Oh, *phhtt*," she said. "The first ten pounds were mostly water."

"You can't be eating enough to be healthy."

"I *am*." For once, she was grateful for the CRON meetings. They made a great cover for a diet. "One of the CRONies showed me a computer program to calculate all my daily nutri-

tional needs so I can be sure to eat the right things. I've been
exercising a lot, too." She'd been exercising with more vigor since
Declan had disappeared; the next time he saw her, she wanted his
eyes to fall out of his head. Her weight loss had been stalled for
a week or so before they'd had their encounter. Since then, the
pounds had flown off. Maybe anger burned extra calories.

"You, exercise?"

"Yeah," Grace said, irritated. "Me. Exercise."

"You aren't turning anorexic, are you? Did Sophia drive you
to this somehow?"

Grace's anger—with judgmental Cat, with despicable Declan;
with prim Andrew, and with her perpetual, aching, crazy-making
state of hunger—all boiled over. "You know, I'd think you'd be
happy for me. Everyone always told me to eat better, to exercise,
that the fat around my middle was going to give me dementia,
diabetes, arthritis, and a heart attack all at once. Now I do what
everyone said and take care of myself, and all I get is a bunch of
crap about being anorexic! Goddamned *anorexic*! No wonder fat
people stay fat. They can't win either way!"

There was silence on the other end of the line. Grace ground
her teeth, fuming.

"Hit a nerve, didn't I?" Cat said at last. "Defensiveness is a sign
of an eating disorder."

"Fuck you!" Grace shouted into the phone. "Fuck. You! Ever
since I turned you down you've been trying to control me, to
keep me to yourself. You don't want me to lose weight because
then I might find a guy who'll take me away from you. You're like
one of those lesbian abusers you work with, trying to keep me
dependent and helpless so I can't leave you. Well, fuck you, Cat.
You have no hold on me."

Silence. Grace could hear her own heavy breathing, her body
shaking with anger, her heart racing. She felt a tingle of dread at

what Cat's response would be, but also felt an eager, almost violent wish for verbal battle.

At last Cat's answer came. "Whoa," she said softly. "I've never heard you this upset before." Her voice quavering with real concern, she asked, "Gracie, are you okay? Is everything all right?"

"I'm fine! Better than ever!" Grace barked back, but without the bite of before. She was vaguely unsettled by Cat's calm, caring response.

"Talk to me, Grace. What's going on?"

"It's nothing."

"It's okay if you don't want to talk to me, but you should think of talking to someone. Professor Joansdatter. Your mom. Or maybe Dr. Andrew?"

"Aren't you afraid he's part of the problem, due to CRON?"

"There's not a lot of choice for someone to talk to in that house. At least his heart's in the right place, and he seems to like you."

"Yeah, he seems to," Grace drawled. "As much as he can."

"What's that mean?"

"It means the guy might as well be a eunuch," Grace groused.

There was a sound suspiciously like a chuckle on the other end of the line.

"What?" Grace demanded.

"Nothing! Really!"

Grace scowled. "You think sexual frustration has caused my bad temper?"

"No, not exactly."

"Then what? Tell me, Ms. Know-it-all."

"I've had a passing acquaintance with unrequited love myself."

An image of Declan sprang to Grace's mind. Declan smiling at her, teasing her, leering at her. Touching her . . . "I'm not in love with him," Grace insisted.

"Mm-hmm," Cat murmured knowingly. "You know what I think?"

Grace didn't want to know.

"I think that you're afraid to admit you love him, because he might not love you back."

"His type can't love." After that night they'd spent together, to leave without even a good-bye . . .

"That's ridiculous. You of all people should know that intellectuals like Andrew—and you—are uncomfortable with messy emotions. It doesn't mean they're not there, though."

Grace started. Andrew. Cat was talking about Andrew, of course, not Declan.

Cat went on, "You and Andrew have to have the courage to face your emotions."

Grace rolled her eyes. "This isn't about courage. He seems more interested in me as a friend than as a romantic partner."

Cat laughed. "Isn't that exactly the same technique you usually use on someone you're interested in? You befriend them and slip in under their radar, because there's little risk of romantic rejection that way."

"No, I do that because that's how you build a relationship with a solid foundation."

"Whatever the motivation, Andrew is probably doing the same with you. Be patient with him. Encourage him."

Grace scowled, not believing what she was hearing. "You're trying to help me hook up with a guy?"

Cat was quiet on the other end of the line. "Grace," she finally said, her voice sad, "I've only ever wanted you to be happy and to have what's best for you."

"So you think Andrew is 'what's best for me,'" she said drily.

"Yes. And I can't tell you how much it relieves me to hear

you being angsty about him. I'd been worried that you might get involved with Declan."

"You think I'm an idiot?"

"I think you're female. Even I could feel the man's sexual aura, so an attraction didn't surprise me. But I'm glad that your true self has shifted your interest on to Andrew, who shares your values."

Grace felt a cloak of "should" settling over her, muffling anger and passion under a layer of reason. Her shoulders slumped and she felt her mouth pursing in disgruntled resignation. She really should redouble her efforts with Andrew instead of wasting thoughts on annihilating Declan. Which path, after all, was more likely to lead to long-term happiness?

"Oh, I meant to ask," Cat said in a sudden shift of tone, "did your mom ever answer your questions about why Sophia is estranged from your family?"

"She doesn't know. And she won't ask anyone, either. She says she sees no point in stirring up old dirt. She thinks it would be intrusive. I think she'd like to pretend that Sophia doesn't exist and that I'm not here with her." Anything positive that Grace had said about Sophia either in an e-mail or on the phone had been met with a decided silence on her mother's side. Her mom was a generous and loving woman, but if someone managed to get on her bad side, they stayed there.

"Have you told your mom about the weight you've lost?"

Grace hesitated. "I want to surprise her."

Cat murmured unhappily. "Is that it, or are you afraid of how she's going to react? You know she'll blame Sophia for making you feel that your body wasn't good enough."

Grace felt a spark of returning anger. "Cat, lay off it. You've never been overweight, so just . . . lay off."

"So I have to have been overweight to understand what damage self-loathing can do?"

"For God's sake, I don't hate myself!"

"Andrew isn't going to suddenly start showering you with affection if you lose another ten pounds. Weight loss isn't a magic potion."

"Sure it is!" Grace snapped, angry now and wanting to goad her. "It always is, where men are concerned. So if I want love and happiness, of course I have to lose ten more pounds. At *least* ten."

"You *are* kidding, aren't you?"

"Am I? Let's get real, Cat. Weight matters. You may be 'more evolved' about it, but the rest of the world is made up of assholes who aren't. Fighting them is a losing battle."

"Grace, this isn't like you," Cat said, worried.

"Says who? You going to start telling me who I am now, too?"

"Maybe you need reminding! The Grace I know isn't a bitch."

The nasty name hit her like a sucker punch, knocking the wind from her. Grace hung up without responding, her hands shaking, her emotions a roiling mess of anger, hurt, and guilt. She flung herself down on the bed, staring at the canopy overhead.

Goddammit, why did she have people like Cat and Declan in her life? She mentally thrashed through her history with them both, working herself into a froth that slowly drained away as her hands rested on her nearly flat stomach.

The pillow of doughy flesh that she used to knead like a kitten seeking comfort had shrunk to the thickness of a summer quilt. She could feel the hard base of her muscles beneath it, waiting to be uncovered. If she could lose another ten pounds by the end of the month, no one would recognize her. She'd be able to wear any pair of pants without wondering if her butt looked like a sack of marbles. She could wear clingy knits without a body shaper. A bikini. If her breasts shrank enough, she could even go braless in a backless dress.

She rolled off the bed and went to examine her face in the bathroom mirror. Her jawline had narrowed, and her neck was thinner, making it look longer. As she turned her head this way and that and lifted her hair into different styles, she caught glimpses of the Sophia in the portrait downstairs.

Grace narrowed her eyes, thinking of how she could use her changing body to make Declan suffer, to give an "up yours" to Cat, and to transform Dr. Andrew into a man with a libido.

For the first time, the face in the mirror was Sophia's. Green eyes stared back at her with calculation and sultry schemes for her own benefit.

Startled, Grace blinked and let her hair drop. Her expression of surprise erased the doppelgänger effect, but the moment she thought of Declan and narrowed her eyes, it returned.

She shuddered. Was she taking on the personality of her aunt? Was she losing herself under Sophia's influence?

Or maybe it was worse than that. Maybe this angry, manipulative person in the mirror had always been inside her, waiting to emerge. Maybe the real Grace had always wanted to control people and be considered a beauty, and crush those who hurt her.

She had the sudden, frightening feeling that her Ph.D. studies had all been an elaborate game of self-delusion to make it the world's fault that she was not adored for being chubby, shy, and lacking in sexual confidence. After all, it felt better than blaming herself for not becoming what the world preferred: a sexually confident beauty who took no guff from anyone.

A knock came at her door, followed immediately by Darlene's cheerless voice. "Fifteen minutes. Don't keep her waiting."

"Okay," Grace called back.

Self-analysis would have to wait. She and her aunt had what Sophia had called a very important engagement, and she hadn't started to dress yet. She didn't even know which shoes she was going to wear. A flush of panic washed over her, anticipating Sophia's displeasure should she choose incorrectly.

With a sense of guilty relief, she shoved aside the conversation with Cat and the disturbing doubts it had raised. Right now, she had to concentrate on looking her best.

She had her $20,000 priorities, after all.

CHAPTER

ɛ 18 ʒ

Grace clopped down the stairs in alligator mules, holding tight to the banister for fear of the slipperlike shoes flying off her feet and sending her tumbling to the marble floor below. Lali was waiting for her by the door.

"Hurry up, hurry up! You're late."

"I know, I know!" Grace said, reaching the floor in one piece and slip-stepping her way toward the door. She could hear the low rumble of a car motor out in the courtyard. "Do I look okay? I was told to put on 'resort wear,' but I'm not sure what that means." She'd settled on an above-the-knee lemon yellow linen skirt, a bateau-neck cream shirt made of a fine-gauge silk knit, and a long necklace of tortoiseshell and citrine. Her hair had been curled, parted on the side, and pulled back into a low barrette at her nape. She'd topped it all with her big straw hat.

"You look great," Lali assured her. "As far as I can tell, in Pebble Beach resort wear just means fake casual. You know, lots of sailor clothes that cost too much to wear on a real sailboat, and cashmere twinsets with pearls, and a skirt that looks like you could play tennis in it."

"I should fit in, then."

"Yeah, except you're about forty years too young for this set."

"You know where Sophia is taking me?"

Lali shooed her out the door and into the sunlight. "No time to talk! Go!"

Grace carefully navigated the steps, watching her feet, then at last looked up.

Stretched out before her was the biggest, shiniest, most ridiculously beautiful vehicle she had ever seen, even in photos. She gaped at the vision in royal blue, cream, and chrome. It was a convertible from sometime before the Second World War, with a long, narrow hood; huge round headlights; and sweeping fenders over the spoke wheels. Chrome pipes curled like whiskers from the sides of the hood and swept underneath the running boards.

Darlene sat at the wheel, dressed in an old-fashioned chauffeur's uniform with a crushable hat and a high-collared black jacket that buttoned down each side. Sophia sat in the backseat, her head swathed in an Isadora Duncan-esque long scarf, enormous sunglasses hiding half her face.

"There you are," Sophia said. "Do come along, darling. It's not kind to keep me waiting in the sun."

Grace shook off her shock and stumbled to the car, opening the back door and slipping onto the cream leather seat beside her aunt. "What is this thing?" she asked in awe.

"This, my dear, is the finest American automobile ever made, a 1929 supercharged J series Duesenberg."

"It's a duesy," Darlene added from the front, and cackled as she put the vehicle into gear and they glided off.

"It's stunning," Grace said.

"It is, isn't it?" Sophia agreed. "I've always felt that a beautiful woman should ride in an equally beautiful car. They set each other off. My second husband bought this for me. It was an extravagant gift even then, but he was an extravagant man."

"How much is a car like this worth?"

Sophia tsked in disapproval. "Grace, you know that's a rude question."

Grace bit her lip, contrite but still curious.

"And besides, the value to me is in the memories of dear Chazz." Sophia canted her head. "That would be husband number two, to you."

Darlene stopped at the top of the driveway and then pulled out onto 17-Mile Drive. As the car smoothly picked up speed, Grace held her hat onto her head with one hand, the brim flapping in the breeze. "I'm sorry, you're right, I shouldn't have asked."

"However, I suppose you'll just look it up online as soon as we return, so if you absolutely *must* know the dollar value . . ." Sophia's lips twitched in amusement. "A few years ago, one sold at auction for one million."

"Excuse me?" Grace gasped.

"It wasn't quite as nice as this one, I don't think."

"One million *dollars*? For a *car*? For *this* car?" Grace couldn't grasp the reality. "And you drive it on the *road*?" she screeched.

"Of course," Sophia said lightly. "It adds a bright spot to people's day to see it. Beautiful things should not be kept behind glass, they should be used. Just as a beautiful woman should live fully and not let herself turn into a hothouse flower, pampered and useless."

"But a million dollars! If we get into an accident—"

"*Pshh,*" Sophia said, waving away Grace's worry. "And so what if we do mar the paint? It's just a car. In fact, I think you should drive us home later."

"No, no, no," Grace said in panic. "Absolutely not!"

"It would be good for you. It would preserve you from ever

overvaluing a man based on the car he drove. You'll always have the Duesenberg in the back of your mind, and know that you've driven better."

"But, but," Grace said, scrambling for an excuse, "but I can't drive a stick shift!"

Sophia turned her head toward Grace, her eyes invisible behind the sunglasses, but the disapproving set of her mouth expressing all. "Did your parents teach you absolutely nothing of use?"

Grace pulled in her chin defensively. "We had only automatics. I've never needed to drive a stick."

"*Every* woman needs to know how to drive a manual transmission."

"Why?"

"There may be an emergency that requires it. But more important, men find it sexy."

Grace laughed. "Oh, come on! Men hate being passengers in cars driven by women."

"They hate being passengers in automatics with frightened, overcautious, or flighty women, yes. But put a man next to a woman in a short skirt who is working the gears with confidence and skill, and all he'll be able to think of is running his hand up to her crotch."

"Oh, like *that's* safe! Talk about distracted driving."

"You don't *let* him, darling. Anticipation is always three-quarters of the fun."

"I guess that's just one trick I'll have to leave out of my bag, then, because there's no way I'm going to learn to drive a stick shift today, in this thing."

Sophia patted her knee. "No, dear, of course not. That would be a wasted opportunity."

Grace sank back in relief, but then was pricked by the

niggling question of what Sophia meant by "a wasted opportunity." Before she could ask her aunt for clarification, Sophia was speaking again.

"We're lunching today at the Beach and Tennis Club dining room; it's open only to members of the club and guests of Pebble Beach Resort. The ladies who will be joining us are all long-standing members of the community here who have formed a charitable organization called the Altruism Society, and I expect you to charm them."

Grace's relief blew away in the passing breeze. "Charm them? How? You haven't taught me anything about charming women!"

"The principles are the same as with men. Just tone it down, as women are quicker to scent insincerity, with the sole exception of any discussion of their children. It's the one topic they will never tire of, and you may keep them on it for as long as you can stand it."

"Great. What if they don't have kids, or their kids are in prison for pushing drugs or something?"

"Then fall back on the skills you already have. The goal in any interaction is to make the other person believe that you thought they were fascinating, witty, and possessed of an unusually warm heart. Women, especially, always like to hear that they're kind, even when they know that they aren't. It comes as a pleasant surprise to them, and they won't want to disabuse you of the notion."

"This sounds like an awful lot of flattery and manipulation," Grace said.

Sophia sighed. "Grace, Grace. It will only come off that way if that is what you believe it to be. Look at it instead as the Buddhists do, and seek to recognize the divine within each person."

Grace gave her aunt a skeptical look.

"I am *trying* to make this easier for you," Sophia said.

They turned off the main road and onto a drive that Grace knew, from the exploring she'd done on a bicycle, to lead to the Lodge at Pebble Beach, a white porticoed building that had been part of the resort since it was founded in 1919. They passed the lodge and went on to the Beach and Tennis Club. Darlene eased the Duesenberg to a stop at the main entrance and shut off the motor. Uniformed attendants rushed forward to open both Sophia's and Grace's doors and help them from the car, Grace less elegantly than Sophia, as she suddenly decided to leave her hat and sunglasses on the seat, realizing it would be ridiculous to have lunch with that enormous brim blocking out her neighbors at the table. Sophia cooed over the young male attendants, who addressed her by name and seemed delighted to see her, the car, or both.

Staff ushered them through the lobby, giving Grace time for only a moment's glance through a doorway to an outdoor pool sparkling in the sun and dotted with swimmers, and then they came into the dining room. It had a simple, airy elegance, but the furnishings were only a stage for the wall of plateglass windows that looked out onto the cerulean waters of Stillwater Cove and the jade green seventeenth fairway of the famous golf links. Grace gaped at the view, the other lunch guests making no more impact on her awareness than murmuring shadows.

The sound of her name broke the spell, and Grace found herself being introduced to eight or nine women who immediately blended together in one well-coifed, conservatively made-up, extremely neat and moneyed phalanx of older women. Flash and bling were out with this set; tasteful neutrals and pastels were in. And reigning over them all was Sophia, dressed today in tones of camel and ivory, her jewelry reduced to a few heavy accents of matte gold.

Grace exchanged smiles with the women, and a few words of

chitchat with the woman seated to her right, named Ellen, who first ascertained that Grace was single and then made mention of her forty-eight-year-old son, presently also single. This prompted a mention of nephews from the woman two seats down, but despite this, it was obvious that something beyond matchmaking was on everyone's mind. What it was didn't come out until after they'd ordered their meals, a half dozen variations on lettuce and low-calorie protein, plus Arnold Palmers—half lemonade, half iced tea—or gin and tonics. An expectant lull followed the departure of the last of the waitstaff, and all eyes turned to Sophia.

"So where are we?" Sophia asked. "Gwennie?"

A woman with white hair in a sixties flip answered. "It's worse than they originally thought. The pipe that broke above the ceiling of the vineyard's banquet hall not only destroyed the plasterwork and warped the floor below but now there's also mold inside the walls. It will be at least a month before the hall can be used."

A gasp of dismay went round the table.

"But it's only three weeks away!" the woman on Grace's right said.

"We have to find another venue," another woman said.

"There aren't any," Gwennie said. "Everything is booked for weddings and conferences. And we simply must have the gala during the Pebble Beach Concours d'Elegance, so we cannot change the date. Everyone will be in town already, and our theme of 'A Long Ago Night in an Enchanted Forest' is too perfect a match for the mood of both the classic car show and this year's special exhibition of the historic auto race on Seventeen-Mile Drive."

Sophia cursed under her breath and muttered, "The organizers of that race should be shot."

Grace leaned toward her aunt and whispered, "What is everyone talking about?"

But Sophia ignored her, her eyes watching the fluster and panic of the women like a fox watching a coop full of hens.

"We'll have to cancel," someone said.

"After all this work . . ."

"We already have two hundred and fifty confirmed guests, including several celebrities, senators, two ambassadors . . ."

". . . all the props and costumes . . ."

Sophia's voice cut through the dithering like a silver stiletto. "The solution is simple."

Complaints broke off midsentence, and everyone turned to the grand dame of the table.

"We will have the charity gala at my home."

The pronouncement was met with a collective indrawn breath of doubt. Glances were exchanged, eyebrows subtly expressed misgivings.

"Er," Gwennie started, looking round the table to gather support, "I worry that your house might not be quite large enough. The guest list is for four hundred."

Grace's eyes bugged. Four hundred people! There was no way they'd all fit in Sophia's house.

Sophia, however, was unruffled. She looked almost bored. "Gwennie," she said in a voice tinged with the faintest trace of condescension, "the secret to a successful party has always been to have too much food and not enough space."

Gwennie tightened her lips but retreated, making Grace wonder if Gwennie had recently hostessed a flop of a party with too little food and too much space.

"My home will be an improvement over the vineyard," Sophia went on, "and we can put the money we save on not renting a space toward additional food and drink."

"But four hundred people," some brave soul cautioned. "And they're to be served dinner."

"Chefs from several of California's best restaurants—I have already spoken with half a dozen—will have their own stations scattered throughout the gardens, serving small bites. Actors and musicians will be dotted through the woods, performing. Strung between the trees will be thousands of Chinese lanterns, glowing softly, like will-o'-the-wisps. Imagine the guests in their historic costumes, strolling the paths of such a venue. It will truly be a Long Ago Night in an Enchanted Forest."

Small discussions broke out among the women, the tone questioning at the beginning but quickly turning hopeful, and even excited.

Their food came, and as Grace picked at her salad—despite her now continual hunger, the thought of eating salad yet again made her gag—and listened to the conversations around her, she began to piece together what was going on. Her neighbor Ellen filled in the blanks that were remaining.

"The gala was Sophia's idea," Ellen explained. "The Concours d'Elegance is a classic car show, as I'm sure you know, and this year there's going to be a special exhibition race re-creating the 1950s races on Seventeen-Mile Drive." Ellen glanced at Sophia and gave a little shake of her head. "Of course she doesn't like that." Before Grace could ask for clarification, she went on, "Sophia suggested that we revive another past tradition. The Carmel Art Association used to hold a masquerade ball every year as a fund-raiser, the most famous of which was at the Hotel Del Monte in 1941. It was called 'Surrealist Night in an Enchanted Forest.' Salvador Dali conceived of the theme and decorations, including burlap hanging from the ceiling to turn the room into a grotto; a wrecked car with drugged, bandaged models lying in it; tigers and elephants and whatnot from a private collection; and his wife wearing a unicorn head. Self-indulgent artistic twaddle, of course, but it was fabulously successful in terms of attendance and publicity."

"And fund-raising?"

Ellen laughed. "Dali spent so much on throwing the party, expenses far outweighed earnings."

"Why not just have people write checks to a charity instead of having them buy overpriced admission to a pretentious party and hope there's something left over for—ow!" Something sharp and hard hit Grace on the ankle. Grace glanced toward her aunt and was met with a look of icy warning.

"Er . . . ," Grace hedged, turning back to her neighbor and seeing the look of carefully controlled offense on Ellen's face. "I mean, I'm sure that's what some people were wondering back in 1941. But it's obvious to me that with this group of women in charge, a charity event will be everything it should be and more. There's no reason that beauty and elegance cannot be part of helping those in need. I think the world is always improved by a display of taste and discernment, and there's no reason one can't enjoy oneself while helping others, is there?" Grace smiled, hoping she'd laid it on thick enough, but not too thick.

Ellen looked at her for a moment, then leaned closer and said under her breath, "Let's not forget the assistance of an open bar for getting bigger numbers written on checks." She winked. "And pretty girls don't hurt, either."

Grace smiled, and gave her a coy look. "I don't suppose your son will be attending?"

"I think he can be persuaded, for the right reason."

"Then I have something to look forward to."

Ellen smiled and patted her hand. The rest of the lunch passed in discussion of details and people of whom Grace had never heard. She played her part as well as she could, never forgetting after that first slipup that it was a part she played, and that her performance was being judged by Sophia.

Grace was exhausted by the time she collapsed into the

backseat of the Duesenberg for the ride home, but the women hadn't been half as uptight or judgmental as she'd expected for a bunch of conservative, filthy rich country clubbers. She'd almost . . . liked them.

"Wow, that was—" Grace started to say. But Sophia cut her off with a raised hand.

"We obey the fifty-foot rule," Sophia said tersely.

Grace raised her eyebrows in question.

"You do not discuss an event or people until you are at least fifty feet away."

"Oh." Grace chewed her lip, and as Sophia waved farewell to Gwennie, who'd just appeared as if from nowhere, Grace admitted that it wasn't a bad policy.

As soon as they pulled onto the main road, though, Darlene broke the silence, speaking over her shoulder, "Did they go for it?"

"Of course," Sophia said, looking self-contented. "What choice did they have?"

Grace laughed. "You almost make it sound like you wanted the banquet hall to flood."

"Darling, there was no flood."

"The broken pipe at the vineyard," Grace reminded her, worried for a moment that her aunt might have lost a synapse or two.

"The only flood was of praise, from my mouth into the ears of appropriate people at Stanford University, which the vineyard owners' daughter will now be attending despite her less than perfect grades."

Grace's jaw dropped. "You wanted the gala at your house!"

"I never liked the choice of the vineyard, but I needed everyone's cooperation for the gala, and I didn't want to force the issue. It's always better to be seen as a rescuer than as a bully, Grace. You not only get your way but also people feel in your debt. It's win-win."

"I don't think 'win-win' is supposed to mean one person getting both wins," Grace said drily.

"Win-win-win, then. At any rate, everyone is happy."

Which made Grace wonder exactly why Sophia was so anxious to have the gala at her house. But she knew if she asked, the last thing she would hear was the truth.

Sophia was like a goddess, moving other humans about like pieces on a game board. And like a goddess, her ways were inscrutable to mere mortals like Grace.

Heaven help her.

CHAPTER
19

"There's no such thing as a Steinbeck cricket, and you damn well know it!" Declan shouted at Andrew, barely restraining himself from tossing the smug bastard off the terrace of Sophia's house.

"Apparently one has been found. It's your unfortunate luck that it was found on your land."

"It's a fake, and you know it!"

Andrew's pale cheeks heated to a raspberry hue. "I don't know why you're blaming me for your problems."

"I'm blaming you because you are a part of that blasted Save Monterey group, and it was one of their members who photographed the supposed cricket. Who gave them the idea to look on my land?" Declan advanced on Andrew, who took a step back. "Who could that have been, Andrew? *Who?*"

"There are probably half a dozen endangered species on that land. I'm sure the EPA will find more than just the Steinbeck cricket, now that they're looking more closely at your abomination of a housing development."

"The Steinbeck cricket?" Grace's voice said behind them. "Someone found a Steinbeck cricket?"

They both turned. Even through his anger, Declan was hit by her appearance. She was in a simple yellow skirt and white top, but her body beneath them had changed. She was still gorgeous, but there was less of her, as if she'd been ill and hadn't eaten well in a couple of weeks. Her breasts were smaller than he remembered when he'd last seen her, naked in bed, exhausted by pleasure.

She didn't look exhausted by pleasure now. In the brief moment their eyes met he thought he saw hurt and accusation; reproach even.

"No one found a Steinbeck cricket," Declan said to her, trying to keep his focus. He kept getting distracted by her body and the hollows of her cheeks, and was wondering why she'd lost so much weight. Was she unwell? Was she unhappy? Was she unhappy with *him*? "Andrew got one of his friends to plant a fake one on my land."

Grace looked confused. "Andrew would never be part of something underhanded like that. Would you, Andrew?"

"You *know* me, Grace," Andrew said. "You know I wouldn't do something I believed to be wrong."

"He doesn't *think* it's wrong!" Declan shouted, Andrew's smug self-righteousness driving him over the edge. "He thinks he's serving a higher good! I'd like to know who put the idea of the cricket in his head in the first place! It's cleverer than I would have given him credit for."

Grace's eyes went wide, and her lips parted.

Declan got a sick, sinking feeling. "Grace? What is it?"

"I may have said something about crickets on your land . . . ," she said, not meeting his eyes. She looked at the doctor. "But if Andrew's environmental group found a Steinbeck cricket, then it's right that the development be halted."

Declan clapped his hands to his forehead in frustration. "There's no such thing as a Steinbeck cricket!"

"Andrew wouldn't lie," Grace said primly, moving toward Andrew as if choosing sides.

Declan felt the betrayal like a stab to the gut. Was she part of the cricket scheme, too? Goddammit! He'd sensed she was out to get him; he should have listened more closely to his own instincts. He'd spent the past few weeks struggling to keep his distance from her, for fear that he was beginning to form a much too real attachment to her. He should have stayed right here and kept his eye on her! Sophia would have been the first to tell him that you keep your friends close, but your enemies closer.

"Grace!" Sophia said sharply from the doorway. She was leaning on her cane, her face stern. "Come here."

"Aunt Sophia, Declan—"

"Grace! At once!"

Her brow puckered, Grace did as her aunt bid. Sophia said something to her in a low voice, which earned a vigorous head shaking and a protestation from Grace. A few more low words came from Sophia, and then with a look of extreme reluctance Grace slipped past her aunt and disappeared into the house.

"Andrew," Sophia said crisply, "help me to that chair. Declan, please pour me a Scotch."

Declan and Andrew both stared at her, held rigid by their anger and unwillingness to quit the field of battle. Sophia rapped her cane on the terrace. "Will you both keep me standing here?" she asked incredulously.

They jerked into motion, Andrew to offer his elbow, Declan to fetch the supportive assistance of alcohol. Five minutes later found the three of them seated at the table under the arbor, ice cubes clinking in two glasses of Scotch and one glass of club soda. Sophia forced them into a conversation about party preparations until Declan caught himself almost smiling at the "God help me escape this" look on Andrew's face, a look he wore as well.

Andrew broke first, making his excuses and promising to see

Sophia the next day. When he was safely gone, Sophia set down her glass and looked Declan in the eye.

"Give me the facts, nothing more."

Declan sighed. "There's been an injunction by the court to stop work on the development, pending investigation of a reported sighting of a new species of cricket on the land, the fabled Steinbeck cricket, to be exact. A member of Save Monterey photographed a specimen on my land, but didn't capture it 'for fear of further reducing an already fragile population.'"

Sophia steepled her fingertips together and tapped them on her lower lip. A smile slowly formed, of the sort she saved for someone who had shown unexpected cleverness. Declan had the bad feeling that the smile was not meant for him.

"Dr. Andrew is full of surprises, isn't he?" she said, confirming Declan's suspicion.

"Unfortunately. He's always hated me. I just never expected him to act on it in such a malicious way."

"But you do know why he did."

"To get his rocks off keeping land undeveloped, and to give me a poke in the eye in the process. How could he resist?"

Sophia chuckled. "You don't really think that that's what this is about, do you?"

Declan frowned, then glanced toward the house, and the balcony to the Garden Room. "You don't mean . . ."

"Of course I mean Grace. He senses that you're a rival, and he's trying to pluck you of your fine professional plumage in front of her eyes. He'll leave you bare as a Christmas goose if he can."

Declan's eyes narrowed as he remembered the way Grace had stepped toward Andrew during the argument and defended the lying bastard. "So you're getting what you wanted," he said bitterly. "Andrew has finally gotten off his ass and started to reach for what he wants. You'll have them engaged by the end of the month."

"Whatever you've been doing with Grace, do keep it up," Sophia said. "She couldn't come to Andrew's defense fast enough. Did she even glance your way?"

Declan scowled.

"We need to keep up the pressure on Andrew, though, if he's going to propose to Grace. Tomorrow I want you to take her out in the Auburn and teach her to drive a stick shift."

"You want me to what?"

"You heard me. It will send Andrew round the bend."

"It will send *me* round the bend," Declan countered. "You really want her to hate me? I taught a friend to drive a manual once, and before we were finished he'd slugged me once and kicked me out of the car three times."

"Wonderful! I want to see her come home agitated, perhaps even disheveled. I'll make sure Andrew is here to see it. It will rouse his protective instincts."

"What's in it for me?"

"I should think my gratitude would be sufficient."

Declan snorted.

"You could steal a kiss or two from her if you're seductive enough; that would at least give you some degree of revenge against Andrew."

Andrew would have heart failure if he knew the things that Declan had already done with Grace, but there were certain things an honorable man never divulged. "I thought I wasn't supposed to lay a finger on Grace."

"That was when I feared she might be foolish enough to fall for you. Her heart is safely in Andrew's hands now."

"Safe in his hands," Declan repeated, but found nothing

reassuring in the idea. Andrew was all wrong for Grace. He had no vibrancy, no passion, no adventurousness. If she married him, he'd suck the life out of her and turn her into a boring, sanctimonious clone of himself.

What a waste.

Grace needed someone who could match her energy and spirit, and who wouldn't be frightened by her sexual hunger. She needed someone who would push her to seek out her limits and surpass them. She needed challenging, and needed a man strong enough to make her feel safe in being herself; a man she knew would never be afraid of her. The last thing she needed was a passive-aggressive man like Andrew who'd never directly confront her. Andrew would make her neurotic, and leave her unsure if he loved her, hated her, or was indifferent to her.

But she wasn't Andrew's, yet. And in Declan's book, no woman was off-limits until she'd said "I do."

Though she probably didn't like him very much, she was physically attracted to him and she enjoyed his touch. If he put his mind to it, he could turn her attention firmly away from Andrew.

And on to himself.

A nauseating, fluttering feeling filled his gut, and he dimly recognized it as fear. Grace's full attention and adoration *was* what he wanted, wasn't it? It was the real reason he'd left town after that unforgettable night with her. He wanted her to give all of herself to him—body and soul—and the intensity of his yearning had scared the bejesus out of him. He wanted her with a hunger he'd never before felt for another woman, but it seemed she couldn't care less about him.

To top it all off, this was Sophia's grand-niece, and Sophia had made it clear that she wouldn't take kindly to him playing with Grace's heart. If he meant to capture Grace's affections, then he'd better want to keep them.

But he wasn't ready to settle down or make lifelong pledges of devotion. He wanted Grace *right now*. What he might want, or what she might want, six months from now was a different story. And did he really even have to worry about that? If they were meant to grow old together, they would. If not, they'd go their separate ways, no harm, no foul. But they'd never find out if they were meant to be together if Grace married Andrew first.

But then he remembered: driving lessons.

They'd probably kill each other before they got anywhere near a bed.

"I want something in return," Declan said.

Sophia's eyebrow twitched. "Oh?"

"You're not going to like it."

"I assume not; you would have asked for it sooner, otherwise, and not waited until you had a lever to use on me."

Declan hesitated, feeling a twinge of doubt. He didn't want to upset Sophia, but this was a rare chance that likely would not come again. "I want to borrow the MG."

Sophia's face went cold. "Do not tell me that you are taking part in that exhibition race."

"It's a once in a lifetime chance. My Jaguar doesn't meet the 1956 age minimum, but the MG does. I'll be careful—you know I will."

"I know no such thing. No man is careful once a competition begins."

"It's an exhibition, not a real race," Declan argued. "This will be the only time I can race a historic sports car through the original route of the Pebble Beach Road Races. I drove in the Monterey Historic Automobile Races at Laguna Seca twice, but that's not the same." The Laguna Seca racetrack, a little ways north, had been built as a rough copy of the 17-Mile Drive race route, keeping many of the turns and hills but erasing the danger of trees lining the road. The Pebble Beach Road Races had moved to Laguna Seca in 1957, and eventually been renamed the Monterey Historic Automobile Races. Now those races were over, too; the last MHAR had been in 2009. "I'm not interested in winning. I'm interested in the experience."

"Bullshit. Winning trumps all."

He reached across the table and put his hand on hers. "Sophia, please. I'll be careful. I've got too much to live for to be careless."

Her gaze sought his, examining. "Do you?"

"Yeah." He grinned. "If I kill myself in the race, I won't have a chance to get even with Dr. Andrew for that goddamn fake Steinbeck cricket he planted on my land."

"Mmm," Sophia murmured noncommittally, and took a sip of Scotch. "Yes, that's obviously the most important thing on your mind." She stared off into the distance, then shrugged. "Take the MG. You're right, you have more important competitions to win than a road race."

"Thanks, Sophia."

Declan sat back, surprised and gratified by Sophia's acquiescence. As usual, though, it didn't take more than a few moments for him to grow suspicious. He glanced over at her and wondered what exactly was going on in her head. Sophia never agreed to anything without having an angle in it for herself.

For a moment, he even wondered if he'd been manipulated into asking for the car.

But no, that was past even Sophia's skills.

Wasn't it?

CHAPTER
20

Sick to her stomach with nerves, Grace stood on the front step of the house and waited for Declan to emerge from the garage with the car.

The night before, Sophia had given her a long lecture on the inappropriateness of choosing sides with men before having received—and returned—a declaration of love.

"When a man has declared his devotion to you, and you have accepted that devotion, then and *only* then do you side with him against all comers. Until then, you remain neutral. You become Switzerland."

"And pretend I don't have a brain?" Grace had scoffed.

"This isn't about who's right or who's wrong, or who you think has the better argument. Have you been listening to anything I've been trying to teach you? This is about recognizing the basic, animal emotions of men. What's the primary reason that males in the wild fight each other?"

Grace lowered her chin and mumbled, "Females."

"Females. And why does Mother Nature make them fight for the right to mate?"

"So that only the best males pass on their genes." Grace scowled. "But we're not lower animals! Declan could beat up

Andrew if he wanted to, but that wouldn't make me want to choose him. Andrew's probably got the better brain."

"If you interfere in their argument, you will be robbing Andrew of his chance to prove himself better than Declan. Grace, they *want* to fight, and they want to do it in front of you. Each wants the chance to prove himself superior to his rival."

"I don't think Declan does."

Sophia rolled her eyes. "Doesn't it strike you as odd that they met and had their argument here, where you were most likely to be a witness to it? Declan could have met Andrew anywhere else."

Grace hadn't bought Sophia's argument about Declan wanting to fight for her, but she could see that she needed to step back if she was going to give Andrew the chance to cut Declan off at the knees and then beat his own chest in victory. A solo victory was always more ego gratifying than one earned while being supported by others.

None of that discussion last night with Sophia had made her feel any better about today's driving lesson. Sophia insisted that it was a necessary counterbalance to Grace's faux pas of supporting Andrew yesterday, but Grace suspected Sophia was using that as a convenient excuse. Grace almost thought Sophia was punishing Declan for an unknown transgression: why else do something so cruel as force him to teach her to drive a stick shift? It would be a teeth-gritting exercise in patience for him.

He was probably dreading seeing her, too. She had no idea what was going on in his head but guessed he might still be smarting after her winning the bedroom bet. It was at least one explanation for his disappearance. At any rate, he had to know she wouldn't be feeling friendly toward him after his vanishing act.

Nerves had her bouncing on the balls of her feet, which were clad in pristine white Keds. They had been Sophia's concession to practicality for the driving lesson. The rest of Grace's outfit said anything but "serious driver": a short white pleated skirt, and a lavender forties-style halter top with a faux knot between her breasts and a broad strap that tied at her nape. A thin tangerine scarf served as a headband, its tail ends draping over one shoulder. Pale green jade dangled at her ears and was strung in chunks on a bracelet at her wrist.

At the moment, she wasn't sure if she was more anxious about spending time with Declan or about driving a manual. She was an adequate driver, just as she was adequate at most physical things she learned, but she was no genius. She knew there were going to be many, many mistakes made in the next hour or two, and she'd be frustrated and Declan would likely start ranting at her, wondering why she couldn't catch on quicker, which in turn would make her more nervous and destroy her concentration.

Grace took a deep breath and tried to calm herself. How bad could it all be, anyway? Millions of people knew how to drive a stick shift. If they could do it, she could do it. She just had to stay calm, keep her wits about her, and pretend Declan was a stranger.

She heard the low, grumbling roar of an engine, the sound so deep that she could feel it in her bones. Somewhere, elephants and whales were trying to answer that subsonic message. A primitive part of Grace wanted to run and hide under a bush.

From the side drive that led to the garages, an antique, cranberry red speedster convertible emerged into the courtyard. Like the Duesenberg, it had a long, narrow hood and enormous rounded fenders over the wheels. It was a two-seater, and where its trunk should have been, the car tapered off into a point that looked a little like the prow of a boat. Big chrome bumpers reflected sunlight like mirrors, and head to tail the car must have been more than fifteen feet long.

Declan pulled to a stop in front of Grace and shut off the motor.

Grace gaped at the thing, immediately forgetting her promise to herself to remain composed. "What the hell is *that*?"

"It's a 1971 re-creation of a 1935 Auburn 851 Boattail Speedster," Declan answered. "Not my thing, really. I prefer survivors."

"What?"

"Original cars that have survived, as opposed to re-creations."

"Why do I have to learn on this?"

"I don't think you'd want to learn on an original 1935 car. The shifting is a little different than on a modern transmission."

Grace waved away his explanation. "No, I mean, why do I have to learn on a goddamn speedster that's probably worth half a million dollars?"

"Half a million? This?" Declan laughed. "No. A hundred thousand, tops."

Grace put her hands over her eyes and breathed deeply. *Calm. Must be calm.* She dropped her hands from her eyes and squared her shoulders. Come hell or high water, she was going to learn to drive that car today.

Declan shut off the engine and got out, holding open the driver-side door for her. Grace made a grimace of a smile and slid onto the tiny bench seat, and then looked in horror over the long, long hood of the car. Forget mastering the stick shift; she couldn't even see the road!

"God help me," she muttered under her breath.

"What was that?" Declan asked, getting in the passenger side, his arm brushing hers in the tight confines of the cockpit.

"I said, 'It's a beautiful car,'" Grace said brightly, trying to ignore the shiver running up her arm from their contact. She put her hands on the wheel and pretended to steer, then put her hand on the shift and mocked that as well, making an engine sound deep in her throat: *RRRRR . . . rrrrrr. . . .* "I can't wait to get going! How fast does it go?"

Something between a soft whimper and a cough emerged from Declan's throat.

Ha! Good! There's no reason we can't both *be miserable.* "What do you say, shall we head straight out to Highway One?" she asked, and put her hand on the key as if to turn it.

"Let's get the basics down first," Declan squeaked, then cleared his throat and continued in a lower tone. "Do you understand the basic principles of how a standard transmission works, as opposed to an automatic?"

"I know you have to use the clutch to change gears," Grace said, her hand still on the key.

"But do you know why?" Declan asked, settling back in the seat. His broad shoulders barely left enough room for her.

"Do I need to know why?" Grace answered tartly.

"I'd think you'd want to understand what it is you'll be learning to do. You should have a concept of what's going on in the car."

"Declan, I don't even understand the mechanics of how burning liquid gasoline makes the wheels turn on a car. I don't think I'm going to benefit from a lecture on clutches and gears."

"Nevertheless, I think you should understand."

Grace heaved a put-upon sigh and sat back, secretly delighted by the reprieve. They could sit here all day discussing gears, if it meant delaying the actual driving lesson. "Fine. Tell me about gears."

"Anyone who rides a bicycle already has a basic understanding of using lower gears to get moving, and for more power on hills. In a standard transmission, there is a positive connection between the motor and the transmission—aka, the gears—which is achieved by using the clutch. A clutch disk, actually. When you put your foot on the clutch pedal, you are disengaging the clutch disk and separating the motor from the transmission. I'm grossly simplifying, of course."

"Of course." Grace frowned at Declan. "Er. What is a transmission, anyway? You always hear about them, but no one ever says what they are."

Declan blinked. "The transmission—again, grossly simplifying—transmits the power of the engine to the wheels of the car."

"Oh! It's what turns gas into motion! Well, look. I learned something."

He narrowed his eyes, as if checking whether or not she was making fun of him.

Grace blinked innocently. Let him wonder if she was as ignorant as she appeared. She *was* that ignorant, as far as cars went, but he needn't be sure.

"Anyway," Declan said. "Disengaging the clutch disengages that positive connection between motor and transmission, and allows you to engage a different gear, either higher or lower. If you shift too far up or down, the motor either won't have the power to move the gear and you'll lug the engine, or will have too much power, and the gear will either slow the motor down, which is fine and is a technique for braking, or you'll kill the engine. And if you don't disengage the clutch entirely when you're trying to shift, you'll strip the gears, which is *not* fine and will mean serious work on your transmission."

"Good to know." She tried to smile but he was starting to freak her out. The last thing she wanted was to strip the gears on a $100,000 car.

"Do you know what kept car companies from developing an automatic transmission much earlier than they did?" Declan asked.

Grace made a face at him. "Is this a *trivia* question?"

"I'm trying to help you grasp and appreciate the workings of the car."

"You sure you're not just wasting time because you're afraid of going out on the road with me?"

"I'm not stalling," Declan insisted, his voice getting a little louder, making her think he truly *was* stalling. "Come on, this is interesting."

Grace tilted her head to the side in an exaggerated "I'm listening" pose and opened her eyes wide. "Tell me, why couldn't they develop an automatic transmission earlier?"

"Smart-ass," he muttered.

Grace made a kissy face at him.

Declan ignored her teasing and became more pompously professorial. "The problem they had was how to keep the engine from dying while the car was stopped. Remember, in a standard transmission, disengaging the clutch disengages the motor from the transmission. So, when you're stopped, if you disengage the clutch you can keep the motor running without transmitting power to the wheels. But without a clutch to disengage, when you're at a stop, how do you keep the running motor from dying while it is physically engaged with a motionless gear?"

Grace thought about it for a moment, could find no answer, and then realized with surprise that she actually was curious. She'd never spared a thought for how an automatic transmission worked, but she suddenly wanted to know. "How?" she asked. She hadn't thought she was someone who could be interested in cars. Would she start asking him questions about football next?

"In an automatic, the motor and the transmission never have a positive physical coupling."

Grace frowned, sure she'd missed something, and also a little disturbed by the word "coupling." It sounded sexual. "So their physical coupling is always negative? Sounds familiar."

He narrowed his eyes at her. "I *meant* that there's no input shaft to connect with— I mean— Goddammit, you know what I meant! There's no physical contact between motor and transmission."

"Then how do you get the . . . car to go anywhere? But I forget. Your best skill is making things go without touching them."

He ground his teeth. "The answer to the question is 'fluid.'"

"Really?" Grace's eyes went even wider. Talk about sexual connotations!

"That's what links the motor to the transmission in an automatic," Declan went on, his face flushing. "The motor spins the transmission fluid, which then spins the desired gear."

"How exciting. I'm getting flustered just hearing about it."

He muttered something under his breath, then continued. "When you're stopped in an automatic, the brake is strong enough to hold the car in place even though the engine is running, but the engine doesn't die because it's not physically, positively connected to a motionless gear."

Grace's lips parted in an understanding unrelated to sex. "That's why an automatic will creep forward if you take your foot off the brake! The transmission fluid is still spinning, trying to move the gear!"

"Yes."

"So in a stick shift, the clutch must be disengaged anytime the car is stopped, or else the motionless gear will kill the engine."

"Right. Or the car has to be in neutral, which means that no gear is engaged."

Grace put her hands on the steering wheel and stared forward, putting the pieces together in her mind. "But—if the car is stopped and I'm trying to get it going again, how does the running motor get a stationary gear moving? I mean, you can't just engage the clutch and connect a running engine to a stationary gear and expect it to work smoothly, can you?" Even as she asked, she was again struck by the sexual connotations, and started to chuckle under her breath. She glanced over at Declan, and saw a look of suspicion on his face.

"The clutch will slip a little at first, as it gets the gear moving," he explained. "Your learning how to smoothly master that moment of coupling, dear Grace, is where you and I are going to have so much fun today."

"Now that *was* meant as a double entendre."

"You're hearing what you want to hear. Can't stop thinking about sex with me, can you?"

"Dream on, big boy," she taunted. "I already know you're not up to the task."

"That was your choice, not mine. If you want to sexually frustrate yourself, have at it."

"Oh, I have no intention of leaving myself unfulfilled."

"You think Andrew is going to meet your needs?" Declan scoffed. "Good luck. He'll run for the hills."

"Look who's talking about running away! You took off like a . . . a . . . like a rabbit being chased by a coyote. You obviously can't handle a woman who's your equal in appetite."

"I took off because I had to get some perspective on what the hell is going on between us."

"I should think it was quite clear," she lied. She didn't know what he felt, and was only half sure of her own feelings.

"Like hell it's clear. This is the strangest damn relationship I've ever been in."

"It's not a re—"

"I know, it's not a relationship," he said, running a hand through his hair in agitation. "But it's something. There's an attraction between us like nothing I've ever encountered, and yeah, it's thrown me off balance. But that's what you wanted, isn't it, Grace? To throw me off balance?" he said with an edge in his voice. He leaned closer to her, suddenly seeming twice as large in the small confines of the car.

"Why would I want that?" she asked innocently, feeling a start of both pleasure and alarm in her chest. She had affected him more than she'd thought, which delighted her, but he might sense more about her angry feelings than she'd intended. It would be much harder to crush the bastard if he knew she hated him.

"Because you want to hurt me, the same way I hurt you that first night."

"Yes, you hurt me," Grace said carefully. "But you also did me a double favor that night. First you showed me how useful you could be for my own sexual entertainment, and then you showed me that you weren't the type of man whose feelings I'd have to care about. My only disappointment has been that you've fallen below the mark, sexually. I'd hoped for so much more."

"Those were the terms of the game! You'd have gotten more if your pride hadn't kept you from saying yes. Believe me, I would have been too happy to oblige."

"Funny, I didn't take you for the type to sit around waiting for written permission."

"The only thing that makes a game worthwhile," Declan ground out, "is having rules to follow."

"And only mediocre players never learn that there's a right time to break them. Risk and reward, Declan. But I guess you like things on the cautious side." She saw the tightness on his face and thought he looked ready to explode. It would take just one more push toward the edge. "Andrew *looks* cautious on the outside, but underneath I'm discovering—"

Declan reached for her, sending a thrill of fear and excitement through her, but almost simultaneously Sophia's sharp voice came from a window on the second floor. "Declan!" she barked, making them spring apart. "Are you going to sit there all day arguing, or are you going to teach Grace to drive the car?"

Grace blushed to her hairline, wondering just how much Sophia had overheard. She looked up at her aunt and waved. Sophia rolled her eyes and disappeared into the shadows of the house. Declan seemed no less disturbed as he fumbled for his seat belt and snapped it shut. Grace adjusted the mirror, then buckled herself in as well.

Taking on an impersonal tone, Declan talked Grace through familiarization with the gears on the stick shift and disengaging the clutch. Using his hands as models for her feet on the pedals, he demonstrated how she was going to start the car and then put it into motion. "Got it?"

Grace's anxiety, so happily forgotten while they were arguing, came back in full force. This was it. She was going to drive the friggin' $100,000 car. She nodded, reached for the key, and turned it.

It made a quarter turn and stopped. No engine turned over. No change in the car was apparent. Grace looked at her feet, checking that they were where Declan had said to put them. She checked the gearshift. Nothing seemed out of order. She looked at Declan.

"It's a re-creation of a 1935 car," he said.

"And?"

He pointed to a red and chrome button several inches from the key. "Starter."

"You could have told me that before," Grace muttered, and pressed the button. The engine growled to life, the power vibrating up the steering wheel to her hands, the whole car gently thumping.

"There's a V8 under the hood," Declan cautioned. "Two hundred and ninety-five horsepower."

"I don't really know what that means," Grace said, sitting frozen with feet on the clutch and brake, and the car in first gear; at least she was pretty sure it was first gear. She looked at the stick to check, looked away, then checked again. She touched it with her hand, making sure it was shoved into place.

"It means that when you hit the gas, the car doesn't just go, it *goes*."

"Fantastic."

"Take your foot off the brake, touch the gas, and engage the clutch."

"I'm going to. I'm just mentally preparing." She mentally replayed what Declan had modeled with his hands, and applied it to what he'd told her about the workings of the engine and transmission. She could almost visualize exactly what needed to happen.

"Do it!" Declan ordered.

Grace took her foot off the brake, hit the gas, engaged the clutch, and the Auburn leaped forward a foot before lurching to a halt and dying, jerking them against their seat belts. "Dammit!" Grace cried.

"Feet on the clutch and brake," Declan said. "Put the car in neutral. Restart the car."

"I know," Grace groused as she obeyed.

Again the car lurched and died. Again she restarted it, and then killed it a third time. She sat still, lowered her brows, and thought. If a motionless gear was what killed the engine, then if the engine seemed like it was going to die, the remedy would be—

"Grace, try again."

"Shh!"

"Feet on the clutch and—"

"*Shh!* I'm thinking!"

"You're never going to learn this by thinking; you need to feel what the car is doing. You'll only learn that by doing. It's a physical thing, not a mental one."

"Just *be quiet. Please!*"

Declan heaved a sigh and crossed his arms over his chest.

Grace gripped the steering wheel and stared out over the hood. The clutch needs to slip a little to get the gear moving—the engine can keep running if the clutch isn't engaged. . . . She realized she had been giving it too much gas and engaging the clutch too quickly. All she had to do if the car started to buck was disengage the clutch a little more.

She started the car, put it in gear, released the brake, gently hit the gas, and slowly lifted her foot off the clutch pedal. The car eased forward, she gave it more gas, and it suddenly lurched. She slammed her foot onto the clutch pedal, keeping the engine alive. "Ha, gotcha!" she muttered, and once again started to ease the car forward. With a few gentle jerks and some play with the clutch, she got the Auburn moving and headed out of the courtyard. With her foot now completely off the clutch, she gave it more gas and with a quiet roar the car shot up the sloping, winding driveway.

Beside her, Declan sucked in a breath, and she herself struggled to maneuver the long car around a bend at too high a speed. As they came around it, a Subaru Forester appeared, half blocking their path. Grace screeched and hit the brake, forgetting the clutch in the process and killing the engine with a lurch. The Subaru swerved and stopped, the two cars coming within a half foot of each other.

Declan swore under his breath. Grace's heart was in her throat, going two hundred beats a minute. She recognized Dr. Andrew's car; a moment later, he inched the Subaru forward, the outside wheels going off the driveway and into the dirt to get by. He stopped parallel to the Auburn and lowered his window.

"Grace? What are you doing in that thing?" he asked, his face tight with worry as his gaze went from her to Declan, so close beside her, to the car.

"Learning to drive a stick shift," she said, barely keeping herself from explaining that it had been Sophia's idea. Sophia's insistence that Andrew must fight for her was still fresh in her mind.

"You're not going out on a public road in that, are you?"

"Of course she is," Declan said before Grace could answer. "Don't you think she's capable?"

"There's capable and there's reasonable. Grace, leave that car where it is and come back down to the house. We'll find an easier car for you to learn on. I'll take you to an empty parking lot and teach you."

Grace's hands tightened on the wheel. She was still scared half to death of the Auburn, and on high alert with Declan sitting next to her, but there was a thrill in the danger that she didn't want to give up. She didn't want to be rescued. "It's okay, Andrew. I'm getting the hang of it already." She gave him a warm smile. "But thanks for looking out for me."

"Are you sure?" Andrew's worried eyes rested on Declan. "I'm a patient instructor."

Declan stretched out his arm, laying it behind Grace's shoulders on the back of the bench seat. "Don't worry, Andrew," he said, "I'll teach her everything she needs to know." He brushed his fingertips over her bare shoulder.

Grace shivered, his touch setting off a cascade of reaction in her body. She rolled her eyes for Andrew's benefit, and shooed him toward the house. "Aunt Sophia's waiting for you. Don't worry, I'll be back before you know it."

Andrew's brow puckered as Declan's naughty fingers shifted to her neck, stroking between her collarbone and ear. Grace grabbed his hand. "Stop that," she scolded, only to find her hand now trapped in his. She smiled again at Andrew as she tugged it free.

"Grace?" Andrew said uncertainly.

"He's just teasing," she said, feigning exasperation. Part of her wanted to see where Declan's roving hand might go next, the rest of her was annoyed that he had to have this irresistible physical effect on her.

"If you're sure," Andrew said.

"She's sure," Declan answered. "How many times does she have to say it?"

Andrew's lips tightened, and with a final nod to Grace he crept the Subaru past them and around the bend of the drive.

"I thought he'd never leave," Declan said.

"You enjoyed that," Grace accused, and shrugged his arm off her shoulders.

Declan brushed his fingertips across her skin as he withdrew, sending a fresh shiver over her flesh. "So did you."

She couldn't deny it, much as she'd like to. "Oh, hush," she said instead, and made a show of getting the car ready to start.

"You're in a tough spot now," Declan said.

"Between you and Andrew? Hardly. I think it's pretty obvious who's the better choice."

"Why thank you, Grace. But I was talking about starting the car on a hill."

"Oh."

"The car's going to roll backward when you take your foot off the brake."

A flutter of uncertainty beat in her chest. "Okay."

"So you're going to have to act with a little more speed, because we're on a bend here and if you roll straight back, you're going to go off the driveway and into a tree."

Was he *trying* to make her more nervous? "Yeah, I get the picture."

"So start the car."

She ground her teeth and started the engine. Once again she stared out over the long hood, mentally rehearsing what she was going to do.

"Grace—"

"Ut!" she said, putting up one hand to stop him. "I'm thinking."

"Gra—"

"Ut! Ut!"

She put her hand back on the wheel, took her foot off the brake, and as the car started to roll backward she tried to get it to go forward. She overdid it on the gas and the car lurched and bucked. She shoved her foot on the clutch, and they picked up backward speed.

Declan made a strangled noise.

Grace slammed her foot on the brake. The car halted and she sat frozen, then dared a peek in the rearview mirror.

A pine tree loomed straight behind them, only a foot or so off the asphalt.

Shaking now, her left leg already feeling the strain of unfamiliar use on the clutch, she started the car again. Canted backward on the slope, she was a little farther from the pedals than was comfortable, and had to point her toes to get the clutch all the way disengaged. Her arch ached. She clung to the steering wheel, trying to hold herself forward as she once again released the brake and hit the gas.

The car lurched and died.

She whimpered.

"Grace," Declan said softly. "You already understand how it works. Like I said before, just feel and do."

"That's not how I work."

"It's going to have to be. Put on the parking brake; I'll take over and get the car somewhere easier for you to practice."

"No! I can do this."

"You don't need to prove anything, Grace. You're learning. Give yourself a break."

"No! Just let me sit and think a minute."

"Grace, for God's sake! You can't think your way out of starting a car on a hill."

He wasn't hearing her; he didn't understand her. The realization hurt and frustrated her. "Declan, I'm not put together in a way that lets me feel my way through anything! I have to think, all the time."

"You could have fooled me. Were you thinking all through the night we spent together?"

"Yes! Always!"

His voice lowered, any teasing or exasperation gone from it. "So it was just a game to you. A test to see how far you could push me."

"Yes!"

He was silent a moment, and then, disbelief in his voice, "Christ, Grace. Are you even human?"

She met his gaze, his accusation and the stress of the moment making the truth spill out from dark recesses she hadn't even known were within her. "You think I *like* being this way? You have no idea how badly I wish I could shut it off sometimes and just be. Yeah, I was testing you that night, but I was also testing myself. Part of me hoped you could push me to where I'd break down and feel so much that thought stopped, pride shattered, and I wouldn't care about or be aware of anything but sex. I wanted to lose myself in sensation. But you couldn't get me all the way there. No one can." She felt tears starting in her eyes, and her voice cracked. "So yeah, I *do* have to think my way through every goddamn thing, including getting this goddamn car to move forward without bashing a hundred-thousand-dollar bumper into a goddamn pine tree! Okay?"

She expected to see anger or impatience in his eyes, but instead saw thoughtful consideration.

"Yeah, okay," Declan said evenly. "If we have to roll up against the tree, it won't hurt the car if you do so slowly."

"Okay."

It took several tries, and finally, coasting and steering backward down the driveway back to the courtyard where she could start again on the flat ground, but eventually Grace managed to get the Auburn up to the top of the driveway. After three tries and some tense moments, Grace pulled the car ónto 17-Mile Drive and eventually shifted into second gear. The speed limit was low enough that she felt comfortable maneuvering the big car, and the sweat of anxiety and exertion began to dry on her skin, lifted away by the sea breeze along a stretch of road overlooking the rocky shore.

Turnouts along the road were packed with the cars of tourists and families getting out to take in the views. People turned to watch as the red Auburn glided by, with some friendly souls waving as if to a passing ship. Declan waved back as Grace grinned.

Stop signs, and cars coming to a stop ahead of her to make a left turn, were her nemeses. She killed the engine a handful of times, but gradually started to get the hang of making the car go. Declan was unusually quiet beside her, offering neither praise nor criticism, and when she sneaked a peek at his face he looked lost in thought. His mental absence was welcome since it kept her from feeling observed and judged, but it was agitating on a different level.

The one thing she'd always been sure of with Declan was that he was fully aware of her whenever they were together. This was uncomfortably like spending time with Andrew.

She scolded herself for being a self-absorbed ninny. She wasn't a child, needing every moment of a person's attention. Especially not Declan's attention, which brought her nothing but grief . . .

. . . and the most thrilling sexual moments she'd ever experienced.

"Turn left at the next intersection," Declan said, jerking her out of her thoughts.

She did as bid, turning onto a smaller road through a residential neighborhood. Declan guided her through several turns and they twisted deeper into the Del Monte forest, past modest houses and past gates that hid other homes from the road. A final narrow, lonely stretch of asphalt wound upward through trees, coming out into a clearing atop a hill. A midcentury ranch house sat alone in the space, with a view over the treetops and a distant line of ocean. The yard was unkempt and the house had weeds protruding from the gutters, the aluminum-pane windows bare of curtains.

"What is this place?" Grace asked as she parked the car and shut off the engine.

"A vacant house," he said, getting out of the car. "I'm working with some investors on buying the land and subdividing it."

Grace got out, too, following him to the edge of the driveway to look out over the meadow and woods. She stretched, her muscles tight from driving. "It seems a pity to fill such a private spot with houses."

"People overrate the virtues of isolation. We're social creatures and like company, however much we complain about our neighbors or communities."

"So why'd you bring me up here? To make sure there are no Steinbeck crickets lurking in the grass to spoil your plans?"

A muscle in his jaw twitched. "No. It was the only place I could think of that was private."

"Private for what?"

He turned, slid his hand behind her neck, and lowered his mouth to hers. She stood frozen in surprise, and then felt a shot of warmth and weakness go through her. Before she could react, he'd wrapped his other arm around her waist and deepened the kiss, her hips pressed up against his, her head tilting back under the force of his tender assault. Her hands gripped his sides either for balance or to push him away, but his lips on hers and the warm, wet thrust of his tongue into her mouth had her loosening her grip and then sliding her hands onto his back to pull him closer.

His slid down to her buttock, squeezing her once and then hoisting her up against his pelvis. She wrapped her legs around his hips and was dimly aware of him carrying her, but it was his mouth that mattered to her as it pressed down against hers, a hungry, devouring substitute for the union of their bodies. She ground her loins against him, seeking contact and sensation.

She felt something warm and smooth against her butt, and as Declan took his arm from around her and lowered her onto her back, she realized he'd propped her on the sloping boat tail of the Auburn. He disengaged her legs from his hips and reached up her thigh, under her skirt, and roughly tugged down her panties, then drew them off her and flung them aside.

A flush of alarm went through her—he was going so fast. Her feet scrambled for purchase, and found it on the chrome bumpers on either side of the boat tail, leaving her thighs parted over the tail end of the car with Declan in the open space. She pushed up with her hands on the sloping metal, trying to sit up. "Declan, what are you—"

His mouth came back down on hers, silencing her. He untied

her halter and let the fabric fall, and she felt his hand on her breast, teasing and arousing, as the force of his kiss lowered her back against the car. His mouth left hers and gently bit a trail down her neck to her breasts. She flung one arm over her head and gripped the back of the seat to keep from sliding downward, and with the other dug her fingers into Declan's hair.

She felt his hands leave her, and heard the clink of metal; opening her eyes she caught the flash of sunlight on his belt buckle, and on a square scrap of color thrown aside—a condom wrapper.

"Declan, I think—" she started to say in shock.

His mouth captured hers again, and his hands slid up the sides of her body, then captured her other arm and raised it above her head. He nuzzled her neck, and as he did he wedged his hips between her thighs. "You think too much," he whispered against her ear. And then he entered her.

Grace gasped, her legs tensing, her feet going up on their toes as they balanced on the edge of the bumper. He wasn't asking permission; he was taking what she had so deliberately obliquely offered him.

He raised his head and met her gaze as he thrust. Her eyes widened, and he held motionless for a moment, as if letting her adjust, and then continued. She felt the dull pain of tight inner muscles forced to stretch, but mingled with it was a hint of an ache just beginning to be soothed. She tilted her hips against him, silently asking for more.

He planted one hand on the car and slid his other arm under the small of her back, gripping her hips, and then there was no turning back. He lowered his face again into the crook of her neck as he took her, his arm at her hips ensuring she met him with as much force as he gave. Grace raised her knees up to his sides and hooked her feet around his back.

"Grace," Declan cried into her hair, "oh God, Grace—" His movements slowed, his grip on her tightened. He held her locked in his hard embrace, and then started to relax. He raised his face from her neck and looked at her, and she blinked against the bright sunlight. She could still feel him, full inside her, and shifted her hips.

"You're *done?*"

He laughed, his belly vibrating against hers. "Only for the moment."

He separated himself from her and helped her off the car. Grace stood on shaky legs, and retied her halter. She was throbbing with unsatisfied arousal, but other than being dazed, she didn't know quite what she was feeling. She'd just had sex with Declan.

With Declan!

She blinked in a sort of stunned shock. She still didn't know what she felt. Her body throbbed and ached and hungered, it shook with exhaustion, but her heart? Her mind? Vaguely stunned, was all she could determine.

Declan cleaned himself up and found an old aluminum trash bin by the garage. Grace looked for her underpants, but Declan spotted them first. He looked at her, then shoved them in his pocket.

Her lips parted. "What are you—"

"I said I wasn't done with you."

A shiver ran through her. "You can't expect me to drive with no underwear."

"What do they have to do with driving?"

"My skirt is short! I can't put my bare . . . *parts* on the leather seat!"

He shrugged.

She pursed her lips and pulled the slender scarf from her hair.

Back at the car, she neatly pleated the scarf on the seat, forming a protective square of tangerine silk. Declan shook his head as she got into the driver's seat, carefully sitting down upon it. The smoothness of the silk felt cool against her tender flesh.

He got in beside her, and she looked over at him. "I never asked for it," she taunted.

"But you did, Grace. In a hundred ways, you did. But most of all, you wanted me to make the decision for you."

"I did not!" she said, offended to the marrow.

He laughed. "It's okay, I get it. It's more of a turn-on for you to have me take control."

Grace sputtered. "It is not! That's, that's . . . a grossly chauvinistic thing to suggest!"

"No, it's a human thing to suggest. We can't help our appetites. You can't help wanting a man who's stronger than yourself, and who will take charge of sex. If I was going to blame anything beyond biology for that, I'd blame your Women's Studies program. It's created a sort of reverse reaction."

Grace gaped at him. "You are unbelievable! You don't honestly think I think that you're stronger than I am in any but a physical sense, do you? Or that I want you taking charge, being a '*man*'?"

"I think we've already established the truth of that, as far as sex goes. Don't you?" he asked with irritating confidence. "But beyond that? Sometimes, yeah, I'll bet you'd like it if the guy you were with took charge and didn't offer you choices."

Grace slapped her hand to her forehead and shook her head. "I'm talking to a Neanderthal. You'd take us back fifty years, to when women couldn't even order their own dinner in a restaurant."

"Hell, Grace. Most of the time, *I'd* rather have someone else order my meal for me. Wouldn't you? Really? Instead of having to decide what you want to eat?"

She shook her head. "It's patronizing beyond belief."

He laughed. "If you feel that way, then it's obvious you've never had any real responsibility in your life."

"*What* are you talking about?"

"If you've never had a chance to make your own decisions, then yes, it's patronizing. But if you're an adult in the real world—as opposed to in school, where you've apparently spent your entire life—then every day you have to slog through endless choices and decisions, about everything from what to eat for breakfast to whether you should rent a home or buy one, to whether the ache in your tooth is worth the money to see a dentist. It's a gift for someone to say to you, 'Hey, sit back and enjoy yourself. I'll take care of things.'"

She shook her head. "It's a trap. A soft, comfortable trap that will slowly disable a person."

Declan looked at her in puzzlement. "Grace, it's not a trap. It's a temporary delegation of duties. Are you so uncertain of your independence that you fear it will be stolen from you if you leave someone else in charge for a few hours?"

"Of course not! But leaving the guy in charge sets the wrong foundation for a good relationship."

"But aren't you tired of *thinking* all the time? Tired of loading every decision with what it says about your personal politics?"

"If you have a brain, you have a responsibility to use it," she insisted, even as she felt the temptation hidden within his words. *Relax, don't struggle, don't strive, let someone else handle the difficult business of life.* But on that route lay a wasted life, with dreams unfulfilled, goals abandoned. She feared that giving in to the lazy pleasure for even a short time would be like taking an addictive drug. She wasn't afraid of someone else stealing her independence; she was afraid she might toss it aside herself.

"Poor Grace," Declan said softly, "always thinking, and having such a hard time letting down her guard and enjoying."

His words hit the vulnerable spot within her, the spot where she feared she might never enjoy the abandon that seemed to come so much more easily to other people. "I can't *not* be this way," she said softly.

He reached over and stroked her cheek with surprising delicacy. "I know." He tucked a stray hair back behind her ear. "Do all the thinking you want, if you must: argue with me, berate me, even chase after Andrew if you must; I can't stop you. But for now, you're going to give up some of your control. Your body is mine."

"You're not even offering me a choice about it?" she asked, a shiver running over her skin.

"Choices are vastly overrated."

"But what would you make me do?"

Amusement pulled at his mouth. "That's not for you to worry about. That's the *point*. Let go, Grace. Just—let go."

Damn the man! To have sensed something about her that she herself hated to admit, that she, of all people, might deep inside be tantalized by the idea of him laying his hands on her whenever he wished, without her permission.

And despite his claim to the contrary, she saw the question in his eyes, and the choice he offered. He talked a good game about taking decisions from her hands, but he was a man who played by rules. He was asking her permission to *not* ask her permission.

There was a kinky sort of honor to it, and a subtle sensitivity, too. For all his posturing, he actually seemed intent on protecting her sense of self-determination. It was a strange paradox.

Grace started the car and they left the vacant house behind

them. The pine trees cast welcome shade on her shoulders as they wound back through the woods and neighborhood toward 17-Mile Drive. Declan spoke only to tell her where to turn, and she wondered if he was giving her time to think.

Her thoughts were in a riot. As she turned onto 17-Mile Drive she was reminded of the day she'd arrived, driving down the same road with Cat and thinking her summer would be spent keeping an old lady company while she watched Animal Planet all day. The last thing she'd have anticipated was that two months later she'd be driving a replica 1935 Speedster pantyless, having just had sex on the back of the car.

What was happening to her?

"Were you ill while I was away?" Declan asked into the quiet between them.

"Ill? No. Why?"

"You look like you lost weight."

"I did," she said, gratified he'd noticed. He'd been back in her life for less than twenty-four hours, and it already seemed as if her former anger belonged to someone else, long ago and far away.

What was happening to her? Had sex addled her brain?

"You're not going to lose any more weight, are you?" he asked.

"Don't you think I should?" she asked, glancing at him.

"I don't know why you lost as much as you *did*."

"If I'm ever going to have a body like Cyndee's—"

"*Cyndee's?* Jesus, why would you want that?"

"She's . . . thin," Grace said, and had the unfamiliar feeling that this simple, obvious reason was inadequate.

Declan snorted. "California's got enough assless women. We don't need more."

Grace blinked. With one idiotic comment he'd made her feel

happier about the size of her butt than she had since she was ten years old.

He's getting under your skin, a voice inside her whispered. *He burned you twice before. Don't let him do it again.*

Grace glanced over at him. His elbow was on the top of the door, the wind ruffling his dark hair, his face set in lines of easy contentment. He caught her looking and grinned, his turquoise blue eyes crinkling with what seemed to be genuine delight in her company. Her stomach fluttered: He was a startlingly handsome man, and when he looked at her like that . . .

"Maybe thinking so much isn't a bad thing," he said cheerfully. "You've picked up driving a stick shift faster than any guy I've taught. And to top it off, besides Sophia, you're the only woman I've known who doesn't fill every quiet moment with chatter. Thinking definitely has its benefits."

"Are you *trying* to be obnoxious?"

His grin grew wider. "You have a hard time accepting compliments."

"You have a hard time giving them in a form a person would want to accept."

He chuckled, apparently not the least dismayed by her prickliness.

Don't fall for it, the voice inside warned her again. *It's the sex clouding your thinking. When a man touches you, bonding starts. It's biology. Don't let it fool you into thinking you like him or he likes you.*

She forced herself to replay her first night at her aunt's house, and the deliberate humiliation he'd caused her after seducing her on the couch.

She made herself remember that he'd left her bed without a good-bye, without a note, without a phone call.

He'd returned to Pebble Beach only because of the Steinbeck cricket. Never mind what he'd claimed about needing space to make sense of his attraction to her; it was a flattering excuse to get what he wanted.

Which was what? Sex? But he'd only want that if he was attracted to her, wouldn't he?

Grace shook her head. He might find her physically attractive, but that had nothing to do with what he felt about her as a person. If she was thoroughly cynical, she'd say he wanted to have sex with her as revenge against Dr. Andrew. Any physical pleasure he got out of it was just a side benefit.

The pain was enough to remind her that she herself was supposed to be in this for one reason: to make Declan fall in love with her, win the bet with Sophia, and then crush his wicked, careless heart.

Any physical pleasure she got out of it would be *her* side benefit.

Or so she tried to tell herself.

Declan watched Grace change gears, her hand confident on the gearshift, her legs tensing and relaxing as she worked the clutch, and a tantalizing flash of tangerine silk appearing under the edge of one thigh as her skirt slid up her leg. His cock stirred. He tore his gaze away from the strip of silk, but couldn't help imagining where it led, and the vulnerable part of Grace it was pressed up against.

A glance at her face showed her eyes sternly ahead, a small crease between her brows. Was she concentrating on driving, or was she thinking about him and what they'd done? He wasn't going to risk asking, not with that look on her face.

Tangling with Grace was like tangling with a tiger. He had to be on guard if he was going to escape with only minor scratches, or have any hope of keeping the upper hand. He was surprised that he'd managed as well as he had today with her; he was even feeling hopeful about his chances of turning her affections away from Andrew and onto himself—which was a minor miracle. He'd been making everything up as he went along.

It was while they'd been trying to get the car up the driveway that he'd had his epiphany about Grace. She all but asked him to push her out of her perpetual, self-inflicted control. Locked in a cage of her own construction, she had handed him the key and asked him to open the door, for she hadn't the power to do it herself.

He'd been half afraid to oblige her. He'd felt her surprise when he kissed her beside the vacant house, then felt the answering hunger in her mouth. He hadn't been a hundred percent certain he had read her correctly about what she wanted, though, and it wasn't the type of decision a man could afford to make a mistake about. He'd watched the nuances of emotion on her face and listened to the language of her body, alert for any hint of resistance, any intimation that she'd offered an invitation she didn't want to honor.

When he'd started to enter her, her eyes had gone wide in surprise, but her body had pressed toward his, seeking more. And when she'd wrapped her legs around his waist, her heels pressing into his back as if kicking him to give her more, the last of his caution fell away.

He'd wanted her for two months, with a growing obsession unlike anything he'd felt before. To finally have her was a feast for a man who had been starving. The sex was as good as he'd hoped, but it was over before he'd had more than a taste of all he wanted. Leaving Grace unsatisfied had been unavoidable, but not regrettable. It meant she was still primed for a second round.

Assuming Grace continued to be willing. The question he'd have to help her answer now was whether escaping the protection of her cage was worth the rewards. Left alone with her thoughts for too long, Grace might chase herself back into the cage and swing the door shut.

Andrew would like that, no doubt. He'd add extra bars and

locks of his own to keep her neatly contained. Andrew was no tiger hunter.

Grace turned down the driveway to Sophia's house and coasted through the turns. She stopped in the courtyard, and Declan pointed toward the garages around the side of the house. Grace shifted into first and headed the car back to its stall.

To keep Grace from closing herself back in her cage, there was only one sure way he knew to distract her.

They pulled into the shaded interior of the six-stall garage and Grace shut off the engine and started to get out. Declan caught the end of the tangerine scarf and pulled it through his fingers, the silk creased and damp.

"Grace," he said, reaching over and catching hold of the hem of her skirt as she stood.

"What?"

He slid over the bench seat to her side and grasped her thighs. A breath of surprise slipped from her; she looked down at him with parted lips and a question in her sea green eyes. Holding her gaze, he wrapped the scarf around her thighs and tied it, pinning her legs together.

She laughed nervously. "What are you doing? I can't walk like this."

"Walking is the last thing on my mind." He got out of the car and took her in his arms, kissing her hard enough that she wouldn't be able to think. His hand roamed down her backside and lifted the hem of her skirt. Her arms went around his neck, her body sagging against his, and a soft moan of hunger purred in her throat.

"I want you standing," he said, his voice low and urgent. "There," he said, turning her toward a support column a couple of feet away.

She hesitated and he saw uncertainty in her eyes. He waited, knowing that she needed a moment to understand that she was truly free, even if she chose to pretend otherwise.

"Grab the post," he told her.

A ghost of a wicked smile touched her lips and then, slowly, as if taunting him, she did as bid.

It lasted longer than it had on the tail of the car, and he put his hands to good use, making sure she got where she needed to go. Her soft moans were his guide and his reward. When they were finished, he untied the scarf from her thighs and handed it to her as she stood up straight, her skirt covering her again.

She looked blankly at the mangled scarf in her hands. "Do I get my panties back?"

Feeling sheepish, he pulled them from his pocket and gave them to her.

"Thanks." Still she didn't move.

"Grace, are you okay?"

She looked up at him, the frown between her brows again. Her hair was a mussed mess, her cheeks were flushed, and her lips were swollen from kissing. She didn't seem to see him, her vision turned to some inner landscape. "I want . . ."

"Yes? You want?"

"I want . . ." She turned and looked out the open garage doors at the white glare of sunlight.

"What do you want, Grace?" He'd get it for her, whatever it was. He'd hand-wash her in a tub of warm water. He'd take her to Paris. He'd carry her to her bedroom, sing her to sleep, anything.

"I really, *really* want a bacon cheeseburger. Can you get one for me?" she asked, as uncertain as if asking him to bring her a bar of gold.

He laughed. "Is that all?"

She shook her head, her expression deadly serious. "With french fries. And a chocolate shake."

"I can do that."

She put her hand on his arm. "And, Declan?"

"Yes?"

"Get extra bacon. Lots of extra bacon."

"Okay."

She left him then, walking stiff-legged out into the sunlight while holding her panties and scarf in one hand. He followed from a distance, and then stopped to watch from the corner of the house as Andrew came out to greet her. The tall man seemed flustered by Grace's somnambulist manner, his questions met by murmurs. As if sensing his enemy, he turned and saw Declan.

Declan held two fingers to his forehead in a mock salute to the doctor. "You're losing her already," Declan said under his breath. "You wanted a fight, so I'm giving you one. And I don't intend to lose."

CHAPTER
ℰ 21 ℈

Research Notes

August 6

Author has clearly gone mad. Starvation diet, extreme exercise routine, and Draconian beauty regime of last two months have exhausted Author of all willpower, self-control, common sense, modesty, restraint.

Ability to obey instructions of Sophia is gone. Control of eating, gone—along with change from semivegetarianism to an unhealthy obsession with cured meats, especially bacon. Exercise routine is gone through with only the barest motions, angering trainer. Author unable to care about trainer's anger, and in a weak moment made rude comment about trainer's lack of ass.

While Author had originally suspected that focusing entire self on becoming beautiful would lead to mental disorder, Author did not predict the form such derangement would take. Author is now obsessed with sex with the despised male, Declan.

Has shallow focus on appearances harmed Author's self-worth to sufficient degree to make Author seek out sex as substitute for self-esteem? This explanation would fit Author's earlier theories.

However.

Author is unaware of any dip in feeling of self-worth. While aware of slight increase in being judgmental re: the appearance of others as Author becomes more focused on own appearance, Author's judgments of herself seem to have improved with increase in own attractiveness.

State of Author's emotions regarding the male is unknown, and at present point may be unknowable. Sexual fever must die back before order can be made from internal chaos. Author is in constant anticipation of next sexual encounter, subsuming all emotion and thought in lust.

August 7
Said male came upon Author in far reaches of garden, and engaged in sexual encounter. Second sexual encounter in D.'s bedroom. Third encounter in Author's bathroom.

August 8
Garden. Garage.

August 9
Author's bedroom. Under piano.

August 10
Author notes that Dr. Andrew is becoming more attentive and protective, and prone to questioning Author about activities and company she keeps. Dr. seems concerned about Author's mental status.

Friend Cat also lately concerned re: mental status.

Mother calling more often, asking more questions, and deeply distressed re: weight loss. Author cannot recall informing mother of weight loss. Suspects Cat has been talking to mother behind her back. Also possible that Cat and Dr. are in contact and scheming.

Note: Possible development of paranoid thinking.

Simple solution is to leave phone turned off.

On bright side, Dr. held Author's hand, a major step forward. For moment, Author thought Dr. might muster courage to kiss her, but the despised male appeared and put the kibosh on that.

Sand dunes.

August 11

Author's period has arrived. Author thanks Trojan for making effective product.

Lack of restraint re: food, exercise has not improved. Five pounds regained. PMS was possibly responsible, but Author recognizes fixation on bacon played its part.

Author unwilling to give up bacon.

As food frenzy and weight gain are contrary to deal worked out with Sophia, Author recognizes she is in danger of losing the $20,000 offered to her in payment for obedience to S.'s instruction.

Author still unwilling to give up bacon.

Alternatives:

Give up $20,000.

Gain control of eating (somehow).

Convince S. to drop diet and exercise from plan.

August 12

Author is outraged by medical establishment and media. In preparing arguments for Sophia re: diet, Author searched medical literature regarding weight and all-cause mortality. For nonsmokers, overweight and obese people have lower risks for premature death than normal weight or skinny people. Skinny people are at highest risk for premature death in all age ranges. Author feeling bitter re: self-restraint for past two months, and unnecessary guilt for past decade.

Also, benefit of exercise beyond minimal amounts (30 min. walking daily, tops) is not clearly established and may in fact be harmful. Author thinks personal trainer should be arrested for assault.

Author has been told for past five years to lose weight for her health, and now finds that she was less likely to die when she was heavier. Confirms Author's suspicion that all "it's for your health" comments are a crock.

Author additionally annoyed to discover that according to research the "most attractive" body mass index for women is 21 (admittedly less than Author's BMI, even postdiet), but that attractiveness drops off much more sharply below 21 than it does above 21

Not only is thinner not healthier, it also apparently is less attractive than plumpness.

Author furious, and in search of bacon.

August 13
Trainer and nutritionist fired.

Sophia claims Author's sheaf of research printouts were immaterial to decision. Of greater import was Author's recent inexplicable improvement in bombshell sexiness. S. claims Author is exuding sexuality, as if sex constantly on Author's mind.

S. likely aware of sexual relationship between Author and despised male (nothing gets past her), but is making show of saying nothing.

August 15
Author's bedroom. Bedroom. Bedroom.

August 16
Dr. Andrew noticed Author's changed eating habits and slight weight gain, and expressed concern. Dr. repeated supposed longevity

benefits of CRON. Author was tempted to wave research papers under Dr.'s nose, but thought better of it, as Dr. being so sweet otherwise. He brought flowers, held Author's hand during walk in garden, and talked about hopes for future: wife, kids, volunteer work for Doctors Without Borders. Again, Dr. almost kissed Author, but obviously gun shy after first disastrous kiss.

Author in dilemma over Dr.

Author very fond of Dr., Author enjoys talking with Dr., and Author finds Dr. physically attractive in gentle way. Author also still tempted to side with Dr. re: Steinbeck cricket, and admires Dr.'s altruism. However, Author strongly feeling guilt of secret sexual relationship with enemy of Dr.

Author unwilling (unable?) to give up secret sexual relationship.

Author unwilling to give up potential for long-term relationship with Dr.

Author can only conclude that diet/exercise/beauty lead to nymphomania, which leads to unsavory, dishonest, sluttish behavior.

Is above considered evidence of decline in Author's sense of self-worth?

Author wonders if attempt should be made to turn sexual hunger from despised male to Dr. All problems solved, if successful.

August 17

Garden. Garden. Garden.

Author obviously has no self-control, no self-respect. Despised male has uttered no word of affection for Author beyond moans and grunts of pleasure. Why does Author continue with him when Dr. is available? Is sexual relationship with despised male interfering with Author's ability to bond with superior male?

Author growing deeply confused over what she wants. At beginning of summer, answer was obvious: write dissertation, get boyfriend. Summer is almost over, and no writing on dissertation has occurred. One intelligent, ideal male is courting her with long-term thoughts. One cretinous lout is banging her (revolting phrase unfortunately apt in circumstances), but never mentions the future. Cretinous lout does show surprising flashes of insight, humor, and protectiveness, though.

Or is Author only seeing some good in the despised male in order to feel better about her continuing sexual relationship?

Sexual relationship clearly messing with head. Confusion abounding.

At beginning of summer, Author was firm in her beliefs regarding validity of her studies and point of view regarding pursuit of beauty and the damage it does to women. Now, Author reveling in own appearance.

Question: Has Author gained confidence with improved appearance?

Answer: Author likes looking better and not being self-conscious about body. Assumes that strangers think better of her now than they did a month ago, and that makes her more comfortable around them.

But.

Author is noticing the weight of other women more than used to. What looked normal before now looks a little porky.

Are fat and body image the real issue, though? Or is it that Author expects world to hold itself to whatever standards she sets for herself, whether standards are being heavy or thin, a rational or emotional thinker, one who lives by feminist or traditional values? Author views the world through lens of her own experience, and judges accordingly.

How grossly unfair.

Maybe what is right and wrong is more fluid than Author thought. As situation changes, so do judgments. Morals, too, to some degree, given what Author has done with D. Author adapts both thinking and behavior to her circumstances.

Ironically, Author notes that values being dependent upon surrounding culture and circumstance is basic tenet of Women's Studies. Apparently Author did not learn as much as she thought in her classes, if truth of said tenet is only now hitting home.

Author doesn't deserve Ph.D.

Stupid Author.

(Author notes additional evidence of decreasing self-esteem.)

If above is true, then how can Author ever form a clear idea of how to live her life? How can she move forward on a path with conviction, when she knows that it is the present environment forming her views as much as either innate or previously learned values? And what trouble might she get herself into, if she has no firm convictions to guide her?

Maybe it doesn't matter how a woman lives her life. She could be a bombshell sex kitten or a spinster with a pile of books, moldering in an ivory tower. One has the same worth as the other, and could be as right for Author as the other, depending on the circumstances.

What is Author supposed to be or supposed to become? "Grace Cavanaugh the Women's Studies Ph.D. candidate" may have just been an illusion created to match existing circumstances.

Maybe there is no unique, eternal "Grace" inside Author, a Grace who was meant to have a specific future, and who, no matter what the surroundings, would have grown up to believe the same things. Maybe there's no unique, eternal person inside anyone.

Present existential crisis is further proof that pursuing bombshell beauty is harmful to women.

August 18

Despised male busy working on MG for historic auto race. Sophia very distressed at any mention of race but refuses to discuss beyond mumbling words like "dangerous" and "foolish." Author beginning to worry about race and risk to despised male.

Why does Author care what happens to said male? Again, sexual relationship clearly messing with head.

Also, Author has been thinking.

If it doesn't matter in which direction she moves—bombshell or academic, low achiever or high achiever, Democrat or Republican or League of Flying Spaghetti Monster—or even if she moves at all, what does she do? She needs to do something with her life, or else why live it?

So, what does Author want to do?

What does Author want, period?

August 18½

Bedroom. Shower.

Sex still good, but Author noted decreased happiness postsexual encounter. While orgasm was reached, still there was . . . disappointment. Author waiting for words of affection from despised male, words that did not come.

Author knows better than to expect them. So why does she want them?

August 19

Author taking ballroom dance lessons.

Gardens off-limits for sex, as workers preparing for gala costume party in four days. Theme: A Long Ago Night in an Enchanted Forest. Sophia to wear green velvet dress from portrait in den. Author to wear vintage strapless black-sequined gown.

Author must immediately halt intake of bacon if gown is to fit.

(But Author still unwilling to give up bacon.)

August 20

Author has been thinking again.

In deepest heart of hearts, Author wants only one thing. The same thing everyone wants. The same thing everyone has always wanted.

Author wants to be loved.

Best chances of rewarding long-term relationship are with Dr. Andrew. But sexual relationship is interfering with bonding.

Therefore:

Sexual relationship with despised male must end.

CHAPTER
22

The Duesenberg rolled down the eighteenth fairway of Pebble Beach Golf Links with Darlene at the wheel, Lali riding shotgun and laughing as she waved to strangers like a homecoming princess on a float, and Grace and Sophia in the backseat, wearing enormous hats fit for a garden party with the queen. They were bringing the car to be displayed in the Concours d'Elegance.

Despite her hat, Grace wasn't feeling festive. She'd been avoiding Declan for two days, ever since she'd realized that if she wanted a real relationship with someone—like Andrew—she had to end the affair with Declan.

She didn't know if she was strong enough to do it. She didn't know *how* to do it. How did you break up with someone you weren't really "with" to begin with?

She knew what would happen. Declan would accuse her of thinking too much: she was having fun, so where was the problem? Then she'd feel like a freak for spelling out her cost-benefits analysis of continuing to have sex with him: the risk versus reward; the profit and loss; the return on investment. And she'd agree that that *was* all too analytical. But it hurt too much to admit the real reason they had to stop.

She was falling for him.

Her heart beat faster whenever he approached, and her face lit up when they greeted each other. She laughed too much at his jokes and slipped his name into conversations with Sophia, Lali, her mother . . . anyone.

Her heart's defenses against him were falling, one by one. If she didn't save herself now, she would be emotionally obliterated when Declan abandoned her. And that day *would* come, she constantly reminded herself. He'd said nothing to make her think it wouldn't, that he'd changed, that *he* was becoming attached to *her*.

There were moments where Grace thought *maybe*. . . . Moments when she'd catch him watching her from across the room, a soft half smile on his lips. Or when he'd catch her mood before she spoke, and ask if all was well, a crease of concern between his brows. Most of all, though, it was the moments after sex that got her, when he'd cradle her in his arms and dot her with tender kisses . . . but never, ever utter a word of what was in his heart. Each time, her hoping heart was disappointed. Each time, the pain of that disappointment grew more crushing.

Sophia had warned that sleeping with Declan would demand too much of her. What had started as a plot to heal her own heart by stomping on Declan's had degenerated into frantically trying to protect herself, while he remained as impervious as ever.

She only had a couple of weeks left in Pebble Beach, and then she'd head back to Seattle. Declan was probably counting on that to end their affair for them. Only it wouldn't. She would still be hoping to hear from him, hoping he'd come visit her, hoping there was a future with him.

The only way to save herself, and have closure, was to end the affair herself. Then, in the weeks that remained to her, she would try to lay the foundation of a long-term relationship with Andrew. It was the obvious, logical, intelligent path to follow.

The thought brought a sinking heaviness to her soul.

She heaved a sigh, miserable despite the beauty of the morning and the luxury of the Duesenberg. To either side of their route down the emerald grass stood white stanchions with catenaries of plastic chain drooping between them, cordoning off the classic cars from the mass of people who would soon be packing the fairway.

Halfway down the fairway an official in a linen jacket and boater waved the car toward its waiting slot amid a short row of Duesenbergs. Darlene turned the car and backed into place, and Grace turned round to look out over the sapphire blue of Stillwater Cove and Carmel Bay. The fairway dropped off in a short gold beige cliff to the water, fifteen feet behind the car. The last of the morning mist had just burned off, and the sun was bright above the hills to the east.

"Thanks for the ride," Lali said, hopping out of the car and slamming the door with enough energy to make Darlene wince. Lali leaned on Sophia's door for a moment, her eyes shining. "My friends are going to be so jealous I got to ride in the Duesenberg."

"If you get a four-point-oh this coming year in school, I'll let you have it—and Darlene—for your prom."

Lali bounced on her feet. "Thank you! Oh, thank you so much, Sophia!" Lali blew her a kiss and darted off to find a friend she'd arranged to meet.

Darlene came round to open Sophia's door, a sour look on her face. "Thanks."

"Every girl deserves to feel like a princess now and then, doesn't she?"

"Everyone always wants to be the princess," Darlene sniffed. "No one wants to be the queen who has to do all the work."

"All the better for the queen," Sophia said. "Fewer competitors for her power." She cast a glance at Grace. "No queen can rule forever, though. A wise one trains her heir."

Grace barely responded, her mind too entwined with thoughts of Declan to leave her bandwidth for verbal sparring with her aunt. She came around the car and offered Sophia her arm. Sophia took it, and they strolled down the fairway toward the Lodge, leaving Darlene to do a final rubdown of the car before the show opened.

"You're quiet this morning," Sophia said, giving Grace's arm a gentle squeeze.

"I was just thinking that the summer is drawing to its close, and I don't see any sign that I'm going to win that extra thirty thousand from you for making Declan fall in love with me."

"And it's only the thought of losing the money that has your face so long?"

Grace didn't answer.

"I warned you it would be dangerous to try."

"I know. But I never thought . . ."

"That you'd fall in love with him?"

Grace closed her eyes against the pain of that truth, not surprised that Sophia had so easily divined her feelings. "Yes," she whispered.

"For God's sake, whatever you do, don't tell him how you feel."

Grace's melancholy fractured under the sharply spoken words. "I wasn't going to! I'm not stupid."

"Women in love are stupid. They give men gifts, they are the first to say I love you, they make sex tapes. Stupid."

"I'm not going to do any of that. I want to end the affair."

"You're giving up?" Sophia asked, her lips curling in disapproval.

Grace's heart ached. "It's a retreat in the face of insurmountable odds. I have to protect myself." She glanced at Sophia's face, looking for some hint of hope, some sign that her aunt, who knew Declan so well, thought differently.

"Hm. And after this retreat, are you going to sit around sulking?"

Grace pursed her lips in annoyance. "No. I'm going to pay more attention to Andrew, as I should have been doing all along. There's certainty of a future with him. I can't fathom why I should have fallen for the uncertainty of Declan."

"Then you need to read up on your behavioral science. Intermittent, unpredictable rewards are always more addictive than sure things. Maybe you've become too much of a sure thing to Declan."

Grace's lips parted in surprise. "You think so?"

"You're right that Andrew is more suitable for you in the long run. Refocusing your attention on him can serve the double purpose of sealing that relationship and bringing Declan to his knees. He won't recognize his feelings for you—if he has them—until he loses you. You've got to make it a real loss, though, Grace. Andrew doesn't deserve to be toyed with, and Declan will sense it if you're only trying to manipulate him with ploys. Drop him for real, and you may yet win that extra thirty thousand."

The thought brought no cheer to her. What good would that money be, when it came at the price of her heart?

She didn't want to give up hope. She wanted, suddenly, to run to Declan and declare her feelings, and beg him to say the same in return.

She imagined the look of repugnance on his face; his glance going to the nearest exit; his hands gripping her biceps, holding her away from him.

Sophia was right. You didn't chase men like Declan. To do so was to lower your worth in his eyes.

"If Declan's appeal lies in his unpredictability," Grace said, "then I'll just have to stop seeing him, cold turkey, as if he were any other addiction. As soon as I see him, I'll end it."

Sophia murmured a faint noise of discontent.

"What?"

"I would ask, Grace dear, that you do this old woman a favor and humor me and my irrational fears, and wait until this evening to deliver your blow."

"What are you afraid of?"

"It's silly . . . I keep telling myself it's ridiculous to think the same thing could happen twice. And Declan is so different from Archie . . ."

Grace was bewildered. "Who's Archie?"

"My first husband, dear. Archibald Townsend the Fourth. A dashing, dark-haired man who loved cars, women, and golf."

"Golf," Grace repeated flatly. Argyle vests and golf knickers didn't fit her image of dark men who loved cars and women.

"It's why we bought our house here in Pebble Beach. We were very happy here, until . . ."

"Until?"

Sophia shivered. "Did the sun go behind a cloud?"

"What happened to Archie?" Grace asked, even as a foreboding certainty grew inside her.

"It was 1955, the final year they held the Pebble Beach Road Races on Seventeen-Mile Drive. Archie had driven in it since the year of its inception, and he had a new MG sitting in the garage, waiting for its chance to challenge the course."

"The same one Declan is going to drive?"

Pain shimmered across Sophia's face, and she nodded. "It survived the race, whereas Archie . . . The car had hardly a scratch on it. A friend returned it to me afterward, thinking I would want the reminder of Archie. It was a generous thought, but . . ."

Grace's throat tightened in sympathy as the disjointed story became clear. "Oh, Aunt Sophia, I'm so sorry."

"He died in that car, at the turn just south of our house. I was standing with a crowd of friends at the end of our drive-way, cheering as the cars went by. I blew a kiss to Archie—" She stopped, her trembling lips closing into a hard line, as if holding back the words could hold back the memories. When she spoke again, it was in a whisper. "And then he was gone."

"I'm so sorry."

"The worst of it was, we had had a fight that morning. The kiss I blew him was for show; I was embarrassed at the thought of our friends sensing something was wrong. But I've wondered ever since if he would have died if we hadn't had that fight, if his concentration had been purely on the road, if he hadn't been dis-tracted by the things I'd said." Sophia shook her head. "I blamed myself. Other people thought the route was too dangerous, with so many trees so close to the road. They said there was too much car and not enough racecourse. They moved the races to a new track at Laguna Seca the next year."

Sophia smiled sadly. "So, although I know it's foolish of me, I would ask you not to end your affair with Declan until the race is finished. I'd hate to think of him being distracted as he passed my house and headed for that curve."

"Of course, Aunt Sophia! A few hours won't matter one way or another."

They reached the Lodge, a whitewashed, white-columned building that had stood at Pebble Beach since the 1910s. A ter-race on the back looked out over the course and the bay. Wait-staff carrying trays of champagne and hors d'oeuvres threaded between the guests in boaters, linen, and tea party hats who were beginning to fill the space. An elderly official greeted Sophia, and guided them to a small cloth-covered table near the edge of the terrace, reserved specifically for her.

"That's better," Sophia sighed as she eased down onto the padded chair. A waiter brought them flutes of champagne and

Grace settled back in her chair to watch the people going by on the grass below. She wanted to ask Sophia more about her marriages, but it seemed neither the time nor the place, and she didn't know how well she could listen even if Sophia did speak of them. Grace's emotions were too distracted with worries for Declan during the race mingling with love, hurt, and the misery of uncertainty. She wanted her relationship with him over, at the same time that she relished these last few hours where there still remained a crumb of hope—however small—that he might yet fall on his knees and declare his love for her.

It was a miserable state to be in. She looked out over the growing crowd and tried not to think about it.

"Grace, dear, go see if you can find Dr. Andrew and tell him where we're sitting. I thought I caught a glimpse of him going indoors."

Grace went in search of the doctor, taking off her sunglasses as she stepped into the lodge. She wore an apricot shantung silk dress with a wide V neck, tightly fitted bodice, and a full skirt that ended just above her knees. Jeweled flat-soled sandals lent a playful touch. As she sidled through the thickening crowd searching for Andrew, she caught the surreptitious leers of older men, their gazes lingering on her breasts. Once upon a time she would have hunched her shoulders in embarrassment, but now she strode by the men without concern. She didn't blame them for looking: her bra cantilevered her breasts before her like Juliet's balcony, an open invitation to adventurous suitors. She would stare, too. They were great breasts.

Which didn't mean she expected to be manhandled. A strong hand grabbed her arm and pulled her out of the crowd, making her squeak in surprise. Her hat blocked her view of her assailant, but even as he dragged her into a narrow hallway her body recognized him.

Declan.

"If I didn't know better," he said hoarsely as he dragged her into a ladies' room, "I'd swear you'd been avoiding me these last few days."

"You're the one who's been too obsessed with car engines and tires and gear thingies to spend any time with me," Grace said, a note of complaint in her voice.

Declan checked the solitary stall and, finding it empty, locked the door to the hallway. The chamber was more a small ladies' lounge than a traditional bathroom, with a carpeted floor and a chaise longue.

Declan ignored the chaise and, grasping Grace by the waist, hoisted her up onto the marble countertop. The back of her head hit the mirror and one hand knocked a jar of lotion into the sink. It was hard to care, though, as Declan's mouth came down on hers and his hands slid up her thighs. His tongue plunged against hers, chasing away all thoughts of breakups and endings. It was as if those thoughts had belonged to someone else, in another lifetime. Nothing mattered but the melting pleasure of his touch and the desire she could feel in the straining of his body.

"Don't make the mistake of thinking I haven't been fantasizing about what I'd do to you the next time we were alone," Declan said into her throat, as his mouth traced down toward her cleavage. His hands found their way up to her panties and tugged.

It was tempting to give in one last time, to let him take her right there on the ladies' room counter. It would be fast and hard and good.

As it would be the next time. And the next, and the next. When would it stop? It never would, unless she took control. She couldn't break up with Declan before the race, but that didn't mean she couldn't behave as if she had.

She grabbed his hands. "Not now. Sophia's waiting for me."

"Let her wait."

She shook her head and forced herself to get down from the counter, even as her body cried out to stay. "I *can't*."

He leaned against her, pinning her to the edge of the counter. "You can."

Anger born of hurt flared to life inside her. She was a sex toy to him, nothing more. It was all she'd ever been and all she'd ever be. "I said *no!*" she snapped, and slipped out of his grasp. A moment later she was out the door.

Seeing Andrew across the room, Grace started toward him, only to have Declan grasp her hand and pull her back. "Where do you think you're going?"

"Aunt Sophia asked me to find Dr. Andrew and take him to her," she said without emotion, trying to hide her anger. "I think her hip is hurting her."

"What's got into you?"

"Declan!" a jovial older man interrupted, slapping him on the back.

As Declan looked at the older man, Grace tugged her hand free and wove through the crowd toward Andrew.

"I've been looking all over for you," she said when she reached him. "Sophia wanted me to tell you where we're sitting."

"That's funny. She sent me to find you."

Smiling to hide the tears that threatened, Grace led Andrew out of the crowd and, on impulse, dragged him into the narrow hallway. Before a question left his lips, she pressed her body up against his and pulled his head down to hers, then kissed him. *Prove you can replace him,* she silently pleaded. *Show me that I don't have to give up passion.*

Andrew was too stunned to respond at first, but as she deepened the kiss, something broke free inside him, as it had that day in the garden. His arms came around her, one hand to the back of her head, and he returned her kiss full bore.

An image broke into Grace's head of Declan finding them and lifting her skirt, taking her from behind as Andrew kissed her. Her moan was captured in Andrew's mouth. Some primitive part of him responded, and she felt the rod of his erection grinding against her belly.

"Dr. Andrew," Declan drawled from the end of the hall, "for shame. Is this how you treat a lady in public?"

Andrew shoved her away, startled mortification on his face.

Grace turned to face Declan, and then slowly, deliberately, licked her lips.

Declan's face darkened, and he swore.

"Andrew, why don't you show Declan where Sophia is sitting?" Grace said. "Now if you boys will excuse me, I must powder my nose."

Without waiting for an answer, she slipped into the ladies' room, locked the door, then sank onto the chaise and wept.

CHAPTER
23

$\mathcal{A}$ndrew drove Grace and Sophia home just before race officials closed off 17-Mile Drive. The race would start in half an hour, and about fifteen minutes after that she could expect to see Declan and the other racers come by Sophia's driveway.

As Andrew turned the Subaru down the drive to Sophia's house, crews were setting bales of hay in place as protective barriers in the tightest turns. Grace turned in her seat to stare at the place where Sophia's Archie had died so many years ago, and felt a stab of guilt and fear that she might have upset Declan enough to lead him to the same fate.

She tried to shake off the irrational thought. He'd been fine the last she'd seen him.

After she'd gone back to Sophia's table, she'd found Andrew in an almost bubbly mood. Declan had met her gaze looking more amused than upset.

Or had he just been good at hiding his feelings? Grace couldn't forget the dark look on his face when he found her with Andrew. For a moment, she'd thought she'd hurt him.

Grace shook off the thought. No. He didn't care about her in any important way. It was only the greedy jealousy of possession that she'd seen in his eyes.

"You have visitors," Andrew said as the car rolled into the courtyard of Sophia's house.

From the backseat, Grace leaned between Andrew and Sophia's heads to see. Two late-model sedans sat parked in the sun, and beyond them was a well-aged, familiar Volvo.

"Cat!" Grace cried.

"You knew she was coming?" Sophia asked sharply.

"No, no clue." Grace frowned.

Andrew parked the Subaru, and when Grace got out she took a second look at the sedans, and saw the small rental sticker on each bumper. Whoever the people were, they had probably flown in.

Grace expected Cat to come flying out of the house, but no one responded to the sound of their arrival. All was silence.

Once they were indoors, Andrew surprised Grace by taking her elbow and leading her toward the living room.

"Andrew," Sophia barked. "What is going on?"

"I'm sorry, Sophia, but this had to be done. Grace has been under some bad influences, and we've all come together to help her save herself before it's too late."

"What—?" Grace started, but then she was in the living room and she saw them: Cat. Professor Joansdatter. And Grace's mother, Alyson. They sat, solemn and homespun, amid the pastel luxury of Sophia's French living room.

"Mom!" Grace said, hurrying toward her. Her mother stood and embraced her, and Grace breathed in the scent of sandalwood and herbs that was as familiar as home. Her mom's loose, crumpled natural-fiber clothes felt rough to fingertips now more familiar with silk, but was no less welcome for that. "What are you doing here? Why didn't you tell me you were coming?"

"It was a last-minute decision. Grace, you've lost a lost of weight," Alyson said, holding Grace away from her and looking her up and down.

Grace stood back and twirled in a circle for her mother to see. "I look good, don't I?"

"You were beautiful before."

"Thank you. But I look better now, you have to admit."

Looking dismayed, Alyson touched Grace's hair, then her cheek where a touch of blush had been expertly applied. "I hardly recognize you. You look like an actress in a magazine."

"You're exaggerating," Grace said, grinning. She turned to the others in the room, and her confusion returned afresh. "Professor Joansdatter? Cat? What *are* you all doing here? Did you come for the Concours d'Elegance?"

"Grace, darling," her mother said. "We came for you."

Andrew led her to a seat and sat her down, then sat next to Cat on the sofa. He sat forward, his elbows on his knees, his face earnest.

"What exactly is going on here?" Sophia asked. The slight flare to her nostrils was the only evidence that she viewed the group as intruders little better than plague-ridden rodents.

Cat answered, a defiant challenge in her voice. "This is an intervention, Sophia. You and Declan have done your damage, but we're here to save the Grace we know and love from disappearing forever."

Grace sprang up from her chair. "You can't be serious! An intervention?" She started to laugh. "What, you think I've become a drug addict? Mom? You know me better than that."

"No, we don't suspect drugs," Cat said, in a tone that suggested it hadn't been off the plate for discussion. "What we've all noticed are the dramatic changes that have been happening to you this summer. Your withdrawal from friends and family, your picking fights with me as if to drive me away—those are both signs of being in an abusive relationship. And you've lost too much weight."

"You've gone from healthy eating habits to bad ones in these last few weeks," Andrew threw in. "That can be a sign of depression."

"Or of having been half starved on your freaking CRON diet!" Grace protested.

"You used to be a vegetarian," Cat said. "I hear you've been eating lots of meat lately."

"So? And how would you know that, anyway?"

Cat and Andrew exchanged glances. Grace's jaw dropped. "You've been keeping tabs on me? I knew it! I thought I was crazy, suspecting a conspiracy, but I was right."

Angry, Grace turned to Professor Joansdatter. Her advisor wore her trademark long scarf wrapped loosely around her neck, and her salt-and-pepper wiry hair pulled back in a low, bushy ponytail. Wooden bangles clacked on her wrist. "What did they tell you that made you think it worth coming down here?" she demanded.

"It was more what I found in your research notes that concerned me. You haven't written a word of your dissertation."

The heat of embarrassment burned Grace's cheeks. "You read my notes?" Though the professor had access to her files, Grace hadn't asked her to look at them. All the details of her sexual encounters with Declan rose to her mind. The bet with Sophia. Her own questioning of whether Women's Studies was a worthwhile field for her.

"You seem to have been derailed from what had been a promising thesis. I wanted to be sure you were all right, and not at risk of becoming one of those students who never finishes her dissertation."

"That could have waited a few weeks, until I was back in Seattle. You didn't have to come down here."

Joansdatter shrugged and looked a little sheepish. "My partner wanted to see Monterey and Carmel."

Grace turned accusing eyes on Andrew. "Why did you arrange this?"

"You are the most perfect woman I know, when you're being the real Grace. The Grace I met the first day you arrived here. The Grace you are when Declan O'Brien is nowhere to be found."

"You'd rather I was fat and dumpy again?"

"I'd rather you cared more about social issues than clothes and makeup, and flirting and teasing so much that a man doesn't know what message you mean to send."

The arrow hit home, and she had no defense to offer. She cast a beseeching look to Aunt Sophia, wondering why her aunt had stayed quiet for so long.

Sophia made a show of looking at her watch. Grace glanced at the ormolu clock ticking on the mantel and realized she had twenty minutes at most before the historic auto race would pass by the end of Sophia's driveway. She wouldn't be able to forgive herself if she missed Declan driving past, and he then was in a wreck at the turn south of Sophia's house. The odds were astronomically against it, yet the seed of fear had been planted and there was no arguing with the irrational certainty that if she was not there to wave to Declan as he went by, he would be distracted and crash.

"Have you all had your say now?" Sophia asked, sounding bored.

"No," Alyson said, coming to stand beside Grace. "I want to know why you've done this to Grace. Why did you invite her down here for the summer? You've never shown the least interest in our family."

"It does appear that way, doesn't it?" Sophia nodded faintly toward the chair Grace had vacated, and Grace offered her arm to her aunt and led her to it, watching with concern as Sophia settled into it with a twinge of pain.

"The truth," Sophia said, "may not be something you're prepared to hear."

Alyson crossed her arms, looking suspicious but intrigued. The others stirred, curiosity bright in their eyes.

Grace looked in puzzlement at her great-aunt. "I'm here because you need a hip replacement, aren't I?"

Sophia shuddered delicately. "Grace, that term."

"Sorry. 'Procedure.'"

"I'm afraid that while true, that was the least of my reasons. You see, dear Grace, you are not my grand-niece at all. Nor is Alyson my niece."

"I'm not?" Grace and her mother said in unison, as breaths of surprise were sucked in around the room.

Sophia shook her head, and left them hanging for several long moments. "No, you're not. You, dear Grace, are my great-granddaughter."

Grace sank in shock to the arm of the sofa, staring with an open mouth at Sophia. "No way."

Alyson shook her head. "That can't be. My mother, Lucy, was your sister. Grandmother said she came very late in life, a surprise, but . . ."

"Did you never question why my mother should have given birth at age forty-six, in that era? I'm seventeen years older than Lucy. I was pregnant at sixteen, and gave birth at seventeen."

"Why the lie, all these years?" Alyson asked.

"I was obviously not going to raise the child. Pretending the child was my mother's was what families did in those days, if the child wasn't given away entirely."

"But . . . who was Lucy's father? Where was he?"

Amusement teased at Sophia's mouth. "He was long gone by the time I discovered I carried his child. He wouldn't have made much of a father, anyway."

"Who was he?" Grace asked, as stunned and curious as her mother. Sophia was her great-grandmother! She was a direct descendant of this woman who had loomed so large in her life these past months. No wonder they looked so much alike. No wonder Sophia had been so interested in her.

"Your great-grandfather was a lion tamer."

Grace laughed, startled. "What?"

"With the circus."

Grace's mother sat down. "You've got to be joking."

Sophia smiled faintly. "You can imagine the romantic figure such a man would present to a sixteen-year-old girl with a hunger for adventure. It was like sleeping with Tarzan."

"You didn't try to find him when you found out you were pregnant?" Grace asked.

"What was the point? I didn't want to raise children in a traveling circus. I had bigger dreams."

"So you abandoned my mother and went to Hollywood," Alyson said.

"It wasn't quite as easy as that. It was a difficult birth, and afterward the doctor warned me that I might never be able to carry another child to term. Leaving Lucy was not easy. It was better for her, though, to grow up with a family, and without the stigma of being a bastard; the times were different then, you know. Once I left, the thought of seeing her or hearing of her was too painful. I resolved never to look back."

"But you did look back," Grace said. "That Easter when you came to Connecticut."

"I wanted to see what had become of Lucy, and I wanted to meet you, Alyson. You weren't what I expected."

Alyson scowled.

"You probably always wondered where you got your amber eyes. They're from the lion tamer."

Alyson crossed her arms over her chest, although Grace could tell that she was intrigued. "Did he even have a name?"

"He went by Gregori, and spoke with a Russian accent. I suspect he may have been no more Russian than a house cat, though." Sophia's gaze softened. "I can see his face in yours, even now."

"A lion tamer," Alyson muttered, still disbelieving but now with a trace of wonder.

"But it was Grace who threw me off that Easter," Sophia went on, and her eyes misted, pain pulling at the corners of her mouth. "I saw myself in her, as I had never seen myself in anyone else before. She reminded me of all I had lost and all I had never had. I came back home sorry that I'd ever gone to Connecticut. I regretted looking back.

"But then, this past Christmas, I received that letter from Grace, and the photo. Here she was, on my coast, struggling to find her way in the world. Her face showed my features, but her life showed that she didn't know who she was."

"She's not you," Cat spoke up. "Her face doesn't make her you."

"But it shows that my blood runs in her veins. How much else of me had she inherited without knowing? What potential lay hidden inside her? What doors could she open for herself, if she discovered and utilized it? It could only help her to find out." Sophia glanced at the mantel.

Grace followed her gaze to the clock, and tensed at what she saw. Crap! The cars would be passing the end of the driveway any minute now. She stood up, anxious to go, but torn by the intrigue of what was unfolding before her.

"You didn't want to help Grace," Cat said. "You wanted to create a clone of yourself."

Grace did a double take, distracted by her friend's words. "Is *that* what you think I am?"

"You look like one, don't you? And lately you've sounded like one."

"I know who I am," Grace said, then caught Professor Joansdatter's wry look. Grace remembered the things she'd said in her research notes, full of questions about who, at heart, she was meant to be, and how she seemed to be so easily influenced by her surroundings. "Or at least I know as much as any of us do," she amended.

"The rest of us haven't rejected our friends, drastically altered our appearance, or changed our values in the space of three months."

"I haven't changed my values." Her eyes went again to the clock, impatient. She didn't need yet another argument with Cat. She had more important things to do.

"Oh, really?"

"I've just explored contrasting viewpoints."

Cat barked out a laugh. "Is that what you call it?"

"Yes, I do. Listen, can this wait? The auto race is about to pass by, and I've got to be there." Was she imagining it, or did she already hear the roar of motors?

"No, it can't wait!" Cat screeched in disbelief as Grace moved toward the door. "You want to interrupt your intervention for an *auto* race?"

"I never asked for a lousy intervention!" Grace called over her shoulder, on the move.

"And they are *historic* autos," she heard Sophia placidly explain behind her. "It would really be a shame to miss it."

Grace ran across the foyer and out into the sunshine. She *did* hear motors; they were going by already! She was missing it! Declan wasn't going to see her. Then he'd crash and die, and it would somehow be her fault, and life would be dark and haunted forever after.

She took off at a run up the driveway, her flat-soled leather sandals slipping on the asphalt. Through the forest of pine and cypress, she caught glimpses of color whizzing by on the road up above. *No, no, no!*

The MG was marine blue. She saw green go by, and white. Just as she reached the end of the driveway she saw a flash of blue, and then the back of an MG, its driver wearing a helmet. Grace jumped up and down, waving her arms, yelling, "Go, Declan! Go!"

Had he seen her? Did he check his rearview mirror? Did he know she was there?

The car disappeared around the beginning of the dangerous bend. Moments passed, and a maroon car zipped by, then a yellow. Andrew, and then Cat and Alyson, caught up to her. Grace noticed for the first time that there were other neighbors at the ends of their driveways, groups of friends, people holding drinks and laughing.

From somewhere around the curve came a low cry of horror from the throats of onlookers, and then deep in Grace's chest she felt a thud of sound. The cry of horror turned into a chaotic jumble of shouts, and piercing it all was a woman screaming.

Grace's stomach dropped. For a moment she saw stars at the edges of her vision. It couldn't have happened. That couldn't be Declan—

She began to run. She heard a shout behind her, Andrew, telling Cat to fetch his medical bag from his car. Andrew kept pace at her side as they ran down the road and around the bend.

A marine blue MG was smashed into a wall of hay bales. People were massed around the car, and between their bodies Grace caught glimpses of a figure lying on the ground.

A thousand possible futures with Declan died inside her as

she approached, her breath catching on sobs of fear. *It can't be over already; we weren't finished; there were things unsaid between us,* her heart wept.

If he was dead, she would be haunted by the unfulfilled promise of this summer with Declan for the rest of her life.

Andrew pushed past the people, Grace following in his wake. When the last of the onlookers stepped aside, Grace looked down.

And saw a stranger.

Every joint in her body went liquid in relief.

Andrew knelt down beside the man and began examining him with cool professionalism. He snapped questions to the crowd about what had happened, how the driver had behaved, how he'd ended up on the ground. As the answers came, the man stirred and his eyelids fluttered open. The sound of sirens approached.

Cat arrived with Andrew's medical bag at the same time the ambulance did. Grace stepped back with the rest of the crowd, letting the EMTs and Andrew do their work. Andrew summarized for the EMTs what he'd learned from the onlookers, and what his own examination suggested. As she watched him, Grace felt a new respect for Andrew. He was a truly good man. A man to count on in a crisis, who had devoted his life to helping others.

Her gaze flicked back and forth between the man she'd thought was Declan and the doctor who tended him—the man who thrived on adrenaline and lived to feed his own pleasures, and the one who healed the wounds such carelessness could cause; the man you'd sleep with, and the one you'd marry and have children with.

The one who'd steal your heart and carry it to the moon, and the one who'd catch and heal it when it fell back to earth.

With the driver safely in the care of the paramedics, Andrew returned to Grace and the others and they walked back to the house, Andrew answering Cat's and Alyson's questions.

"They said it looked like he started to pass out just as he came to the corner. He hit the bales and then opened the car door and tumbled to the ground."

"Drugs?" Alyson asked.

Andrew shook his head and ran through the possible diagnoses.

Grace heard with only half an ear. Her heart had died when she thought it was Declan on the ground, but it had risen again while she watched Andrew. She could live her life chasing after a man who offered nothing but heartache, or she could turn her affections toward a man who had made it his life's work to help others. She could be with someone who had his own best interests at heart, or someone who had *her* best interests at heart. It was all so clear.

And yet . . .

And yet.

They reached the courtyard and Andrew went to put his bag in his car as the others headed back into the house. "Grace, a moment?" he said, catching her hand as she went by.

She nodded and waited while he put his bag away.

He shut the car door, turned around, and took both her hands in his own. "Grace, I'm sorry if it seems like I went behind your back in talking to Cat. Please believe that I only did it out of concern for you. I've been watching all summer as a transformation seems to have been coming over you, and while there have been some advantages—like your weight loss—I've also seen some behaviors that concerned me. I was losing sight of that principled, opinionated, intelligent woman I first met. I thought that *you* might be losing sight of her, too."

Grace bit her lip, a sense of shame rising within her. She *had* betrayed herself, to such a degree that the woman Andrew spoke of seemed a dream from a different life. "Maybe," she admitted.

"Relationships are supposed to make us better people, not worse."

She felt her cheeks heat and tears sting her eyes. She'd known that, once upon a time.

"I thought he had corrupted you completely. But then today, at the Lodge, when you kissed me . . ."

Grace ducked her face, embarrassed..

"I felt such passion in you, Grace. Passion for *me*. It was as if you were crying out to me to save you, and I realized that you'd been asking that of me all along, and I'd been too scared and blind to see it. It woke me up, and laid to rest the doubts that had been lingering in my mind. Grace," he said, and dropped down on one knee. "Will you marry me?"

CHAPTER
24

Grace stood on the balcony of her bedroom, staring out over the dark gardens and the moonlit sea beyond. She was trying to find a space of calm amidst the tumult of her mind and emotions.

She'd sent Andrew home with a promise that he would have her answer tomorrow. "The intervention, the crash, Sophia . . . ," she had said. "I can't think straight."

He'd been apologetic and solicitous, and until he left an hour later he doted on her like a mother with a sick child, while Grace cringed under his care, feeling undeserving of the attention and affection.

Sophia, meanwhile, had managed to convince Alyson and Professor Joansdatter that every big bad tale they'd heard about her was a misunderstanding, and she was actually a softhearted, lonely old woman who wanted only the best for her long-lost family. Guest rooms were made up, and even Professor Joansdatter and her partner—her husband, Gary, although she always used the gender-neutral term "partner" for him—found themselves ensconced in a room. Sophia had made sure that Grace kept her own room private, though.

"The last thing you need is one of these people in your ear all night, yammering at you," she'd said.

To which a grateful Grace had answered, "Andrew asked me to marry him."

Sophia's gaze had sharpened with interest. "And?"

"I don't know. There's so much going on, I can't think straight."

"This is where I'm supposed to say that you make this decision with your heart, isn't it?" Sophia said. "But we both know better than that. This is a decision to be made with both head and heart together. Anything less invites disaster. Too many women have destroyed their lives by following their hearts against their own better judgment.

"Look at Darlene. Do you think she would be so bitter now if she hadn't been a flighty romantic young girl who chose her mate based on dashing good looks and grand gestures, and ignored it when her head pointed out that he was a drunk?"

Surprise had made Grace blink. "*Darlene,* flighty and romantic?"

"It shows you what disillusionment can do to a loving heart."

As Grace stood alone now in her bedroom, though, she didn't know what either her head or her heart was telling her. There was too much internal noise, too much confusion, too much emotion. Andrew's proposal; the crash; the revelation that Sophia and a Russian (maybe) lion tamer were her great-grandparents; the arrival of Professor Joansdatter, her mother, Cat; the acknowledgment that under the influence of Sophia and Declan she *had* lost sight of her moral center and become . . . someone else.

She took a deep breath of pine- and sea-scented air, wishing it could clear her soul of confusion as easily as it cleared her lungs.

Someone rapped softly at her door.

Grace cursed under her breath. "Leave me in peace, will you?" she muttered to the night.

The rapping came again. "Grace? It's me," Declan's muffled voice said. "I know you're in there."

Grace closed her eyes for a long moment. Before she could see clearly enough to give Andrew an answer, she had to end her affair with Declan. Her heart didn't want it, but the head did: he was bad for her. Continuing with him, when he so clearly didn't love her, was killing her. Love wasn't supposed to hurt like this.

A moment of clarity hit her, striking like sunlight through her clouds of confusion. It wasn't really Declan she had to break up with, it was her own childish fantasies that she had to let go of. It was time to grow up and be an adult. She could no longer live with the Grace who pretended to be Declan's sexual toy. She had to break up with *herself.*

If she was strong enough.

She strode across the room.

On the other side of the door, Declan waited impatiently for Grace to open it. He had a terrible sense that this day, which had started so well, with so much promise of excitement, had tumbled toward irretrievable disaster. Everything had gone wrong, and in the gap between morning and now, when he had been away from Grace, people had stepped into her life and, he feared, ushered her back into the cage of who she used to be.

But maybe they hadn't succeeded. Maybe she was still free.

Maybe she was still . . . his.

If she ever had been. His stomach turned with fear.

The door opened a crack, and Grace peered out. "Declan, I—"

He pushed through the door and shut it firmly behind him, then stalked into the room. "Sophia told me about the 'intervention.'" He laughed. "Good God, I'd have loved to have seen that!"

Grace crossed her arms over her chest, holding herself.

Declan caught the movement, then looked at her strained face. His eyes narrowed even as his gut twisted. "They didn't get to you, did they?"

"I'm sorry I missed you going by in the race," she said flatly. "I tried to get away in time to wave to you, but I was too late."

"No one told you? I wasn't even in the race. The damn car wouldn't start! If I didn't know he had an alibi, I'd suspect Andrew of sabotage."

"But you spent all that time making sure it ran," she said, puzzled, her arms dropping to her side.

"I know. Suspicious, isn't it?"

"So it never *could* have been you," Grace said softly, wondering.

"Excuse me?"

She shook her head. "You heard about the crash? It was a blue MG just like yours."

He was glad of the distraction, glad to avoid a deeper subject. "Yeah, it looked almost the same to a layperson, but it was a completely different car." Then a light dawned in his head. She'd been *worried* about him! A shot of hope eased the clenching in his gut. "You thought for a minute that I had crashed?" He laughed. He came forward and wrapped her in his arms and stroked her hair. "Were you worried about me?"

"No," she said into his chest, her body stiff and unyielding.

Obviously she *had* been worried.

Feeling reassured, he kissed her cheek and released her, then dropped onto her bed and leaned back on his elbows. He grinned at her. "Hey, pretty lady, wanna take a ride?" he joked.

Grace's lips tightened.

Uh-oh.

"Declan," she said, "I don't want to see you anymore."

His grin faltered, a sense of unreality coming over him.

Her arms crossed over her chest again, and she gripped her

elbows so hard her fingers dug into her flesh. "We've had fun, but it's time to move on."

He sat up, flushes of heat and cold going through his body. For a moment the room spun. Then the fear and disbelief were burned away by a blind, unreasoning anger. "Time for you to move on to Andrew now—that's what you mean, isn't it?"

"Andrew's got nothing to do with it."

Declan sprang to his feet. "Like hell he doesn't!"

Grace shook her head. "Ending this has been inevitable. You know it, and I know it. People like you and I were never meant to be together; we're too different."

"Says who? That group of ninnies who came after you today?"

"One of those *ninnies* is my mother!"

"They want you to be with Andrew, don't they? They probably sat around discussing what a nice young man he is, so perfect for you, so intelligent, a *doctor*."

"They didn't say a word about him. It was all about how I've changed."

Declan approached her, and lowered his voice. "Yes, you've changed. You've freed yourself from that goddamn ivory tower you'd locked yourself away in. You would have withered away into a sexless old hag if not for me."

Grace snorted. "You don't know the half of it."

"What don't I know?"

Her gaze slipped away from his. "Never mind. None of this matters. Maybe I *have* changed, but I don't think it's for the better. Being with you hasn't made me a better person, Declan. I'm not happier or kinder. I haven't pursued my goals. Being in lo—Being *with* someone should make you want to be a better version of yourself, don't you think? It should make your heart feel bigger, and make you feel that anything is possible. But with you . . ."

His throat was dry and tight. She wasn't joking around. This wasn't just sex she was talking about. She was talking about something deeper, and she was saying that she found him lacking. "With me, what?" he asked hoarsely.

"Playing these sex games with you, I'm less than myself and less than I could be. I'm less than I *want* to be. It was fun, it was an experience, I learned some things, but it isn't enough anymore. I need more. I need something . . . more meaningful." Her big sea green eyes gazed at him, a question in their depths.

Was she asking if he understood?

Fuck, yes, he understood. The sex had been great, but hey, buddy, time's up, out you go. You were only good for one thing to me.

She'd never liked him or respected him. So what had he expected? That screwing her six ways from Sunday would change her mind, and make her think him worthy?

Yeah. Maybe he *had* thought so.

He nodded to her, his jaw clenched. He would not humiliate himself in front of her by betraying how badly he hurt. He accepted his fate even as he felt the searing pain of something breaking loose inside him, as if a dagger had been dragged through his guts. "Okay. Yeah. It's been great, but summer's almost over. It's time to go back to the real world, isn't it?"

The question in her eyes died. She blinked, then looked down. "Yes. Thank you for being so reasonable about this."

Reasonable? He wanted to throw her on the bed and make love to her until she changed her mind. He wanted to shake her and tell her not to be a fool. He wanted . . .

He wanted *her*.

But she didn't want him. Raging against that one incontrovertible truth would gain him nothing and only hurt her. He went to her and gently lifted her chin with his fingertips. "Be happy, Grace," he said, using every ounce of his control to make it sound like a parting between friends, nothing more.

Tears shimmered in her eyes, and her lips trembled. "Andrew asked me to marry him," she whispered.

The blood left his head, and for a crazy moment he thought he would faint. He held himself rigid and took a deep breath. He'd kill the bastard. Kill him! But Grace was still gazing up at him, taking in every nuance of his expression. He swallowed hard. "The world is yours for the taking, Grace. Don't exchange one ivory tower for another. You deserve more than that."

A small frown pinched her brow, but before she could say anything more, he dipped his head and gently kissed her, feeling the petal softness of her lips for the last time. "It'll be okay," he whispered against her mouth, and only realized as he turned away that it was himself he was trying to reassure.

As he opened the door, the sound of glass smashing came from the marble staircase down the hall, then a shriek of pain and surprise, cut off short.

Declan bolted down the hall, his heart in his throat, Grace on his heels. When he reached the head of the stairs he saw Sophia sprawled halfway down the staircase, a shattered decanter of Scotch sending its alcoholic fumes through the foyer.

"Sophia!" Grace shrieked, and rushed toward her.

Declan grabbed her arm and shoved her back toward her room. "Call nine-one-one! Call nine-one-one!" She raced away, her face white.

Declan ran down the stairs to the woman who had been like a mother to him for his entire adult life. There was blood on her forehead, seeping into her white hair, and her limbs were canted at an unnatural angle.

He crouched down beside her, his world breaking apart. "Oh God, Sophia. What have you done?"

CHAPTER
25

Five of them sat tense and silent in the small waiting area down the hall from Sophia's hospital room: Grace, Alyson, Darlene, Declan, and Andrew. Andrew had tried several times to get information for them on her condition but had been shut down by claims of confidentiality, the hospital staff inexplicably uncommunicative with Sophia's primary care physician. They'd taken information from him but offered none in return, leaving him to hunker, ignorant and embarrassed, with the nonmedical peons.

"I still can't believe it," Alyson said quietly to Grace. "My grandmother. Your great-grandmother. It explains so much, but I still can't believe it."

"I know," Grace agreed. "Does it make you think any differently about yourself? About who you think you are?"

Alyson slowly shook her head. "I couldn't say. It makes me understand my mother a little better, though, and some of her attitudes. She must have always known. And I suppose I understand Sophia a little better now, too. I used to hate her, but now I feel more sorry for her than anything else. What a lonely life of regret she must have led."

Grace felt a twinge of doubt on that, but kept quiet.

A nurse appeared. "Grace?" she asked the group.

"That's me," Grace said.

"Sophia would like to see you."

"She's awake?"

The nurse started to answer, then stopped. "Room 322," she said, and left.

Grace exchanged a puzzled look with the others and got up. Behind her, Darlene and Alyson decided to go in search of coffee.

She walked down the carpeted hall with its wide oak chair rail, beige pink paint, and medical supply carts. The muffled sounds of televisions came through partially opened doors, with patients, white sheets, and railed beds half visible inside.

The door to room 322 was ajar, leading into a small foyer formed by a pastel curtain mounted to a track in the ceiling. Grace came around its edge prepared to see her aunt—her great-grandmother—hooked up to tubes and machines, with a monitor softly beeping along with her heartbeat.

Instead, she found Sophia with the head of her bed raised, a small bandage on her brow, and Ernesto sitting beside the bed, holding her hand. No tubes. No monitors. Just a remote control on the rolling bedside table, and a pitcher of water.

Sophia looked the worse for wear, however. Her skin was tinged with gray, her lips bloodless, and her eyes and cheeks seemed to have sunk into purple shadows. She looked a half hour from death.

Seeing Grace, Ernesto murmured something to Sophia in Spanish and kissed her hand, then left them alone.

"Grace, darling," Sophia said weakly, and raised her hand toward her.

Grace rushed forward to take it, sitting where Ernesto had been. "Sophia! Are you okay? What did the doctors say? No one will tell us anything!"

"They don't know yet what happened, what's wrong," Sophia

whispered, and took a deep breath, as if exhausted by the effort. "It could have been a stroke, a heart attack, a brain tumor . . ."

"They don't know?"

Sophia patted her hand. "They'll figure it out eventually. I don't want you to worry about that, though. I want you to do something for me."

"Anything," Grace said, her heart feeling as if metal bands were squeezing it tight.

"Tomorrow evening is the gala."

"We have to cancel it."

Sophia shook her head. "No. After all my hard work? I want you to take over my role. I want you to hostess the party."

"Me?"

"Who better?" Sophia said with a faint smile. "Darlene knows all the details. She'll fill you in. You'll wear my green dress, of course."

"It'll never fit."

Sophia ignored her. "There's a tableau vivant you'll be in, and you'll be led out onto the dance floor in an opening dance. And of course you'll need to welcome everyone. You can do that, can't you?"

Dread grew in Grace as each duty was spelled out, and she imagined herself trying to step into Sophia's shoes—literally—as the grand dame of the fête. "Maybe one of the other women who organized the gala would be better—"

"You, Grace." Sophia squeezed her hand. "I have taught you all I know. Consider this your final exam."

Grace bit her lip, uncertainty washing over her.

"For me, Grace. Do it for me. It may be the last thing I ever ask of you."

Grace sucked in a breath as tears stung her eyes. "Of course. Don't worry, I'll make you proud."

Sophia smiled and closed her eyes. "Thank you." She was silent for a few minutes, and Grace started to wonder if she'd fallen asleep. Then her eyes opened a slit and she spoke again. "You can send Ernesto back in. And then tell Declan I'd like to talk to him."

"Okay." Grace moved to leave, then looked back at Sophia with a half smile. "Ernesto is devoted to you, isn't he?"

"Stubborn old fool."

"Stubborn for loving you?"

Sophia's eyes opened fully. "Stubborn for never marrying me. He thinks I have too much money to ever respect him as a husband. He insists on being my lover, but nothing more." Sophia laughed hoarsely. "Don't look so shocked, darling. One's love life doesn't stop at eighty."

Grace blinked, and went to fetch Ernesto, who was waiting just outside the door.

He read the surprise on Grace's face, and his eyes crinkled with amusement. "She doesn't really want me to marry her," he said softly. "My power comes from being unattainable, and that excites her. We are both happier this way."

Grace nodded dumbly and watched him slip back into the room. She'd known there was affection and flirting between them, but never suspected how deep their emotions ran. She'd thought Sophia alone, but right under Grace's nose she had a lover devoted to her, who valued their bond above a chance at millions.

Still stunned and amazed, she wandered back to the waiting area, only coming back to herself at the sound of Declan's voice.

"You goddamned greedy prick!" he cried.

Grace came around the corner just in time to see Declan's fist connect with Andrew's nose. Andrew yelped and stumbled, and fell on his butt. Blood flowed from his nose, his hands going up to staunch it.

"Declan!" Grace screeched. "What the hell are you doing?"

She rushed forward and dropped down beside Andrew, who was feeling the bridge of his nose, testing it for breaks. "What the hell?" Grace demanded, glaring up at Declan.

Declan's face was red with anger, his breath heaving, his fists clenched at his sides, but he didn't answer. Alyson and Darlene hadn't returned from their coffee quest, so there was no one to explain what had happened.

"She wants to see you," Grace told Declan harshly. "Go. Get out of here."

Declan and Andrew locked glares.

"Sophia's waiting," Grace said.

Declan's hot stare went from Andrew to her, and then he tore himself away.

When he'd gone, Grace started to help Andrew up. "What happened?"

Andrew shook his head. "He's a menace. I mentioned you, and he went ballistic."

"What did you say?" Grace asked, intensely curious.

He shook his head, feeling his nose. "I should press charges."

Grace gripped his arm. "With Sophia in this condition? It would distress her. Don't."

Andrew gritted his teeth, but nodded. He went to a cart parked nearby and found a towel. He pressed it to his nose, then squeaked in pain. "Goddammit! Christ, he deserved to have that fake cricket planted on his land."

Grace rocked back on her heels. "What?"

Andrew's eyes darted to her, wary.

"The Steinbeck cricket was a plant, like Declan said all along?"

Andrew held out his hand toward her. "In a good cause. You said yourself, it was a shame to see such beautiful land fall under a developer's bulldozer."

"But you *lied?* To me, to Sophia, to everyone? You made up an animal that doesn't even exist! Declan is going to court about it."

"It's all in a good cause. I thought you would understand that. Doesn't the environment matter to you?"

"Not enough to lie about it. How is that honorable?"

"The end justifies the means."

Grace shook her head, staring at Andrew in disbelief. "I didn't think this was who you were."

Andrew rolled his eyes. "So you're not going to forgive me one fake cricket, when I can forgive you for behaving like Declan's whore all summer?"

Grace's eyes went wide, and she felt her cheeks flame. *"No."*

He snorted. "Figures."

Grace shook her head. "No to everything, Andrew. There's no way in hell I'd marry you now."

The color drained from his face. "Grace, wait. Let's talk about this."

"About what? Why would you even want to marry 'Declan's whore'?"

"I'm sorry, I didn't mean that." He reached out toward her.

She backed away. "You're not who I thought you were."

Darlene and Alyson appeared, paper cups of coffee in their hands. Their conversation cut off as their surprised gazes went from Andrew's bloody face to Grace.

"Mom, we're going back to the house," Grace said, taking Alyson by the arm. "C'mon."

"What—"

"I'll explain in the car." If she ever could explain. Today it felt as if the world had turned upside down, and there was no end in sight to the chaos and upheaval.

*   *   *

Declan stomped down the hall to Sophia's hospital room, rage still flooding his veins. If Grace hadn't appeared, he'd have pounded the crap out of Andrew, and he was of half a mind even now to go back and finish the job.

Goddamned fucking little nitwit prick.

After the women had left the waiting area Declan had tried not to even look at the jerk who'd proposed to Grace, but then Andrew had started flapping his lips.

"Quite a revelation about Sophia being Grace's great-grandmother, eh?" he'd said.

Declan had grunted.

"It makes it even more likely now, doesn't it?"

Curiosity had made Declan turn unwilling eyes on his enemy. "Makes what more likely?"

"What you've been counting on. You thought you could screw Grace into marrying you, and then when she inherited Sophia's fortune in a few years you'd have it all to yourself. Looks like you miscalculated, though. Looks like Grace is going to choose substance over style, just like I knew she would. You'll never see a dime of Sophia's money. I win."

"That's why you asked Grace to marry you?" Declan said in disbelief. He'd always suspected Andrew was hoping for an inheritance from Sophia, but it still shocked him.

Andrew shrugged a shoulder. "It's not a burden. She's intelligent and pretty. It's good genetic material for children. And it should be fairly entertaining making them, as long as she doesn't gain too much baby weight between each one." He grinned.

It was the grin that sent Declan over the edge. The smarmy little prick. He had Grace in his net, but he had no idea of the treasure he held. No damned idea.

He stopped outside Sophia's door to get control of himself.

He was dimly aware that the rage felt better than what was waiting for him beneath it: a bottomless, black sense of loss.

He went in, and Ernesto came over to tell him in a low voice that the doctors didn't yet know what had happened to Sophia. With a silent, sad nod Ernesto left him alone with her.

Declan approached the bed, the last of his anger draining away. The sense of loss welled up to take its place, filling his soul with a desolation like none he'd ever known.

He took Sophia's frail hand in his own. It felt as fragile as a butterfly's wing.

"Declan," Sophia said, opening her eyes.

He sat, and leaned close. "I'm here."

"Surely you don't look so woebegone over me?"

"That shouldn't surprise you."

"It's flattering, but I'm too wise to believe it. It's Grace, isn't it?"

Declan ducked his face, and to his shock, felt tears in his eyes. One fell free, soaking into the sheet and making a small, dark spot.

"Poor Declan," Sophia sighed. She slipped her hand free of his and touched his bent head. "I warned you that you might have to come by love the hard way, that you'd have to lose it before you could ever understand its worth."

"I've made a muck of things," he breathed through his tight chest. "I didn't even know I was destroying my chances at something that would mean so much to me."

Sophia chuckled. "So what are you going to do to clean up your mess?"

Declan raised his head. "It's too late. Andrew asked her to marry him, and then she told me she didn't want anything to do with me."

"And what did you say to her then?"

"What could I say? I tried to be a gentleman and accept it."

Sophia's hand slipped from his hair down to his ear. She twisted it sharply, with surprising strength.

"Ow!"

"Idiot."

"What would you have me do? She made it clear that she doesn't want me."

Sophia's hand reached toward his ear again, and he shied away. Deprived of her target, she said, "Do you really think that a girl like Grace would spend all summer having sex with you if she didn't care for you at least a little?"

Declan gaped at Sophia, embarrassment flushing through him. "You knew?"

Sophia rolled her eyes. "Did anyone not know?"

"Did she say anything to you about how she feels about me?"

"I don't betray confidences."

"Sophia! Please!"

"You're a coward, Declan. It's Grace you should be talking to, not me."

"She already made herself clear."

"Are you sure about that?"

"She said I wasn't enough. She said she needed more."

"And you said what?"

"That I understood."

Sophia narrowed her eyes. "That's it?"

"Yeah."

"God help me. Did you ever tell the girl that you love her?"

"No, of course not. I . . . I didn't know I loved her. But she's never hinted that the feelings might be returned."

"Forgive me for being a senile old woman hopelessly behind the times, but are the ways of women so different now that it is now *their* job to declare their affections first?"

"You mean . . ."

"If Grace is half as smart as I give her credit for, why the hell would she make herself vulnerable by letting you see what was in her heart? What reason did you ever give her to trust you?"

"None," he said. "Not a damn one."

"Even Andrew had the guts to propose to her—which means you owe me a bottle of Johnnie Walker Blue, by the way."

He nodded in disbelief. She was on her deathbed, collecting a debt?

"Are you going to let Andrew have her?" Sophia went on. "Are you going to let her spend her life with him? Are you going to let him take her to his bed every night, and plant his children in her belly?"

"No. No, by God, I'm not!"

"That's my boy." Sophia sighed, and seemed to deflate, as if she had used the last of her will and energy to get her message across. She closed her eyes, and vaguely waved him away. "I'm so very tired. Let me rest now."

"Of course." Worried, and flushed with guilt over taxing her strength with talk of his screwed-up love life, he squeezed her hand and kissed her forehead. "Sleep well. You'll be home soon."

"God willing . . . ," she murmured, and drifted off to sleep.

Sophia heard Declan leave, and Ernesto returned to her side. She popped open an eye to check that they were indeed alone.

"The coast is clear, my wicked dear," Ernesto said.

"Thank God." Sophia sat up. "Sweetheart, could you get me a washcloth? My vanity is offended by this makeup that turns me into a corpse. I'd rather not have you see me this way until I'm dead."

"You are a bad, bad woman, *mi amor*. So many lies you have told this summer, so many schemes you have put into play. I did not think your plan with the MG crash would work, but I was a fool to underestimate you." Ernesto went to fetch the washcloth.

"I may be a bad woman, but I'm a brilliant actress," she called after him. "With any luck, I can stop pretending that my hip hurts so badly, too. Those steroid injections were a high price to pay for the facade." When Ernesto returned she patted the bed beside her and raised her brows seductively. "I did pay for the room through tomorrow, you know. Care for a bit of necrophilia before I wash off the paint?"

"*Dios mio*—a very bad woman," Ernesto said, but the light in his eyes said anything but.

CHAPTER
ɛ26ȝ

"Was this altered to fit me?" Grace asked in puzzlement the next day as Darlene zipped her into Sophia's green velvet gown. It closed perfectly over the vintage merry widow undergarment, the cut of the dress conforming to every curve Grace had reinstalled on her body with her consumption of bacon.

"It's the original, unaltered gown," Darlene said. "Sophia was heavier when she was younger; it's only age that has made her so thin."

"Son of a bitch," Grace muttered. "She was telling the truth all along."

"Hm?"

Grace shook her head, not wanting to explain how Sophia had insisted it wasn't the weight that made the difference in sexiness, it was the attitude.

She went to look at herself in the mirror. Her hair was parted on the side and curled in the waves that were Sophia's signature style. Thick black swoops of eyeliner turned her eyes sultry, while her newly arched brows had been darkened with pencil. Bright red lipstick contrasted with the green of her eyes.

She looked almost exactly like the Sophia in the portrait.

There were subtle differences, but to all except close associates, she was Sophia's youth brought back to life.

How ironic that she should finally reach the pinnacle of all that Sophia had wanted her to achieve while Sophia lay in a hospital bed at death's door.

Grace bit the inside of her lip, using the pain to force back the threat of tears. Sophia would want her to put on a happy face. For these few hours, she would be the bombshell Sophia had claimed she could be. She could fall apart afterward, when the gala was over and she was alone with the empty spaces in her heart that had until so recently been filled by Declan, Andrew, and Sophia herself. They were disappearing from her life even as she slipped her feet into Sophia's black satin, rhinestone-studded shoes.

"Five after seven," Darlene reminded her. "Come down and I'll take you to your place in the tableau."

Grace nodded and searched Darlene's face for some show of emotion. "Any word about Sophia?"

A muscle twitched in Darlene's cheek and then, awkwardly, she patted Grace's bare shoulder. "Try not to worry. She's a tough old bird."

There was a knock on the door. Grace's heart turned over, absurdly hoping it might be Declan. Darlene opened the door to an unexpected face: Professor Joansdatter.

"Mind if I come in?" The professor asked. She was wearing a red fringed flapper dress and a feathered headband that looked like it came from the same costume shop Grace knew her mother had used for a gown for tonight.

"Not at all," Grace said.

Darlene slipped out, leaving the two of them alone.

Professor Joansdatter looked Grace over, then whistled low and long. "Holy cow. I would never have thought it."

Grace shifted, feeling a flicker of uncertainty.

"You look exactly like that portrait of your great-aunt. Er, great-grandmother. You're the spitting image of her."

"I know. I'm doing this for her."

"And for yourself, too, I hope."

Grace sat down, perching lightly on the edge of a chair seat. The dress and undergarments didn't allow a slouch.

Joansdatter took a seat on the edge of Grace's bed. "I wanted to see how you're doing. There's been a lot going on around here, and an awful lot of it seems to center on you. How are you faring?"

Grace felt a quiver of threatening tears, and bit down again on her lip. "I'll make it through, one way or another."

Joansdatter nodded, her eyes locked with Grace's. "Your research notes make a lot more sense to me after meeting the players involved. This has been a transformative experience for you, hasn't it?"

Grace laughed and gestured toward her body. "You could say that."

"I meant more than skin deep."

Grace's smile faded. "I feel as if the person I used to be has been broken apart. I'm not sure I can put all the pieces back together again."

"Good."

Grace blinked. "Good?"

"It looks to me like you've found some new pieces of yourself. Maybe, before you came down here, you were in danger of becoming too crystallized in one way of being. Sometimes we need shattering. It's the only way to build anew, on a firmer, wider foundation."

"It doesn't feel like a good thing."

"I imagine not. But from where I sit, Grace, I see a woman who is going to have a much more interesting life than I would have predicted three months ago." Joansdatter smiled and left.

At 7:05, Grace took a deep breath to settle her nerves and went to meet her duties. From her balcony she had seen the guests arriving for the past half hour, their voices rising from the gardens below, mixed with the strains of a string quartet deeper in the gardens. The sky was still light, but beneath the trees it was just dim enough to make the fairy lights glow, as if the forest were indeed enchanted by will-o'-the-wisps, luring guests down intriguing paths.

As she opened her bedroom door she was hit by the louder thrum of voices as people passed through the foyer below. She went to the other end of the hall, where a smaller carpeted staircase led to the back of the house. Darlene was waiting for her by a side door that led out into the garden, near the terrace.

"You have the welcome speech?" Darlene asked.

Grace nodded and flashed the note card hidden in the palm of her hand.

"This way. Mind your step."

Darlene led her out to a narrow wooden walkway hidden by a curtain from the view of the crowd. A short flight of temporary wood stairs led up to a small stage around which had been built a huge gold frame. The stage held a recamier with a faux leopard skin draped over it, and red velvet drapes in the background.

Only for you, Sophia, Grace said silently. With Darlene's help she arranged herself on the sofa in the exact attitude of the portrait. She could see the dark shape of the real portrait in front of her, silhouetted on the stage curtain by the spotlights aimed upon it.

"Okay?" Darlene asked.

Grace nodded.

Darlene squeezed her shoulder. "Sophia will be so pleased."

"I wish she could see it."

Darlene flashed a rare smile, and disappeared down the small staircase.

Grace closed her eyes, breathing deeply. *For Sophia. I can do this for Sophia.*

The string music from in the gardens stopped, and the big band thrummed to life. Trumpets blew and then a drumroll started. The hubbub quieted, and as the lights on the curtain threw the portrait into even higher relief, Grace knew that her moment was here.

The portrait lifted straight up and away, raised by cables. The curtains followed, and Grace held perfectly still, playing her role as a portrait as the spotlights and hundreds of eyes turned upon her.

One one-thousand, two one-thousand, she counted silently as the drumroll grew louder and louder. At ten, the roll stopped with a crash of cymbals and Grace stood and spread out her arms. The crowd cheered and applauded.

Shaking in her heels, Grace waited a moment while a microphone was lowered toward her, and then spoke the welcome she had practiced for hours.

"The Altruism Society welcomes you to a Long Ago Night in an Enchanted Forest. We hope the magic of this night will inspire you to create a little magic of your own at Children's Hospital. Until the witching hour comes to spirit you away to a more mundane world, we invite you to partake of hidden feasts and pleasures in our gardens of wonder and delight. We, and Children's Hospital, thank you for your generosity and kindness, which is always where the true magic lies."

She bowed her head and the crowd applauded again, and the band struck up Rodgers and Hammerstein's "Some Enchanted Evening." Grace stepped to the edge of the stage, where she'd been told her dance instructor would be waiting to help her down the stairs and onto the dance floor.

A masked man in white tie and tails was waiting for her, but the moment her eyes met his through the mask, she knew it was Declan.

"'Some enchanted evening,'" the bandleader sang, "'you may see a stranger, you may see a stranger, across a crowded room . . .'"

She put her hand in Declan's white-glove-clad one, his strength sustaining her as she stepped down to the dance floor. With masterful confidence, he put his hand on her waist and swept her into the dance.

"'And somehow you know,'" Declan sang in his baritone along with the bandleader, "'you know even then . . .'"

"What are you doing here?" Grace asked, her heart in her throat.

"I thought it would be obvious."

She shook her head, tears starting in her eyes. It was all too much. This, on top of everything else. "It's not."

"I'm dancing with the woman I love."

Grace tripped, but he caught her and swept her across the floor, his movements so smooth that she doubted anyone had seen. "Don't tease me," she said.

"I've never been more serious. Grace Cavanaugh, I love you. I love you with every fiber of my being, and going through life without you would be dying a new death every day that I wake without you beside me. I love you," he said, sweeping her in a dizzying spin. "I *love* you, Grace. I love you."

Disbelieving joy started to rise inside her. "Truly?"

"Marry me, Grace. Please marry me!"

She tilted her head back and laughed, her joy overflowing. "Yes! Yes, yes, yes!"

"My Grace," he whispered, and she heard the crack of emotion in his voice. He stopped and wrapped her in his arms, bending her backward and kissing her thoroughly as the crowd erupted in cheers.

As Grace came up for air, a light caught her gaze. Up on the balcony of Sophia's room, her great-grandmother stood beside Ernesto. "Look," Grace said, nudging Declan.

He followed her gaze and laughed.

"What's that in her hand?" Grace asked.

"She's toasting us with Scotch."

Grace laughed, and Declan spun her back into the dance. "Remind me to tell you about the fifty thousand dollars she owes me," Grace said.

He looked at her in surprise. "I will."

Other dancers joined them, and from the corner of her eye Grace caught sight of Cat . . . dancing with Cyndee, the personal trainer. Grace's eyes widened, but Cat met her gaze and winked.

"'Once you have found her, never let her go,'" the bandleader sang, the voices of Declan, Cat, and every man present joining in.

"'Once you have found her, never . . . let . . . her . . . go!'"

EPILOGUE

The North American Journal of Womens Studies, volume 3

The Belle of the Ball: It's Her Party and She'll Only Cry if She Wants To

Cavanaugh, G. S., University of Washington, Seattle, Washington

Abstract

Beauty is only skin deep, we have all been told. But for women who are perceived as beautiful, do the effects of this perception reach deeper into their lives than a reflection in the mirror? If so, is it for good or for ill? And whose perception is it, exactly, that declares a woman beautiful in the first place? After thirty-five interviews with attractive women of all ages and stations in life, as well as a three-month makeover experiment, it is proposed that being perceived as attractive can be a powerful tool in social interactions; that the effects of using such a tool can be good or ill depending upon the wisdom and motives of the woman in question; and that it is the perception and attitude of the woman herself that is most responsible for the beauty that others see in her outward face and form. Rather than being an arbitrary judgment placed upon her from outside sources, beauty is a tool within the reach of every woman—should she dare to develop and use it.